Sinister Connections

By Anna Browne

Acknowledgments

Thinking about all my family and friends back in Stoke on Trent, where I decided to set the scene for this psychological thriller story. Also thank you to my husband Dr Johnny Browne for his patience allowing me to be sometimes absorbed in my writing, and his help and encouragement in getting this published. Finally I want to thank my lovely and faithful readers, you know who you are.

Copyright

Copyright © 2017 by Anna Browne

All rights reserved.

Chapter 1

Jennifer Sudbury kicked of her shoes and turned on her computer. She had just poured herself a nice glass of Chablis French wine, one of her favourites. She had had a long and tiring day at the office, and was now about to unwind. The computer had become her escapism, and proved to be a great source of relaxation, her drug. She was now totally addicted to one of the chat rooms that she frequently logged onto, and had been for the past nine months or so. Of course she had always been very careful not to give out any personal details, knowing that it would have been far too dangerous. She even had a pseudonym name that she called herself while online which was 'Katie.'

Jennifer took a long sip of her wine and logged on. This was the moment when she would no longer be Jennifer Sudbury, personal secretary to a well known firm of solicitors and divorced. Instead she would now be Katie carefree and single and never been married.

No sooner had she logged on to the chat room justforfun.com there were messages flashing up onto the screen and all seemed to cry out to her to answer them. But this time she decided to ignore them, and instead went straight through the list of names to see who she would click on. One in particular caught her eye - Prince of Mystery - then she clicked on it with a smile, before she took another sip of her wine.

'OK Prince of Mystery who ever you are let's give you a chance' she said out loud to herself, and hoped he would not turn out to be like the rest she had previously clicked on during the times she had been in the chat room. Not that they had all been that way. Some she had found interesting in a strange sort of way, but others had been sleazy and she wondered which Prince of Mystery would be.

'Hi Prince of Mystery do you want to chat' she typed and then clicked send. A minute or two went by and other messages continued to flash up onto the screen, but there seemed to be no reply from him. Disappointed Jennifer decided to click on another name, Foxy guy, but just as she did so came the reply she had been waiting for from Prince of Mystery.

'Hi Katie...been waiting. How are you?'

Jennifer frowned with a sort of half smile when she read out his answer, but knew it was all part of the game that people liked to play, and so often said things like that. So she typed back her reply.

'Oh really Prince of Mystery, and have you another name?'

Soon his answer flashed up on her computer screen again. ' Nope. Mystery by name and Mystery by nature. Now do you mind if I ask you a question Katie?'

'OK what sort of question?' Jennifer quickly typed back, wondering if the question would turn out to be something sordid as they often did. She had been asked what she was wearing or what colour was her underwear, and always when that happened Jennifer would cut the other person off.

'What colour would you choose, black or white?'

Jennifer rolled her eyes and wondered to herself what kind of question that was, and why he had

—

asked it in the first place, but decided she would humour him and play along at least for the time being. After all she had nothing better to do, she had not even had a proper date since her divorce from David, her one time lover, companion and husband. It had been quite a short marriage in reality only lasting a few years, three to be exact. But it had started to go wrong at an early stage, and before she knew it the marriage was over, followed by a very painful divorce. But as there were no children involved it had thankfully been dissolved quite quickly, although Jennifer had been left with hardly anything. Not that she had taken much into the marriage, and so she really couldn't complain. It had been David who had the higher paid job, and David who had paid the deposit on the semi that they had decided to buy.

Jennifer had fallen in love with it instantly, almost as quickly had she had fallen in love with David. Then they had taken their vows together on that lovely day in June, standing side by side on a beautiful picturesque beach in Marmaris, she had felt the luckiest person alive. She had thought then that they would have been together forever.

She had worn a short lightweight ivory lace off the shoulder dress, which had shown off her lovely figure and tan, and she had felt and looked beautiful. They had both decided that they would make up their own vows to each other, instead of sticking to the more traditional ones, and neither had known what the other had pledged to say, until the very day they had said them.

It had been the perfect wedding, or so Jennifer had thought at the time. Everything had gone to plan from the word go. The only people that had been present were Jennifer's father Clive Beaumont and her older sister Nicole, and on David's side were his parents and one of David's best friends, and lastly Jennifer's best friend Francesca who she had known nearly all her life, or at least since infant school.

In fact Francesca was exactly the same age as Jennifer and she had also shared the same birthday. She had proved to be a great source of help after she and David had split up, but their friendship had started to cool a little bit since Francesca had started to date a guy she had met from work. Jennifer knew it was going to happen sooner or later and it was understandable since it had also cooled when Jennifer had met David. However they would still make time for each other, and met up at least once a week for coffee, or to go to the cinema.

Jennifer typed in an answer to what Prince of Mystery had asked her.

' Lets see' she said to herself out loud. 'I will go for white.' Then she clicked the send button.

' Thought so. My choice would have been black of course....may I ask another?' he typed back almost instantly.

'OK go ahead' Jennifer replied finishing off her glass of wine. She was starting to relax now and just hoped this conversation would not turn sordid. After a few seconds his second question popped up on the computer screen.

' Would you rather be stuck in a lift or lost in a forest?' he had typed.

Jennifer sighed deeply and rolled her eyes, and

wondered where all this was leading to. But as strange as the questions were, she saw no real harm in them, and so she continued to humour him.

She had been very tempted to reply neither, but instead she replied 'lost in a forest' simply because she had a dreadful fear of confined spaces, and although she certainly did not like the idea of being lost in a forest, she knew that she would dislike being stuck in a lift ten times more.

She remembered the time in complete horror, when she had been in fact stuck in a lift, and although it had not been for that long, maybe just for less than ten minutes, those ten minutes had seemed like hours. By the time that the door of the lift had opened again, she had had visible beads of perspiration on her forehead, and her heart had been pounding so hard that she had thought it was going to explode. She had felt sick to her stomach and been close to tears. There had been two other people in the lift at the same time, an elderly man somewhere in his late seventies, and David who she had not known at the time. In fact that was how they had met.

David had been aware of the affect it had had on Jennifer, and when the door had opened eventually after a couple of attempts at sounding the alarm he had asked her if she would like to go for a cup of tea or coffee to steady her nerves, but all she had really wanted to do at the time was to go home, and so they had gone their separate ways only to meet up again by chance three weeks later.

Jennifer had been on her lunch break from the firm of solicitors that she worked for, and had decided to treat herself to something different than

—

the sandwich pack she usually had. She had stopped by a small restaurant that was family run in the heart of Hanley in Stoke on Trent. She had also been there many times with Francesca. It was a lovely place, and all the staff were always very polite and would often engage with her in pleasant conversation.

She had ordered herself something nice to eat, macaroni cheese with jacket potato and salad. This made a nice change from sandwiches, and she had just started to tuck into it when she caught sight of David, who was heading her way and their eyes instantly met.

'Why hello again. May I sit down here with you' he asked with a big grin on his face, and then stopped when he saw Jennifer hesitate.

'We met that time in the lift......remember?'

Jennifer had nodded and muttered a reply in between mouthfuls. The lift had been something she had wanted to forget, but instantly she had remembered him with his lovely smile, that seemed to light up his face. And despite the fact that it had scared her half to death at the time, she had felt strangely pleased to meet up with this guy again.

'Oh sorry' he had said holding out his hand 'David Sudbury. Pleased to meet you again.'

'Me too, and in more pleasant circumstances I might add' she replied returning the smile and shaking his hand. He had a nice hand, firm yet tender she had thought. They had chatted for quite a while, just like old friends, until Jennifer had suddenly checked her watch, and was shocked to see that she was at least ten minutes over her allowed lunch break.

Muttering her apologies she quickly got up and paid her bill, leaving a confused David looking on. She almost ran the short journey back to the offices.

The following day Jennifer had been drawn to go back to the restaurant again secretly hoping he would be there too and she had been pleasantly surprised to see him as she had walked through the door. She had smiled and he had waved and beckoned her over. This was how they had continued to meet until on the third day David had asked her out on a proper date which Jennifer had excepted. They found they had so much in common. They both liked watching action movies, or rather David did. Jennifer secretly liked the soaps too but never admitted it, since David had already told her he loathed them. She decided that he was more important than any soap, and besides she could always watch catch up on the days they did not meet.

Francesca thought she was mad that she didn't tell him about the soaps, but Jennifer only laughed and told her he did not need to know everything about her. They would have a girly night in and Francesca would bring a bottle of wine and a DVD to watch, but Jennifer had already got the catch-ups on and so to her dismay Francesca had to watch them all over again.

Jennifer read Prince of Mystery's reply.

'That is what I thought you would answer. It's not nice being stuck in a lift is it Katie?' he had typed.

As she read it a shiver ran down her back. I am being silly she thought, and it was just a silly game he was playing after all. He did not know her, how could he? Neither did she know him it was all a coincidence, all part of the game and if she chose she could just as easily end the game and the conversation, anytime she wanted to. Then he would be gone just like the rest of the people she had spoken to. And so that was what Jennifer decided to do.

'There Prince of Mystery whoever you are' she smiled smugly to herself, and ' Hello Peter.' A nice sensible name is Peter, she thought as she proceeded to strike up a conversation with him, while she could see that Prince of Mystery made several attempts to speak with her again, each time she avoided him and continued to chat to Peter, until he eventually decided to give up and she could see that he went off line.

Peter turned out to be the usual boring guy, and even before they had been chatting for five minutes, he was asking her for her personal email address, which Jennifer was not willing to give. To be friends online was one thing, it was a bit of fun, exciting to her now boring mundane life, but she had no interest in taking things any further, at least for now.

She wondered if she would still be logging onto chat rooms in another couple of years or so when she hit thirty. She was almost twenty-eight, the same age as her friend Francesca. They planned to celebrate together, or rather that had been the plan. But now Francesca had Paul and she was almost sure he would be taking her out instead. She suddenly felt down at the thought of celebrating alone.

When she had married David she had been twenty-four and had thought that they would have been together forever. They had even planned to start a family soon, although David had wanted to wait a while longer, until he had got established in the Insurance firm where he worked. He was due for promotion any time or so he had kept telling her. That was his excuse for all the long hours he had started to put in lately. She did not know exactly at what point their marriage had started to go wrong. All she had known was he had gradually changed and seemed to be spending more and more time away from home.

Even Francesca had commented on it. But Jennifer had been so naive and had believed what David had told her. She had not thought he had been the cheating type, but in hindsight what did she really know? She had been devastated when he had eventually told her that their marriage was over. She wondered what had gone wrong, and if it had been her fault. He told her at first, that it was not her, but him. He had changed and that was why it was not working anymore. He told her that there had been no one else involved, and like a fool she had believed him, because deep down inside she wanted there to have been no one else. She had loved David unreservedly. He had been her everything, and she had thought she had been his but she had been wrong.

And now this was her life. Living in a private apartment because the semi they had lovingly decided to buy together had to be put up for sale. David had told her that he had not intended to continue to pay his share of the mortgage, and there

13

was no way she could have afforded to pay his share as well as her own. It was only after a month of their split that Jennifer had found out that he was seeing someone else. In fact he had been seeing her all along, which hurt more than ever. He hadn't even had the backbone to tell her. Instead he had sprouted his excuses, his lies.

It was almost eleven pm when Jennifer turned off her computer. She suddenly felt tired and needed to go to bed. She noted that the guy that had called himself Prince of Mystery had suddenly come back online again, just before she had shut down, and she briefly wondered who else he would be speaking to tonight. Then she shuddered as she had thought about his strange reply about the lift. It was a strange world out there. The computer screen only allowed you to see what a person wanted you to see, and anyone could put a picture of themselves or what they would like to think was themselves up. She had joked to Francesca that she was thinking of making up a profile and going onto the chat rooms, but all Francesca could say was to be very careful. Francesca was more mature minded of the two, and although they both had social media profiles with Facebook the profiles they used there were the real thing. The chat rooms were something else though. Before she got into bed Jennifer checked her mobile.

There was a missed call and a message from Francesca asking if she could contact her tomorrow. Jennifer frowned. She had not heard it come through at all, and she checked to make sure that her phone was not on silent, but it wasn't. She decided that she would text her first thing since the time was now nearly eleven thirty, time she was asleep. She had work again tomorrow.

Chapter 2

The following day proved to be really busy at work for Jennifer. She had to type out two sets of agreements both for a local letting agency. Then there was an affidavit to do, and all before lunch. It was not helped by Mr Stone, one of the solicitors being in a bad mood.

She had sent an early morning text message to Francesca before she had left her apartment but had not received a reply yet. And as usual had been greeted by one of her neighbours. She did not know his name, but the very sight of him simply gave her the creeps. He always seemed to be leering at her in an inappropriate manner, and strangely this seemed to happen just as she was leaving for work in the mornings. He would pretend to be looking outside his door checking for something and it was as if he knew she was about to go out. She had even tried to leave earlier than usual, but to no avail, he was there before she had time to close her apartment door.

He looked like he was in his mid-fifties and always looked like he needed a good shave, and he had longish hair that was going gray. In fact Jennifer often wondered how he could afford to be renting his apartment at all, since they were privately rented and this guy looked like he didn't have a penny to his name. But what did she know; he might be a rich eccentric. Whatever, she did not like the look of him or the way he seemed to stare at her as if he was undressing her.

The rest of the afternoon was just as busy, and Mr Stone's mood seemed to get even worse. She would be glad when it was time to go home. She checked her mobile again to see if Francesca had left a message as she had set the setting to silent and so she would not have heard it come through if there had have been one. Just as she was checking, Mr Stone came out of his office and saw her, which seemed to make his mood worse.

'Ms Sudbury please do that in your own time, and not in ours' he told her crossly. And Jennifer could only mumble an apology.

'I have more files I want you to copy as soon as possible, and I will be having a client arriving at three o clock. So when he arrives can you please buzz me and let me know' he told her.

' Yes sir.....and I will get to work on those files straight away ' she told him, feeling slightly peeved.

She eventually managed to speak to Francesca who told her that there had been a guy asking questions about her to Paul.

'What sort of questions?' she asked looking puzzled.

'Just the usual ones, if you were single or married and if you lived in Stoke.'

'Fran I hope he did not give him any details. I mean he could be anybody' she replied starting to panic.

'Relax Jen he hardly told him anything. Just that you were divorced.'

'Thank goodness. Let's hope it stays that way too. He could be a axe murderer for all we know, besides I have enough to contend with from the creep next door.'

'Oh, is he still bothering you Fran?'

'I would not say he is bothering me exactly. I

mean he never does anything. In fact he never says anything either, just stares at me in a sleazy manner that gives me the creeps' she explained, and her friend could only sympathise.

'Maybe you should look around for another apartment if it bothers you that much.'

'I don't want to do that though Fran. I rather like where I am. It's just across from the lovely park and besides it took me ages to find it. I just could not be bothered to flat hunt again.'

'But if he is bothering you' she continued.

'That's just it though, the guy says nothing but just stares, sometimes I think he isn't all there.'

'Right! In that case, maybe you should try talking to him. You know, just say hello or it's a nice day, or anything to break the ice. Maybe he is just shy or something Jen.'

But Jennifer did not think so somehow and told her so.

'But how do you know if you have never even spoken to him?'

'Believe me Fran I know! It's the way he seems to look right inside me. He just gives me the creeps. Now can we please talk about something else. Like our birthdays, which happen to be in three days time' she told her.

'Ah yes. I was meaning to get to that. Look Jen, duck. I know we always celebrate together and always have done, but Paul wants to take me out this time. In fact he told me that he booked a table. I am really sorry. But listen I have an idea, we could still celebrate together and go out for a meal but on a later date. What do you think about that?'

Jennifer half knew that this would happen so

18

was not in the least surprised, only disappointed that it had

'OK that's fine. I will just stay in and wash my hair or something, don't you worry about me, after all it's only a birthday and another year older' she told her feeling very sorry for herself.

'Oh Jen don't be like that. You know that there would have been nothing better than I would have liked to have done, but I can't let Paul down can I? Besides I think he may be going to pop the question or something.'

'Pop the question? Oh I did not know it was that serious between you two. I mean you have not really known him that long have you?'

'Long enough to know I love him Jen, besides I am not getting any younger am I? I would like to have children some day' she told her.

Jennifer felt a slight pang of jealousy rise up within her at that statement that had surprised even her. She had so much wanted to start a family with David, but of course he had had other ideas.

'Will you go and visit your father? I know Nicole is in France, but you could maybe go to see your dad?'

Jennifer shook her head.

'He is far too busy, besides he sent me a card yesterday with a cheque inside. I think I will just have a quiet day alone. Maybe watch some TV or go online or something.'

Francesca felt bad at letting Jennifer down as they had always celebrated their birthdays together. Even when Jennifer had got married they still managed to have lunch together and then they would each go their separate ways until the next time they met. She did not like to let her down, but Paul was important to her, and he had gone and booked a table so there was no way she was going to let him down. Jennifer would just have to understand.

Jennifer let herself into her apartment and put the kettle on. She decided she needed a coffee. The day had been simply awful, what with Mr Stone's mood and then Francesca telling her that they had to delay the celebration that they had together. Even though deep down she knew it would happen, she still could not help but feel disappointed. Francesca was the only good friend she had, and now that friendship looked like it was cooling. She knew she was being selfish and that it was only fair that Francesca would want to go out on her birthday with Paul, yet she just could not help herself. She suddenly felt very lonely.

She turned on her computer and then went to make herself a cup of coffee and a sandwich. Then she updated her profile on Facebook and noted she had two friends' requests. Both of them were from women who she had never heard of, so she deleted both. You could not be too careful. Profiles were always getting hacked, and Jennifer had to change her own password more than once. She checked on newsfeed, nothing interesting there, then decided to look at her friend Francesca's profile. There was a lot of talk about her new boyfriend and the places they had been to. The way she was talking about him sounded so lovey-dovey somehow that Jennifer felt another pang of jealousy. She only hoped for her friend's sake that if they did get married, the relationship would last longer than her own had.

She thought about David then and what he was doing. He had deleted his own profile just as soon as they had spit, or else she would have been tempted to go onto his page and have a nosy too. She imagined he would have moved in with the other woman he had been seeing, but did not know for definite. Jennifer knew she would have to stop thinking about him if she was to move on, but it was so hard sometimes. She logged off Facebook and finished her coffee.

'OK justforfun.com lets see who is online' she said out loud.

She saw that it was mostly the same people as before. Peter was there, so was Foxy guy and someone called Lusty Kim. But there was no Prince of Mystery, not this time.

All at once a message came up from Peter.

'Hello Katie. Do you want to chat again' he said, but Jennifer could not be bothered. She had been bored enough the last time she had spoken to him. This time she needed to unwind and forget all about her past.

Just then Prince of Mystery logged on and flashed a message up making Jennifer's heart suddenly beat faster.

'Ah Katie you are back. I am sorry if I scared you off the other day. I hope we can still be friends?' he typed.

Jennifer's first instinct was to ignore him, but she felt bored and wanted to speak to someone. After all it was only a bit of fun, what harm could it do anyhow? He did not know anything about her, or where she lived and so she decided she would answer him.

'Hello Prince of Mystery. How are you? It's fine you did not scare me off.'

'I am pleased about that. You have to excuse me sometimes I like to ask strange questions, but don't mean any harm. It's all part of the little games I like to play. And thank you for asking how I am, I am fine and I hope you are too. Now would you like to play some more games, that's if I did not scare you off.

'I already told you, you didn't scare me off, so OK I am up for it, ask away.'

'Would you rather be single or married?' he asked.

Jennifer smiled to herself. That's simple I would rather be married any day, especially to the right person she thought, but instead she typed back single. To which Prince of Mystery in return typed his reply.

'Ah so you are married or divorced even?'

What on earth! Jennifer thought when she read it.

'How does saying you would rather be single mean you were married or divorced?' she typed.

But Prince of Mystery decided to ignore it and instead asked her if he could ask her another question. But before she got his question her landline phone started to ring. She quickly left her computer to answer it, wondering who it could be. Nearly everyone contacted her via her mobile, except on rare occasions her father would call her on it.

Jennifer answered on the third ring.

'Hello' she said, waiting for the other person to speak. But instead she was met by silence, except she knew somebody was there because she could hear their breathing. It was a sort of faint breathing, but nevertheless someone was there she knew that and it was starting to spook her out.

'Hello is there someone there?' she asked again. Then before she could say anything else, she heard a faint click, where the other person had replaced the receiver. That's strange she thought to herself going back to her computer. There had been someone there she had been sure of it. Maybe it was just a wrong number, which happens all the time. She was being silly she thought. She had left the computer online when she had got up to answer the phone, and there were messages appearing everywhere except from the guy called Prince of Mystery who was now reading offline.

She decided she would give Foxy guy a go and typed 'Hello do you want to chat' but there was no reply. Instead she got someone called Lusty Kim who wanted to know what colour knickers she was wearing! Enough of that she thought and logged off.

She turned the TV on to great her favourite soap, she had forgotten all about it. Being single did have some advantages after all, she thought. At least you got to watch what you wanted, when you wanted.

Yet thinking about things, it did not outweigh the advantages that marriage had, like having someone to come home to, going to bed together and cuddling, walking hand in hand, and basically having someone to share your life with. She actually envied Francesca she had all those things, or would have if Paul asked her to marry him. Whereas unless she did something about it she would stay lonely and single for the rest of her life, and all she would have for company would be her TV and computer. She didn't even have a cat or a dog for company. Not that it would be practical to have one, since she was living in an apartment, also the fact that she was out at work all day. Maybe she should sign on to a dating agency, she suddenly thought, but she wasn't sure. That might prove to be a disaster too, and yet people she had known had done it. So it might be worth a try. She need not give her real name, at least not at first. She could make a pseudo name up on her profile and then if she liked any of the guys and got to know and trust them, then and only then would she be willing to give her real name. Anything was worth a try.

Just as the ending theme music to the soap she was watching started to play, the telephone rang once more. Jennifer hesitated at first and thought she would let it ring out, but then she thought better of it and went to answer. She was being silly, maybe even starting to get a little paranoid. It was all this talk from Prince of Mystery. The last phone call was probably a wrong number, or someone who could not get through. She wondered then if it was Nicole, her older sister who was staying at her grandparent's house in Agay in France. She had been there for most of the year, and had been able to work from there. Maybe it was Nicole and she had phoned to wish her a premature happy birthday but could not get through, and though she and Nicole had never really been close as sisters go, she would still phone up and wish her a happy birthday the odd time.

'Hello' she said again speaking into the phone, but was greeted again by the eerie silence apart from a faint breathing at the other end.

'Nicole is that you?' she asked, but again no answer. Then just as before whoever it was replaced the receiver. After a while the phone started to ring again, but this time Jennifer decided not to answer. If it was important whoever it was could ring her mobile.

Chapter 3

The following day Jennifer mentioned to a colleague about the silent phone calls she had started to receive. Lizzie was thirty-two and about the same age as her sister Nicole. She had only been working at Stone & Watson for less than a year compared to Jennifer's eight, but she was a nice girl, easy to speak to and Jennifer liked her.

'If it were me I would have a whistle ready and blow it into the phone' she told her, and Jennifer smiled.

'Maybe it was just a wrong number and nothing sinister though' she told her, after all she had never had them before. She told herself she was just being paranoid because of other things that had started to happen. This morning when she had closed her apartment door she found an empty beer bottle just in front of the door. She wondered at the time if one of her other neighbours had let someone in on the intercom so that they gained access to the hall but then dismissed this. Then she had seen Mr Sleazy looking at her again with that look that gave her the creeps and she hurried away with the bottle in her hand, only discarding it when she came to a rubbish bin on the way to the bus stop.

It was Saturday, the morning of her birthday, and Jennifer was not looking forward to spending a day in. In fact she decided she would go out. Francesca had phoned earlier to wish her a happy birthday, and reminded her that they could have lunch together sometime, but as both of them would be working all week it would have to be the following Saturday, which Jennifer was not too pleased about.

'Maybe we could do dinner instead then next week' she offered.

'But what about Paul? Won't he mind?' Jennifer replied.

'He will be fine about it Jen, come on let's plan it, what do you say?'

So Jennifer had agreed. They would meet up around lunchtime maybe go to a cafe for a bite to eat and then go shopping. Later on they would meet up again and go out for dinner and maybe have a drink or two to celebrate.

There had been no more strange phone calls in the last two days, and so Jennifer was beginning to relax and think that it had just been a wrong number after all. She decided that today she would treat herself and buy a new dress. Then after she could get a coffee at the family run restaurant Laceys. She showered and dressed casually in jeans and jumper and brushed her shoulder length dark hair. She had felt happier now that Francesca had suggested meeting up the following week.

Last night she had even joined a dating site online and uploaded a photo of herself. It had been one of her favourite ones taken a year ago. Maybe she would get lucky, she thought, as she looked for her handbag, jacket and keys. They were here somewhere, she thought, going back into her bedroom again, and she found them on her dressing table.

Just at that moment her intercom buzzed. Someone was outside and asking to come in. She had not been expecting anyone. Oh well, she thought to herself, I am going out anyhow so I will see who it is, instead of answering the intercom.

Jennifer locked her door and let herself out. She glanced to see if Mr Sleazy was outside like he usually was, but was pleasantly surprised to see there was nobody there. She smiled to herself as she opened the main door and was shocked to see a bunch of dead flowers lying on the floor. They were clearly dead but still in the polythene wrapping and there was a card with just one word, KATIE.

Jennifer was visibly trembling as she let herself back into her apartment. She could hardly get the key into the lock, she was so upset and now she did not have the heart to go shopping. In fact she did not have the heart to do anything. She was so shocked that she had left the flowers there on the floor where she had found them; she could just not bear to pick them up, even if it was to throw them into the bin. She felt totally confused. Who on earth could have sent them and why? The thing that had shocked her the most was not because they were dead flowers, but it was the card that was attached with the name Katie on it.

No one knew she called herself Katie. No one, except the people she spoke to online in the chat rooms. But they did not know her from Adam, let alone where she lived. It was just not possible, she told herself.

She had also used the name Katherine for her dating agency profile, but again all that she had given away was her personal email address. She thought about ringing Francesca and telling her what had happened, but did not want to spoil her day. It was her birthday also and she knew if her friend thought she was upset she would insist on calling down to see her. Yet she just could not settle, so in the end she picked up the phone and rang her.

'Jennifer calm down and tell me again what exactly happened?' she said.

'It was awful, someone rang the intercom buzzer, and when I went down all that was there was a bunch of dead flowers. It's really spooked me out' she explained in between sobs.

'But how do you know they were meant for you. Was there a card?'

'There was a card with one word written on it.'

'Right, OK, look, I will be over just as soon as I can' and before Jennifer had time to protest she had put the phone down. It seemed ages before Francesca arrived when in fact it had only been less than thirty minutes. She lived only a few miles away in a town called Longton.

Francesca buzzed the intercom and Jennifer opened the door. Francesca held out the flowers.

'Are these them?' she asked. Jennifer could only look on in amazement .The flowers that Francesca held were not dead at all, far from it, and strangely enough there was no card.

'I think you need a cup of coffee or maybe something a little bit stronger to settle your nerves' she said going through to the kitchen and putting the kettle on. Shall I put the flowers in water?'

'What! Certainly not. I don't want them anywhere near me' she told her friend who only shook her head and told her that she probably had an admirer who sent them for her birthday.

'Listen to me Fran, they were not the flowers that I saw earlier. I don't have a clue where the ones you bought up came from, all I know is they were definitely not the ones. Besides there was a card attached with the name Katie on' she explained.

Her friend started to look worried for her now. Jennifer looked very pale and her eyes were red and swollen where she had been crying.

'Look Jen are you sure, I mean you could easily have been mistaken, and surely if the name Katie was on a card attached to the flowers, then maybe it's all a mix-up after all. Maybe they were meant for someone else, someone named Katie and they just got the address wrong, it does happen you know.'

'That's just it Fran. Katie is the name I have been using online, in the chat rooms' she explained.

Francesca's eyes grew wide. Now she was really worried about her friend. She had known that she used the chat rooms because she had told her, but she did not realise she had given out any personal information, like where she lived. She knew that was dangerous and thought Jennifer would have had more common sense than that.

'Oh Jen you have not gone and told anyone where you live have you? If so you are playing with fire.'

'NO of course not, what do you take me for, an idiot. I am not that stupid as if! ' she told her getting cross.

'Then how does anyone know where to send flowers to?'

'That is just what I am telling you. No one knows. I have never given out any personal information online.'

'OK, OK....let's think about this sensibly. You have never given any information out to anyone, even regarding your online pseudonym, yet you have a bunch of flowers delivered with the name Katie on, that appears now to have lost the card you saw attached.'

'Dead flowers too may I add. They were dead when I saw them' she insisted.

But Francesca could only look at here with a strange expression. She just did not know what to believe.

'But not dead now as you can see for yourself can't you? ' Francesca added pointing to the flowers.

'Whatever Fran, they were dead when I found them, I tell you.'

Francesca shrugged.

'I don't understand it either Jen but you did actually tell me that your online name was Katie, so who else could you have told? And you need to think about this one very carefully.'

That's just it though Jennifer thought to herself she had told no one her online name. In fact she could not even remember telling Francesca. She shuddered at the thought that she may have told someone else. If Francesca had known her online name had been Katie, then who else knew? It made her feel sick inside just thinking about it.

Francesca had left soon after, so that she could get ready for her date with Paul and she told Jennifer to ring her if anything else untoward happened, no matter what time it was. She had also taken the flowers with her, because Jennifer did not want them in the house. Just the look of them gave her the creeps. She needed to forget what had happened, and like Francesca had said it could have been a genuine mistake, but if that was the case then why were the dead flowers changed when her friend had bought them in, better still where was the card with the name Katie written on it? It all did not make sense, unless someone was trying to scare her.

Wait she thought, trying to remember the flowers. The ones she had first seen were dead carnations mixed in with chrysanthemums or some other sort of flower. Yet the ones that Francesca had found were definitely roses, they were not carnations, and so someone had to have swapped them over in the thirty minutes or so that it had taken Francesca to arrive at her apartment.

She shivered at the thought. Whoever had rung the buzzer to her apartment and put the flowers there, must have been watching her. They could have been hiding somewhere in the park, maybe in the bushes. But who would do such a thing and why?

Jennifer decided she needed to relax her mind, and so logged on to her computer. However this time instead of going to the chat room, she decided she would log into her email, just to see if there were any replies to the profile she had set up as Katherine. Sure enough there were three replies. Two of them she decided were not for her, although they were both eager to meet her, but the third one looked promising.

According to his profile he looked around the same age as Jennifer, give or take a few years. He had a lovely face with thick dark hair and an olive complexion. In fact he could easily have been mistaken for Spanish or Italian except for his name, which was definitely English. She read it out aloud to herself. 'Luke Miller...OK Luke Miller you look nice' she thought to herself as she read his profile. Professional guy that likes long walks and romantic meals out. It gave his age as twenty nine. Just right she thought, just a year older than she was. She decided she would reply to him, but would take it slowly and certainly not give much information out. Just as she was about to reply the telephone began to ring.

Jennifer got up to answer it. She was feeling more like her old self again now. Logging onto the computer had relaxed her. She might even go out later after all, and treat herself to that new dress, and then a meal in Laceys.

'Hello' she said but was greeted by an eerie silence just like before, not even the breathing that she had heard before. But she knew there had been someone on the other end of the phone, because like the times previously after a minute she heard the click of the receiver as they replaced it.

Jennifer did not know what to think. She went back to her computer and with shaking hands she decided to type a quick reply to Luke Miller, anything to take her mind off what had happened. She decided to keep it short and sweet, thanking him for his interest and asked for more personal details about him. She asked what his profession was and said she was interested in talking to him and maybe if they found each other interesting they might meet up sometime. Then she pressed send and logged out, put on her jacket and decided to go shopping, after all this was her birthday and she might as well make the most of it.

She decided to go to the Potteries centre in Hanley one of her favourite places. It was always buzzing with shoppers especially on a weekend. She just loved all the different shops there, all under the same roof and she was sure that she would find a nice dress. If not she could always walk further into town and look there and besides Laceys was only just around the corner.

Jennifer found two dresses that she really liked, but after trying both on she decided on the second one. It was a lovely fitted dress in beautiful sapphire blue. Blue was her favourite colour, and David had always said it was a colour that suited her well. It brought out the colour of her blue eyes and he had always liked to see her in blue. She suddenly felt choked inside when she thought about it. Then she decided to put it back on the rails and picked up the first one again. She needed to think beyond David now and what he had thought.

It was her life, and David was no longer part of it whether she liked it or not. The first dress was shorter and looked the more glamorous of the two, a typical little black dress number with diamantéé around the neckline. She held it up beside herself again and looked in the mirror. It cost more than she wanted to pay, in fact much more, but decided that it would be worth it and besides it was her birthday after all. If she couldn't treat herself now when could she? So she walked out with her purchase and walked around the corner to Laceys. Her mobile phone rang just before she reached the little restaurant. She could see that it was Francesca before she picked it up.

'Hello Jen just wanted to check that you were OK duck. I hated to leave you like that.'

'I am fine Fran, I have done a bit of shopping and now I am about to go into Laceys and get something to eat.'

'Ah that's good. I am glad you decided to go out. It's what you needed to take your mind off things. I have been thinking Jen, do you think that guy that lives near you in the apartment has got anything to do with the flowers, I mean you said he gave you the creeps and maybe it was him. I think you need to be very careful anyhow, just me being concerned about you. I am sure the flowers are nothing' she continued.

'I really don't know Fran. I never thought of him, simply because the name Katie was written on them, and there is no way he would know I call myself Katie' she told her.

'I suppose, but you do need to think who else you could have possibly told. Anyhow Jen I had better go, I have a date. Paul is picking me up in less than an hour. I will probably ring to catch up after the weekend.'

'OK Fran and happy birthday again. We can exchange presents next week.'

'Happy birthday Jen and yes that will be just great. Have a nice meal.' Then they both ended the call.

She smiled to herself as she slipped her mobile phone back into her bag, and looked at the menu that Rebekah had handed to her. She decided that she would have the special of the day, fish pie with mixed vegetables and fries, and a glass of water just for now.

It was typical of Francesca; she had always been the thoughtful kind. Maybe that was why they had always stayed friends. She and Francesca had known each other since they were five years old, although Jennifer had grown up in Stoke on Trent in a place called Trentham. Her father had been half French and she had never even known her mother who had died giving birth to her, leaving her father alone with two little girls. He had never wanted to speak about her mother, except to say that Jennifer was his special little girl and that she was his wife's last gift to him. She had seen lots of photos of her mother, but because she had no memory of her, found it difficult to feel anything except sadness that it had happened at all.

She had also felt that at one time that her older sister Nicole had blamed her for her mother's death, simply because they had never really been close at all as sisters go. At one stage when they were growing up Nicole had bullied her, but when she had reached her teens she had seemed to change a little towards her. Maybe it was because she had matured and realised it was not her fault at all, but where as she lost out with Nicole, she had gained both a friend and a sister with Francesca.

She was glad that she had decided to go out, and hoped that she had been wrong about the flowers and they had been delivered to her by mistake, but deep down she did not think so somehow.

Chapter 4

Jennifer looked at herself in the long bedroom mirror. Not bad she thought to herself, and the dress looked lovely too. It was a good choice, and she looked more like the Jennifer pre David.

There had been no more strange incidences since the flowers and the phone call, and Jennifer was beginning to think that maybe the flowers had been a mistake like Francesca had said, although it was odd because the flowers that her friend had brought into her were certainly not dead ones. Could she have imagined it all? She did not know, except that it was probably the chat rooms and Prince of Mystery whoever he was, that had been freaking her out.

She had had a reply from Luke too. Not too pushy, just to give a few more details about himself. It turned out his profession was in medicine and he was a male nurse. He told her that he always wanted to become a doctor except he did not pass the grades he needed because he was not clever enough. When Jennifer had remarked how foreign he looked, he just emailed back and told her it was in his genes from way back. Most probably his great grandfather who had been Spanish, which made sense although Jennifer would have thought parents not great grandparents, but what did she know. He seemed nice anyhow. They had been chatting through emails almost every day, sometimes twice or three times a day for a week when Luke asked for her mobile phone number. By this time Jennifer thought that there would be no real harm in giving it to him, after all he still did not have her address or her real name.

Francesca had changed their meeting time for their celebration to the evening. At first they were meant to have met up around lunchtime and spend the day together, just like old times and maybe doing a spot of shopping. She had told her that she was seeing Paul for a few hours in the afternoon, and asked if she minded. Reluctantly Jennifer had agreed and told her that she did not mind, not really. After all she could not say otherwise could she? Jennifer had booked a meal in a restaurant just outside Hanley for around seven pm and Francesca said she could pick her up, but they both thought it might be better if they caught a bus and then shared a taxi home. That way they could maybe go to a club after and have a drink.

Francesca had her own little car and had been driving since she was eighteen. It had been something that Jennifer was meaning to do, to get herself a car. She had passed her driving test just before she had met David and always meant to got a little mini when she had enough money saved. She had also liked the look of the new Volkswagen Beetle and fancied one in red. But then she had met and married David and he had told her that he had thought it was pointless having two cars, and she had agreed, especially since there was a good bus service nearby, and even where she lived now the buses ran regular as clockwork.

She looked at the clock, still ten more minutes before she needed to go out to meet Francesca. She applied a little more eye makeup and put on some lipstick. It was a new berry shade that she thought she would experiment with and then she ruffled up her hair with her fingers to give it a little more body.

She was feeling quite pleased with herself as she slipped into her shoes that had classy silver high heels and then put on her short black Karen Millen jacket which just complimented everything she wore. It had cost her an arm and a leg when she'd bought it over a year ago, and she had only ever worn it once before. One final check through the mirror and she thought, 'perfect!' which she said out loud to herself. Then after she had checked that she had her purse, keys and her mobile phone and most importantly Francesca's birthday present she let herself out of the apartment closing the door behind her. She would make the most of tonight. It felt really good to be going out with her friend, and she intended to have a good time and let her hair down, she deserved it.

Francesca was waiting outside the restaurant when she got there and waved as Jennifer approached.

'Hello birthday girl good to see you. How was your week?' she said giving her a big hug.

'Good to see you too Fran, my week was good, and there were no more funny things happening so far thank goodness' she replied, and then they went inside to wait to be seated. They were shown by the waiter to a table for two by the window. It was a pleasant restaurant that they had both been to many times before. A little upmarket but not too snobby, and the staff were always nice and friendly.

'Love your dress Jen, it really suits you' Fran told her as Jennifer took off her jacket and put her bag under the table

'Thank you! Glad you like it, I bought it last

week, especially for this night. I decided that I needed a treat, especially since last week and the mysterious flowers.'

'Yes that was a bit strange wasn't it, but if nothing else has happened since it must have been just something or nothing. They were probably delivered to the wrong address, duck. That's what I think happened anyhow, just a coincidence, they do happen' Fran told her picking up the menu to read.

'I know that Fran. It was just a bit scary seeing them and the card with the name Katie on it. It gave me the creeps. Now enough of that, what about you? Have you anything to tell me regarding Paul?' she asked with a smile prompting a reply.

Francesca put the menu down and shook her head and sighed deeply.

'No nothing at all. Do you know Jen I was almost certain he was going to pop the question to me. I just can't understand it, all the signs were there, or rather I thought they were, but nothing!' She picked the menu up again and began reading it.

'Oh right, I suppose you were disappointed then Fran. Can I ask why you thought he was going to ask anyhow?'

'Well it was about a week before when I mentioned that I usually celebrated my birthday with you and you should have seen his face Jen. He looked really sneeped, and said that he had booked a table for a special surprise. Well I just thought by surprise he might mean....you know? Anyhow I was wrong' she told her.

'Oh I see, but Fran he might have meant by the special surprise the booked table for your birthday.'

'I know that now don't I, but it wasn't just that

Jen, we seemed to be closer than we had ever been these last few weeks, and he was also talking about us moving in together. I just put two and two together and made six, which was silly of me.'

Jennifer nodded to her friend in agreement and looked at the menu to see what there was.

'Do you really feel he is the one for you though? I mean you have not really known each other that long have you, what is it six months or less?'

'That's just it, I do really love him, and it's actually been a bit longer than that more like eight months. I think I will order the beef' Francesca told her deciding.

'I did not think it was that long Fran, in fact I thought it was less than six months myself. I think I will have the beef stroganoff too, it sounds quite nice....are you having a starter? We could share one if you prefer, what do you fancy?' Jennifer asked putting the menu down.

'I think I fancy a prawn cocktail' she decided, as the waiter came back to take their orders. They also ordered a bottle of the red house wine.

'For starters' Jennifer laughed and then her mobile started to buzz to let her know a message had come through, she took it out of her bag to check who it was from, as Francesca looked on inquisitively.

'Who is it Jen?'

Jennifer smiled when she saw it was from Luke but just put it back into her bag.

'It's just someone I have got to know' she told her.

But Francesca was not letting it go. 'Come on Jen spill! Tell you what, you aren't half a dark horse. Is it someone from work? Are you dating someone? Someone you haven't told me about,' she continued in a teasing manner.

'No nothing like that. OK I will tell you. I made a profile up on a dating web site and this guy.......'

But before she could finish Francesca looked at her like she had grown two heads or something.

'Jen I really don't believe you.....a dating website! I mean and after the things that have happened.'

'It's nothing like you think Fran, besides I have been careful, I only gave him my mobile number recently. It's not like he knows where I live or anything.'

Francesca shrugged and put her hand on Jens.

'Just be careful, that's all I can say, I just worry about you.' Then the waiter brought them the bottle of red wine that they had ordered and poured each of them a little in their glasses to taste. Jennifer nodded her approval and he left them.

'Here's to us' Francesca said and poured out more of the wine for both of them. They clinked glasses and then she handed her a small gift bag.

'For you Jen. Just a little something.'

'Thanks Fran I have yours here too.' she told her taking it out of her bag.

Jennifer looked inside the gift bag and took out the little box which held a pair of lovely diamanté earrings.

'They are really beautiful...thank you, and look they match my outfit too' Jennifer told her, holding them up for her to see. In fact she decided to take off the ones she was wearing and put the new ones on. Jennifer had bought Francesca a Pandora charm for her bracelet, one that looked like a bouquet of flowers that read happy birthday on it. She knew that her friend was a great fan of Pandora and as she suspected she was over the moon with the gift. She was wearing her bracelet at the dinner and so took it off to put the charm on. She smiled as she held out her wrist for her to see and showed her another charm. It was in the shape of a heart.

'This one's from Paul' she told her, and Jennifer smiled back and took a sip of her wine.

They ate the starters first and had another glass of the red wine and no more was said about Luke. Instead they talked about old times, ex boyfriends, and work.

'I really do need a holiday. Work has been so stressful these last few weeks, and Mr Stone is a pain up the bum' Jennifer told her finishing off her prawn cocktail.

'I know what you mean....maybe you should just take a week off if you have holidays due and go and see your grandparents in France. Where are they, Agay?'

'That's an idea, but Nicole is still there. I don't want to put them to too much trouble and besides I have not spoken to them for quite a few months. I got fed up of them asking me about David and if I am OK' she told her then continued

'Don't get me wrong. I love them both dearly and I know that they only ever have my best interests at heart. But I find it's hard for me when they mention David. I know they liked him and hoped we would have been very happy together.'

'I wish my grandparents lived in France instead of Manchester. I would be there in a flash....just

43

think of all that sunshine. I really think you should consider going to visit' she said taking a long sip of her wine. 'If I hadn't got Paul I would offer to go with you' she told her cheekily.

'How are your grandparents anyhow?' Jennifer asked

Francesca looked into her glass of wine with a sad expression on her face.

'My granddad is not doing so well actually. He has diabetes and a few other things wrong with him. They both had to move into a warden controlled flat a few months ago. Granny does her best to cope with him, bless her, but according to my dad she looks and sounds shattered most of the time. They have a nurse who comes in once a week to give him injections and other stuff, and I think they have meals brought in too, but they don't cope so well or so I hear. I really should go down to visit I know. Well I went a month ago with my dad it was awful seeing him like that, he can hardly walk now either. Old age hey? Best do what you can and when you can.'

Jennifer looked on sympathetically agreeing with her friend.

'I suppose I am lucky with mine. They are both in their early nineties but still quite independent and active. I think granddad still goes for his long walks. They have a dog that he takes out every morning before breakfast. I probably should ring them. They sent me a lovely birthday card with a cheque inside and so did my dad. I got nothing from Nicole though, not even a birthday card. Mind you I wasn't surprised really because she never did send me one, so I am not missing anything.'

'When did you last speak to her?'

'To be very truthful I forget, but it's got to be at least a few years easily.'

Francesca looked amazed.

'A few years? You never did get on with your sister though did you? I remember how she used to be with you when you were little, like you were a burden or something she would prefer not to have. She hung around with those older girls, and you used to ask to go with her, but she would not want you around her.'

Jennifer sighed deeply and agreed, wishing this had not been the case, but there was no love lost between her and her sister.

Then the waiter appeared again with their main courses. They ate almost in silence and both of them finished at the same time.

'That was delicious Jen. Glad I ordered the beef' Francesca told her wiping her mouth on the napkin.

'Yes me too...this is a nice place,' she said looking around. 'And the staff are really pleasant, don't you think? Do you want to order a desert or coffee or shall we just get the bill and go and find a nice club somewhere?'

'Oh I think we will just go, I don't know about you but I feel stuffed. We will just divide the bill and go I think' Francesca replied rubbing her stomach and Jennifer nodded and got out her purse.

The club they decided to go to was heaving, probably because it was a Saturday night. Jennifer tried to remember the last time she had been there, it had got to be before she had met David because he had hated clubs with a vengeance. With David her life had changed completely, and at the time she had thought for the better. She never missed going out dancing then, all she wanted was to be his wife and one day have his children.

'It's buzzing in here, just like old times, what do you want to drink?' Francesca asked as they both headed for the bar.

'Think I will have a Prosecco what about you? I will get these Fran.' Jennifer caught the eye of one of the barman, but he held up his finger and mouthed to her one minute.

'It's pretty lively in here and the music is good. I am enjoying tonight so far, how about we get our drinks and sit over there until the dancing gets underway?' she told her friend who nodded in agreement and then turned to talk to a girl that Jennifer did not recognise. It must be a work mate or somebody she thought to herself looking around. They headed for the table and were both laughing and joking when Jennifer came back with the drinks and handed Francesca hers.

'Jen this is Lucy a friend of a friend of mine from way back' she said and the girl with the short cropped bleached hair and tattoo smiled at her, then she got up and was gone into the crowds.

By the time they had finished their drink Jennifer was beginning to feel a bit tipsy but good. The night was still early and they were both enjoying the music and dancing and a couple of guys came over to ask if they wanted another drink to which Francesca told them no, they were waiting for someone. They bigger guy of the two shrugged and after glancing a half smile at Jennifer moved on.

'Why did you say we were waiting for

someone?' she asked trying to make herself heard over the boom of the music.

'Because I did not like the look of them, besides I may as well tell you while you were getting the drinks Paul sent me a text and said he may call in later.'

'But Jen, this is our night remember, and where does that leave me, I mean I don't want to be a wall flower' she said as she was beginning to feel annoyed

'Calm down Jen if he comes it won't be for another few hours or so. Besides he can give us a lift home. It's not like I am planning to leave with him or something....chill out' she explained, but Jennifer did not see it that way, and thought her friend could be a bit insensitive at times. It was their celebration that had been put on hold for a week and she thought the least she could do was spend all the evening with her. Anyhow she was not going to let it bother her and decided to go to the ladies and touch up her makeup. Just because Francesca refused a drink from a guy did not mean she had to. She was here to enjoy herself and that was what she would do.

When she came back Francesca had another drink waiting for them both and had a sorry look on her face.

'I am sorry Fran, look I will text Paul back and tell him not to come if you like' she said.

But that only made Jennifer feel bad for objecting so she smiled back and said it was fine. They finished their drinks and danced some more and then the girl with the short-cropped bleached hair appeared again and asked Jennifer if they were having a good time. This time she was with a tall stocky guy with a beard. Jennifer nodded but the music was beating out so loudly she could hardly hear herself speak never mind them, and when she turned back around again she could not see Francesca at all. They all went to sit down in the corner, and Lucy asked Jennifer what she had been drinking and if she would like another one, and before she could answer no the stocky guy went to fetch her one.

'Nice dress' she told her, looking her over admiringly.

'Thank you, Lucy, isn't it? Francesca said you were a friend of a friend.'

'You could say that. Yes I know her boyfriend or rather Billy here does' she answered smiling up at the big stocky guy who winked back at her.

'Oh right....I see, I wonder where my friend's got to?' she asked scouting the room to see if she could see her.

'I think she popped out to the toilets' Lucy told her.

'Do you live near Fran?' she suddenly asked.

'Not that near, maybe a few miles away that's all.'

Jennifer took another sip of the drink they had bought for her, thanking them again. The girl seemed nice, but there was something about her and the guy that made Jennifer feel uncomfortable. Maybe the way the guy kept whispering in her ear every now and again, or perhaps it was because it made Jennifer feel a little jealous that she had no one that did that to her.

'I think I had better go and find my friend' she

told her, but when she stood up the room seemed to swim in front of her, that she had to sit back down again.

'You OK duck?' Lucy asked putting a arm around her.

'I don't know just felt a little bit lightheaded then' she replied taking another sip of the drink they had brought her.

It suddenly felt very hot and stifling in the club and if the place had been heaving before it seemed ten times worse now. Maybe she had just had too much to drink. Jennifer looked around for Francesca again willing her to appear. She could not understand where she had got too. She could hear Lucy speaking and then there was the stocky guy that appeared to be saying something to her and smiling, but it all sounded as if they were both speaking underwater or something. It felt strange and it was beginning to turn into some kind of nightmare, with the beat of the music and different faces that kept appearing then disappearing in front of her. Some she seemed to recognise and others were strangers, and then she thought she heard Francesca's voice before blackness overcame her.

Chapter 5

Jennifer stirred and for one fleeting moment did not know where she was. When she opened her eyes everywhere was in darkness, and at first she thought she was dreaming. Her head hurt and felt heavy and all she wanted to do was go back to sleep again. She wondered what the time was but did not have the energy to even look, her eyelids felt so heavy that she closed them. She must have drifted off again because the next thing she remembered was looking at the alarm clock besides her bed and the red luminous dial. She was back in her apartment and the time read eight am.

She sat bolt upright and shook her head. She could remember going out to meet Francesca last night, them both eating a meal together and going to a club. She could remember dancing and having a few drinks but that was all. She could not remember coming back home, or getting into bed. In fact looking at herself she still had the black dress on she had worn the previous night, minus the jacket. How strange she thought, why could she not remember? She struggled to get up and looked around for her bag, which she eventually found on a chair in the living room along with her jacket and bag. She needed to ring Francesca and ask her what had happened and how she had got home, so took her mobile out of her bag, feeling relieved that it was still there and she had not lost it. Three missed calls from an anonymous number and a few text messages from her friend. She frowned as she read all the messages in order.

'Hi Jen where are you?'

'Jen pick up.'

'Jen I have got to go, call me when you get home.'

She decided she needed to ring Francesca and find out what had happened, because she didn't have a clue and was starting to feel worried. She found her number in contacts and pressed dial, and it just seemed to ring out and then the phone went dead. Looking at the battery content it looked like the phone needed charging and had run out of battery power. She would try again later, but for now she needed to take a shower. She stank of stale alcohol and cigarettes, and she hurt like mad. She felt like she had been through the mill and back.

Why couldn't she remember how she got home, unless Francesca and her boyfriend had brought her, but she did not think so somehow, because of the messages that her friend had left. She tried her best to think but her head was hurting so much, it all seemed like a haze. She plugged her mobile in to charge and dragged herself to the bathroom where she took a shower.

The warmth of the water felt good washing over her aching body, and she started to relax a little, until she saw the big bruises on the top of her thighs.

'MY GOODNESS' she shouted to herself, and grabbed a towel, 'what the hell has happened to me?'

Jennifer got out of the shower and put on her bathrobe. She decided to try Francesca's mobile on her landline, but there was still no answer. She needed to know one way or another how she had got home. She felt sick inside and just hoped that whatever had happened it had been her friend that had brought her home and not some stranger. It just did not bear thinking about. She tried in vain to re-run the events of the previous night in her mind, but all she could remember was going to the club and having a drink and both of them dancing, everything else was vague. Just as she was about to try Francesca again, the phone rang and she picked it up, expecting to hear her friend on the other end that was returning her call.

'Fran.....' she began then froze when all she could hear was the same eerie silence as before.

'WHO IS THIS?' she shouted down the phone. But whoever it was just remained silent until after a minute Jennifer heard the click of the receiver being replaced. She felt sick and shaky and just did not know what to think. How on earth had she got home? She just did not remember at all, she must have knocked back some drink in the club for this to happen, and she knew she needed to get hold of Francesca to find out.

Nearly all morning she kept trying her number, but to no avail. Wherever Francesca was she was not answering her mobile. Maybe there was a simple explanation in all of this she thought, maybe her friends mobile had also ran out of charge, and she had not bothered to charge it back up yet. She might even be spending the day with Paul. She needed to stay calm, it would all be explained, she thought when she eventually got hold of her friend. But how could the bruises on the top of her thighs be explained? She could not remember falling down. There were also a few bruises on her wrists, like she had been held and had struggled. She shivered as she touched them then she decided to log onto her computer. She would type an email to Luke to take her mind off things.

After she had written it she pressed send and went to make herself a cup of coffee and a piece of toast. If she had not heard from Fran by the morning she decided that she would call at her house to see her after work. She knew that she still lived at home with her parents, but no longer had their landline number. It was strange really, Francesca had initially moved out of her parent's house at almost the same time that Jennifer had met David. She had found herself a flat which she decided to share with another girl, not far from where she worked in a printing firm which had been handy. Then when she lost her job it had been almost impossible to keep up with her share of the rent, and so she had had no other choice but to move back home again, and there she had stayed.

Jennifer took a sip of her coffee and a bite of her toast and went back to her computer to see if Luke had answered her message. There were three messages in her inbox. Two of them were from guys that had viewed her profile from the dating website, that she had set up and there was one that clearly said that the email she had just sent was being returned because the address was not recognised.

Strange, she thought to herself, ignoring the other two emails she went back to the message she had sent to Luke in her sent box, and then resent it. Maybe it just had not sent right the first time she told herself, but after about five minutes or so it came back again that there was an error and that it could not be sent to the email address she had tried to send it to.

With shaking hands she went onto the dating website to try and find Luke's profile. She could easily check his email address from there....problem solved, or so she thought but she just could not find his profile at all, no matter how much she looked. It seemed to have vanished completely. Nothing made sense. Why would Luke suddenly take down his profile on the dating website? Unless he did not want any more emails from anyone else, maybe that was it. After all they had both been exchanging emails regularly and in fact she had also given him her mobile number. Maybe that was the reason he had taken his profile down, but that would not explain why her email to him had been undelivered. She decided to get her mobile and check his mobile number. She could always send him a text message and ask him why he had removed his profile and ask him to text her his email address to her again. She remembered that he had sent her a message while she had been in the restaurant with Francesca, just a simple one that had read 'this is my number no excuse now for not texting.'

Yet there was no message from him in her inbox, neither were there any messages in her trash box. In fact there were no messages at all except for the messages her friend Francesca had sent the previous night. Could she have imagined the message on her phone? She felt like she was losing her mind. How could this be? Had she imagined Luke? It was like he had never existed. Something just did not feel right, she knew that but did not know what. All these silent phone calls, the dead flowers that she had found the week before, and the fact that when Francesca had arrived at Jennifer's apartment they had been swapped, and the card that she had seen along with the dead flowers with the name KATIE had completely vanished too. She now had no evidence of Luke ever having existed. With trembling hands she rang her friends mobile again. This time after a few rings the phone turned onto the answerphone and she was able to leave a message. Thank God, she thought as she spoke into the phone.

'Fran it's me Jen can you give me a call when you get this. Please I need to speak with you urgently, its about last night.' Then she rang off.

Jennifer got dressed and decided she would ring her grandparents in France. She needed to thank them for her birthday card and cheque. She had meant to do it a few days ago, but had forgotten.

'Hello Grandpa it's Jenny here.'

'Ah Jenny mon amour.....How are you? Did your birthday go well?' he asked pleased to hear her voice.

'Yes grandpa it went well, and thank you so much for the card and money. I am sorry I did not ring before now.'

'Ah it not matter, so long as you got money from me and your nan. You can buy something nice.'

'I will and how is nan?'

'She is here and waiting to talk to you....look after yourself and come when you can to see OK' he told her handing the phone over to his wife.

'Hello Jenny, how are you love?' she asked.

Maryanne Beaumont had never lost her English accent even though she had lived in France for a long time.

'I am fine, still working away at the solicitors, and living in the apartment' she told her.

'But how are you really love, I mean it can't have been easy when you spit with David...sad in fact' she continued and Jennifer rolled her eyes.

'I am fine, I promise' she continued.

'You will have to come to France and you can to stay with us, your grandpa would love that. Do you think you can get time off?' she asked.

'I would love to, but don't you have enough with Nicole being there I mean .....?'

'Nicole? Nicole is not here love, she has not been here for months.'

'Oh right! That's strange, dad told me Nicole was staying with you. Maybe he had got it wrong. Oh well perhaps I will book a few weeks off work, I will let you know OK, but before I go how are you?'

'As fit as a fiddle. We go walking every day me and your Grandpa, and we swim in the pool and your grandpa has his cycling.'

Jennifer smiled as her grandfather was at least 92 and she thought that her grandmother must be at least 90. It was incredible how active they still were. She thought it had got to do with the healthy lifestyle that they led in France, all that walking and cycling had to be good for you. Plus the sunshine, and she suddenly yearned for sand sun and sitting around their pool in the magnificent villa they lived in. It would be lovely to fly out to see them even for just a short while. Agay was a lovely place in the South of France, and this time of the year would usually be hot. She would try and book some time off from her work, because she was owed some. She promised to let them know a week or two before she went then ended the call.

Jennifer felt much better having spoken with her grandparents; now all she needed to do was speak to her friend. She thought of ringing her dad and asking about Nicole, but decided not to. It had been strange that her father had said that her sister was staying with them; maybe he had got it wrong. Anyhow she and Nicole had never been close which was a shame, it would have been lovely to have a sister that she discussed things with as they had grown up, but that had never been the case.

It was after four pm when her mobile rang and Jennifer was relieved to hear Francesca on the other end.

'Fran, I am so glad to hear your voice' she told her

'Jen, what's wrong? Are you OK duck?' she asked sounding cheerful.

'No Jen I really need to ask you something, it's about last night?'

'Right well I could ask you the same thing. I mean you are a dark horse.'

'Dark horse...what do you mean dark horse?'

'Going off like that' Francesca continued

'But that's just it Fran I can't remember what happened, I can't remember how I got home. It's obvious I did, but I have not got a clue how....really I don't .'

'You can't remember Jen!! How much did you

drink last night? 'she tutted.

'Drink! Well I only drank as much as you did. Do you know what happened last night?'

'Jen as far as I remember we were having a good time dancing and then I nipped out to the toilet, and when I came back, I got sidetracked because some girls from my work were talking to me, but I saw you talking to this guy at the other side of the room, so thought you were OK.'

'What guy? I really can't remember at all.' Jennifer told her anxiously.

'To be honest Jen I had never seen him before, but you seemed happy enough, you were both laughing together like you were old friends or something, and when I eventually got away from the girls from work I came to look for you, but you had disappeared.'

'Good grief Fran don't say I went home with some stranger that I can't remember. You are scaring me now'

'I am sorry duck I really am but I thought you must know the guy.'

'That's another thing I want to ask you, do you remember me talking about a guy named Luke, while we were in the restaurant?'

'Luke yes why do you ask?'

'Oh thank goodness and do you remember me telling you the text message that had come through was from him?'

'Yes of course, and I told you to be careful.'

'Yes you did, but guess what, his text message is no longer on my phone, and I sent him an email that was returned to me, and another strange thing is that his profile is no longer on the dating website.

I just do not understand it' Jennifer explained.

Francesca sighed deeply.

'I told you that you had to be careful didn't I Jen, you just don't know who you are speaking to, or giving out information to.'

'That's just it I only ever gave him my mobile number.'

'Well you say that, but it's easy to let something slip.'

'I didn't though Fran, in fact I didn't even speak to him on the phone. It was his first text message to me. I really don't know what's happening to me, but I don't like it at all.'

'Did you get my text messages from last night Jen? I would not have left you I promise but Paul came for me, and Lucy said she thought you had left with that guy and ....'

'Speaking of Lucy who is she Fran? I know you said a friend of a friend, but how do you know her really? Do you think she will know what happened to me?' Jennifer asked feeling worried. She vaguely remembered Lucy now, and speaking to her, then everything else was a blur.

'I really don't know. Like I said she is a friend of Paul's or rather her boyfriend is. I shouldn't think she would know what happened to you more than I do. Do you really have no idea how you got home?'

'No honestly. I was at the club and then the next thing I know is I wake up in my bed in the apartment.'

Francesca went suddenly quiet.

'Jen you were not undressed were you? I mean no one....'

'No I was still wearing my black dress I wore the

night before, but I really have no idea how I got into bed, but another strange thing is I have some bruises I only noticed when I got into the shower.'

Francesca gasped.

'Bruises? You have some bruises....where Jen, where are the bruises?'

'On the top of my thighs and on both wrists. Fran I am frightened now, I really am' she told her friend starting to sob.

'Oh duck maybe you should not have had a shower. I mean I think you should go to the police, I really think you should report this' she continued which made Jennifer cry even more.

'Promise me Jen you will report this?'

'That's just it though I don't know anything, what will I say to them? Only I was out in a Club and the next I know I am back home in my own bed?'

'But the bruises! I mean if there were no bruises then I would just say you must have had far too much to drink and that's it, but if you have bruises, how do you know you were not raped? I think you need to report it.'

Jennifer had not really thought that rape had been a possibility, simply because she had woken up with her clothes still on, but thinking about it her friend had a point, and she felt sick to the stomach at the very thought of it.

When she had finished speaking to her friend on her mobile, she immediately picked the phone up again and phoned the police to tell them what had happened to her. Francesca was right she needed to report it, and should have done so first thing that morning even before having a shower.

Chapter 6

After speaking with the police she decided that she would rather go down to the station instead of them having to send someone out to see her. She had briefly told them what had happened, and the police officer she was speaking to advised her to bring whatever she was wearing last night with her. She explained that she had had a shower without thinking but they did not comment apart from telling her to bring the clothes she was wearing the previous night with her. So after she put the phone down she rang Francesca back. She offered to go with her, but Jennifer thought it might be better if she went herself.

'Well OK if you are sure Jen, but promise you will let me know what happens the moment you get back home again' she told her.

'I will Fran, I just feel a bit nervous about the whole thing you know. If only I could remember, but you are right. I have to report it don't I because of the bruises, and first thing tomorrow maybe I should consider getting the locks changed to my apartment.'

There was a sharp intake of breath from Francesca.

'Yes definitely!' she replied, and after asking again if she wanted was sure she would be OK they ended the call.

The nearest police station was in a town a few miles away called Longton, but since Jennifer had spoken to someone from another branch, she decided to go there. She felt nervous as she walked through the door carrying her clothes in a carrier bag. It looked quite empty as she approached the main desk to give the desk Sargent her name.

'One moment please' the guy told her, and asked her to take a seat while he fetched someone.

Jennifer sat down and looked around the small waiting room, with its magnolia walls that looked like they needed a splash of fresh paint. There were posters on the walls here and there, some about the dangers of drink driving. One poster was about domestic violence and how you could report it anonymously. There was a crime report number underneath.

Jennifer must have been waiting for fifteen minutes when a young woman police officer came into the waiting room followed by an older man.

'Hello Miss Sudbury is it? Would you like to follow us please' the older man told her and the policewoman just smiled and held the door open for her.

They led her into a separate room that had written on the door Interview Room 2. The older man who looked somewhere in his late thirties held a chair out and beckoned for her to sit down. The young Policewoman remained standing, while the man sat down behind a table opposite her. Jennifer thought initially he looked miserable but then when they were seated he smiled the most amazing smile, or so Jennifer had thought. He had with him some papers and a note pad and pen. She looked at the name badge on the front his shirt but before she could read it, he introduced himself.

'I am DC Alex McKenna, and this is Police Constable Sofia Rayner,' he said with a gesture of his hand, and the policewoman smiled putting Jennifer at ease.

'Now before we continue I want to ask you if you wish to make a formal complaint. I will take a detailed statement about everything that happened when was it last night? But I have to tell you that it will be your choice if we take the report any further, but you do need to do so as early as possible to facilitate the investigation process' he told her.

To which Jennifer nodded that she understood, and did wish to make a formal complaint. She felt she needed to get to the bottom of what had happened to her, one way or another. He asked her to confirm her name, address and date of birth before he started the interview.

'So Ms Sudbury you went out for a belated birthday meal with a friend of yours. Can you give me your friend's name and address please' he asked her, pen in hand ready to write.

'Francesca Davis, 33 Freeman Street. She lives with her parents' she told him and he wrote it down.

'Where was the restaurant exactly and what time did you both leave?' was his next question and Jennifer explained what had happened in the restaurant. She also thought about the text message she had got from Luke, and whether to mention it or not, but at this stage did not think it was irrelevant so did not say anything.

'Did you meet anyone else while you were in the restaurant?' he continued 'or did anything strange or unusual happen.'

To which Jennifer answered no.

'Now the club you went to afterwards where was

it, and what time did you arrive?

Jennifer told him the name of the club and where it was situated and what time to her knowledge they had arrived there, to which he nodded and smiled to the policewoman who was still standing and said yes they knew of the club she was talking about. He wrote all the details down and then when she told him about the bruises at the top of her thighs and showed him her wrists, he frowned.

'I was coming to that Ms Sudbury, we think it would be be your best interest if you would agree to be examined by one of our female nurses. Would you agree to that?'

Jennifer felt suddenly tearful and the policewoman noticed and nodded to her gently.

'OK but I did shower as I told the policeman over the phone, but I have brought the clothes I wore last night with me' she told DC McKenna handing him the bag which contained her dress, underwear and shoes. He in turn handed them to policewoman Rayner, and got back to asking more questions which he promptly wrote down. After he had written out the statement, he got Jennifer to sign it and then stood up and was just going to ask the policewoman to take Jennifer along to see the nurse when Jennifer felt she needed to tell him about the flowers she had found the previous week, also about the mysterious phone calls she had been having. She knew if she was going to make a formal complaint she needed to tell them everything and so she did, while DC McKenna looked on with a serious expression when she told him about the dating website and her user name of Katie.

'I see' he said making an amendment to the statement, and signing his name to say he had done it.

'OK PC Rayner will take you down to see a nurse now' he smiled at her with his kind grey eyes that seem to sparkle, and for some reason she felt herself blush.

The nurse that she saw was really nice. She was around fifty and had a kind face. She asked Jennifer about her medical and also sexual history and wrote what she said down in her report. She also told her that she needed to examine her and run some tests, but she could opt out anytime she wanted. The Nurse then asked her to change into a paper gown and left her for a few minutes while she did. She used some cotton swabs to collect any potential DNA, and then asked if she could take a blood and urine sample. When Jennifer asked what it could show, she replied that because Jennifer had passed out at some stage of the night the blood and urine sample would prove whether or not any date rape or other drugs were used and whether she might have been the victim of sexual assault. She also looked at her fingernails but they looked perfectly fine and still manicured. Then she asked if she could collect another swab from the inside of Jennifer's cheek, this was so the lab could differentiate Jennifer's DNA from that and any other she might find. She then checked all the bruises, being careful to photograph and file her report. Lastly she examined her internally and checked for any tender spots, taking a few more swabs to test for semen.

After she had finished the examination, the

Nurse told her that she could then get dressed again. Then she sat Jennifer back down and told her if she wanted to she could receive emergency contraceptive or medication to prevent a number of sexually transmitted diseases. She also asked her if she would like to see a counselor, to which Jennifer nodded that she was OK

It took a fairly long time and she was relieved when it was all over. All she wanted to do was go home, and maybe phone her friend. Her head was banging again. Before she left the station DC McKenna had another brief word with her and handed her a card with his name and number on it, which Jennifer put into her bag. He also told her that he or someone else would get in touch during the course of the following week, and he strongly advised her to change her locks, which she agreed she would do. He told her not to hesitate to get back in touch at any time, if she remembered anything else, or if anything else unusual or sinister happened and she said that she would. He then shook her hand and she left the station.

It was a lovely evening for walking, but all Jennifer could think about was getting home and putting her lock on the door. Tomorrow she would phone a locksmith up and get the lock changed. She planned to phone into work sick so that could be done. She did not want anyone knowing what had happened so she would just say she had a stomach bug or something and that she would be in the following day. Her priority was to get the locks changed, she knew that.

When she got home and let herself into the

communal hall she was greeted by her neighbours sleazy look. He was doing something or nothing to his door, but she was in no mood for him so just gave him a dirty look as she passed him. He mumbled something obscene that Jennifer did not quite catch as she opened her apartment door and she quickly went inside and she bolted the door. It was only then the ordeal she had been through fully hit her, and she burst into tears.

'Fran it's Jen, just to let you know I have been to the Police station and made a statement. I had to have an examination and they did all kind of tests on me. They asked for your name and address and so I gave it to them, hope you don't mind....oh and I told them about the flowers and the silent phone calls, anyhow just to let you know.'

Then she put the phone down, and after only a short time it began to ring and she was pleased to hear that Francesca had returned her call.

'Hi Jen sorry I missed your call. What do they think might have happened to you?' she asked sounding concerned.

'That's why they did all the tests to find out. I don't think I will know anything until everything comes back from their lab. They took all kinds of swabs and stuff, I thought the nurse was never going to finish.'

'Have you remembered anything else since?. I mean I mentioned it to Paul and he thought it was strange too' she told her.

'No! Not a thing. I was wondering does your Paul know Lucy's address by any chance and also the guy she was with?'

There was a long pause and a few mumbled

words in the background before Francesca replied and Jennifer thought she had got cut off at first, but in fact she had been covering the phone with her hand and speaking to her boyfriend.

'Paul says he does not know where they live Jen. He also says its best if he stays out of it all as well since he was only there to give me a lift.'

'Oh...right! And what about you Fran? I did give them your address.'

'Look duck it's not that I don't want to help you, but I don't see what I can tell them. Anyhow, it's not like I saw you go off with that guy or something is it' she told her.

'But Fran I thought you were my friend! If the shoe was on the other foot I would be there for you.'

'I don't think that's fair of you Jennifer. I am just saying I don't know a thing, and to be honest with you neither would Lucy, and Paul certainly doesn't.'

'Oh thanks a bunch Francesca, it was you that thought I should report it and now you don't want to get involved.....thanks a bunch!'

'Don't be like that, I tried to warn you about messing around on the internet in those blooming chat rooms or whatever you call them didn't I? You must have given out more information than you are saying, that's all, but you were always a soft touch.'

'Fran what are you saying? That everything that's happened to me is my fault? That the flowers and the silent phone calls were also my fault?'

'No I am not saying that, but you must admit it's all a bit strange. The flowers I brought up were certainly not dead, and neither was there a card with the name Katie on them, and then we go out last night and you disappear and conveniently can't remember what happened that's all I am saying!'

'Are you saying that I imagined those flowers were dead now, and I imagined that there was a card with the name Katie on them too. I don't believe you! And I thought you were my friend.'

'Look all I am saying is you have been under a lot of stress just lately and then you have been dabbling with all kind of things on the internet. I....'

'No Francesca you look! I have not been dabbling with all kind of things, just a few harmless chats online, where I never once gave any information out, and whether you believe me or not those flowers I found were dead. The flowers you found when you arrived were not the same ones.'

'OK Jennifer if you say so, but I don't really want to get involved OK.'

'Well I am sorry you feel like that but whether you like it or not you are sort of involved, we went to that club together remember?'

'And that's were it ends, you left alone and as far as I know the last time I saw you were having fun with a guy' Francesca told her getting a bit cross, and again Jennifer heard someone in the background talking. She was tempted to just end the call and put the phone down, she was so disappointed in her friends attitude to the whole thing.

'Anyhow I have to go now, Paul and I are going out soon.'

'OK I think I get the message' and this time she did put the phone down. She was so upset with Francesca's attitude that she burst into tears again.

She half wished she had not bothered to go to the police after all. It looked like her friend would not be supporting her in this.

Chapter 7

Jennifer had a terrible night tossing and turning and she dreamt that she was being tied to a chair and all kind of strange faces kept appearing calling her a slut and a whore. Then she saw Francesca in her dream laughing at her and pointing. She woke up in a sweat and turned on the bedside lamp. She looked at the clock, It was only 4am but she needed to get up and make herself a drink which she did.

Francesca had really upset her by saying she did not want to get involved, and tears sprang up into her eyes again. She had known her since she was about five years old and she had classed her as her best friend. It was so out of character of her to be saying these things, maybe it was because of Paul her boyfriend's influence. Also she had not liked the look of that other girl in the club named Lucy and she just vaguely remembered speaking to her and someone else she was with. That was why she had asked her friend for Lucy's address, just in case she knew anything. She shook her head to try and clear the muzzy fog that seemed to have filled it, but try as she did she just could not remember anything else and certainly not how she got home.

She also found it a mystery how Luke's text message had vanished from off her phone as she could not remember deleting it. She only wished he would send another message, that way she would have his mobile number again. But when he had asked her for hers, he had not sent his mobile number by email like she had done, but had instead texted it to her.

Then a thought occurred to her, Luke's emails and her emails to him would still be on her computer in her inbox. Frantically she logged on and went to her email account to see and sure enough they were still there. In fact there must be at least twenty of them. It somehow gave her comfort that she still had them, at least they had not been deleted like the one on her phone and she now had proof that he existed. She decided that she would have another go at trying to find his profile on the dating website, but like before it was nowhere to be found. Jennifer frowned and logged off. She was starting to feel tired again and needed to get some more sleep. She would phone her workplace up tomorrow and tell them she was unable to go in. Then after that she needed to get a good locksmith to change the lock. Then she needed to drop a spare key off with the Estate Agent that dealt with her apartment since the landlord was living abroad.

First thing the following morning Jennifer phoned her workplace and put on a feeble voice telling them she had woken up with a tummy upset, but that she hoped to be in work as usual the following day. She hated to lie but knew that if she had told them that she had been out celebrating over the weekend and could not remember how she had got home it would not look too good. Besides she did not want anyone else knowing. It was bad enough that Francesca was not going to support her in all of this and in fact she was still stinging over her attitude. She would have thought her friend would have stood by her. She had checked her phone to see if Francesca had sent her a text message relenting but was sorely disappointed to see that she hadn't. Oh well, it looked like their friendship was over, which hurt Jennifer more than anything else. She wondered what she would tell the police if they contacted her. She knew that they most probably would since it was Francesca that she had gone out with and she just hoped what she told them would not make her look a fool, but she would not hold her breath about that.

Jennifer managed to get a locksmith to fit another lock. He was an elderly gentleman and he came a few hours later and fitted the new lock in hardly anytime at all. Although it had proved more costly than she had first thought it would, at least he had not asked any awkward questions. In fact he was quiet and got on with his job, and when it was done Jennifer breathed a sigh of relief, because now she felt safe again. Another good thing was that Mr Sleazy her neighbour had not been hanging around the communal hall like he usually did.

It was the middle of the afternoon when Jennifer's landline started to ring. It always made her nervous since she had been receiving the silent phone calls and so she answered it warily. Not a lot of people contacted her that way anymore since they all had her mobile number except maybe her father or grandparents but she had recently spoken to them.

'Hello could I speak to Ms Sudbury please' the polite male voice on the other end of the phone said.

'Speaking' she replied not recognising the voice, but felt glad it was not another silent call.

'Ah Ms Sudbury it's DC McKenna here. Just a

follow up from yesterday to let you know that the various swabs and urine and blood samples have been sent away to the lab for the purpose of a toxicology report to establish levels of alcohol or drugs, and to say all this could take between five to ten days or even longer. In the meantime we will continue our investigation and speak with your friend or anyone else you think could be helpful in our inquiry' he told her, then added 'is there anything else you have remembered that could be helpful to us.'

'I appreciate that, but try as I have everything is still a bit vague to me. I did have the locks changed though, first thing this morning' she told him.

'That's good. In the meantime if you remember anything....anything at all give me a call.'

'I will, can I ask when you will be speaking to my friend Francesca?'

'Someone will go and see her or contact her during the course of this week' he told her.

'Okay thank you.'

'We will be in touch just as soon as we have any news. Thank you and like I say if there is anything you remember, however small, or if anything else happens get in touch.'

'OK and thank you for letting me know.'

When she put the phone down Jennifer made herself some coffee and logged onto her computer to her Facebook account. She just had not got the heart to put anything on. Then she went onto her friend's page to see if she had written anything about Saturday night, but there was nothing at all, only things about the previous week about her and Paul. There were a few photos of where they had been and a lot of likes and comments, which she read. Hang on there was a comment from Lucy the girl with the short-cropped bleached hair saying 'Great to have seen you both, here's to lots a fun next time.'

She decided then to go onto Lucy's page and have a nosy. Lots of photos of her partying but it did not say much about her personally except her name was Lucy Jo, with no surname displayed on her page. It gave her age as twenty-five and single from Stoke on Trent. She half considered adding her as a friend, but decided against it. She logged off her Facebook account and logged into one of the chat rooms. Lots of messages flashed up on the screen but none she recognised, until there he was, Prince of Mystery again. She was just about to log off when a message from him came.

'Hi Katie, where have you been? I have missed you' and although she knew he had freaked her out the last time that they had spoken she was curious and decided to speak to him. She was feeling lonely and still hurting from Francesca's attitude. She could not see what harm it would do, just so long as she did not give any information out.

'Hello Prince of Mystery how are you?' she asked and pressed send. And as before his message came back almost straight away.

'Oh I am fine Katie, all the better now you are here' he told her.

Jennifer smiled to herself, this is more like it. Just harmless conversation, so long as it does not get sleazy or scary it would be fine.

'What's the weather like where you are?' he asked.

Well talking about the weather beats talking sexual or scary any d,ay she thought as she typed out her answer. 'Weather is fine....what about where you are?'

'Oh you know up and down' he replied. She wondered then if he was in the UK, but did not want to ask in case he asked her where she was too. Instead she typed.

'Yes I know what you mean.'

'Katie' he typed back 'would it really upset you if we asked each other questions again?'

Here goes she thought, although he was being polite so she typed back her answer.

'It depends on the questions you ask.'

'It's just that I like to play games sometimes, but don't want to frighten you off. So how about we play a little game, and anytime you want to stop we will' he wrote.

Mhmm Jennifer thought with a big frown, it couldn't do any harm, and besides she was bored.

'OK but just for a short time' she told him.

'Right then my first question is what country would you prefer to live in France or the UK?' he typed.

Jennifer wondered why he should have mentioned France, then shrugged it off and thought it's got to be a coincidence. There was no way he knew that she had grandparents living over there, or that she had spent lots of holidays there too. She quickly decided to type UK, even though France was her favourite country.

'Ah the UK, good choice' he replied. 'Although it's probably because you live in the UK' he continued, but Jennifer was not saying.

'Can I ask another question please? '

'OK go ahead.'

'What is your biggest fear being buried alive, or locked in a dungeon? ' he typed.

Well thinking about it neither she thought to herself. Both sounded horrendous, but she knew that he was expecting her to answer just one. She wondered why he got his kicks from asking all these strange questions and almost asked him, but didn't instead she gave him her answer.

'It would have to be locked in the dungeon. But my answer would be neither' she replied.

'Ah Katie, play the game right please. Which would you prefer and only one answer is allowed.'

Jennifer sighed and wondered where this sick game was going and if she had not been so bored she would have just logged off.

'OK Prince of Mystery my answer is locked in a dungeon' she typed.

'Interesting, interesting, and my next question is would you prefer to be tied up or made unconscious?' he replied?

Well after her ordeal at the weekend she did not want to play the game anymore. She thought it was sick....he must be sick, and he had hit a raw nerve, but instead of just going and logging off she sent him her reply.

'I don't want to play this gave anymore Prince of Mystery whoever you are' she typed sounding braver than she actually felt.

'Tut tut Katie you are not afraid are you?' he typed back.

Jennifer not wanting him to know he had hit a raw nerve told him that she was not afraid, why should she be.

'Good because fear can also be your friend' he replied.

Well that's a funny thing for him to say. How on earth can fear be someone's friend. It just didn't make sense, in fact nothing the guy said made sense at all. Why she had answered any of his questions in the first place she didn't know except she was bored. She decided to ask him to explain how fear could be someone's friend.

'What do you mean explain?' she asked him.

'Well fear can be a great friend to the person that's the perpetrator' he replied.

What kind of answer is that Jennifer thought? If anything it's a sick answer.

'I disagree, and the person that finds that inflicting fear is their friend then they are sick.'

'OK Katie you have a right to your own opinion and I respect that. You have spirit, I like that' he typed back.

'Good because that is exactly what I think.'

'Another question for you which requires just one answer a yes or a no please. Have you ever been so scared you wet yourself?' he wrote.

'No not really, have you?' she replied suddenly deciding to pass the question back.

'Tut tut Katie I am the one asking the questions remember, you are not playing the game right. In fact I bet you have felt fear so great that you did wet yourself.'

'Why do you say that Prince of Mystery?'

'In fact I can almost feel your fear right now. Admit it you are afraid? And I am right about you wetting yourself aren't I Katie?'

His last message was too much that Jennifer decided she had had enough. This guy whoever he was, was really weird. So she logged out of the chat room altogether. What sort of person was he, and his last question had hit a raw nerve.

Her mind went back to when she was around 5 years old just before she had met Francesca. She had been playing hide and seek with a few other children in some deserted buildings. In fact she had not meant to have been there, her father had warned her to keep away from the area. But three older children along with her sister Nicole had gone and this one time Nicole had allowed her to tag along, although she had initially objected. One of the boys who was almost ten had said she could and that it would be fun. When it came to Jennifer's turn to close her eyes and count to twenty, she could not find any of them, until the very last place she saw which was this small dark building. Then that was when it happened, someone locked the door and left her there, until after almost an hour had passed, and poor Jennifer had become so afraid that she wet herself. It was so dark and cold in there and she never did find out who had locked her in or who had in fact let her out again either.

She shuddered at the memory of it, and she cursed herself for ever playing games with Prince of Mystery. She should have learned her lesson from the last time she had spoken to him. He had left her with a bad feeling then. He must be a right sick person to think that fear could be anyone's friend. She knew that there were people that liked inflicting pain and fear on other people, she also knew that that was how some people got there kicks.

She decided that it would be the very last time she spoke to him and in fact she did not think she would log on to the chat rooms again either.

She thought about her grandparents then and how nice it would be to go and visit them. She loved them dearly and loved their little villa in Agay. She could imagine sitting around the pool and relaxing and going for walks down to the beach. Their villa was situated high up and it had a sea view. She had always loved going there, even when she was little. She had such fond memories of the place, and her grandpa and nan were gentle kind people. She had spent most of her school holidays with them and Nicole had gone too. Their dad had been far too busy with work, even more so than now. In fact she hardly saw her dad because he was a workaholic, not that he did not care for them, she knew he did, and she often felt and thought that he favoured her more than her sister Nicole. Maybe it was because she had been the youngest and last one since he had never remarried. She had often fantasised about having a new mother and maybe a new brother or sister, but it was not to be. She was suddenly looking forward to work tomorrow to take her mind off things.

Chapter 8

The following day was a busy one at work for Jennifer. There were a lot of files to type out for Mr Stone, but at least it took her mind of what had happened to her during the weekend. She was just glad she had Lizzie to talk to, because Mr Stone's mood had not improved. She wondered if he was having some kind of problems, because he had not always been this hard to work with. She knew he had a big case coming on dealing with drugs, and he had to represent a client who was also a well-known businessman with plenty of power and money. She knew a little about the case but not everything.

She decided to ask Lizzie if she wanted to go for her lunch break with her, and she gladly accepted.

'It's only sandwiches I'm afraid. I have brought a packed lunch and thought I would eat it in the park around the corner since it's a nice sunny day.'

'Thanks yes, I would like that and I am only having sandwiches too' she replied with a smile. Jennifer thought how easy she was to talk to, and thought about telling her about the weekend, but since she hardly knew her, thought better of it.

'Glad you are feeling better. A stomach bug was it? There's a lot of it going around apparently' she said to Jennifer who nodded sheepishly. She felt bad at carrying on the lie, but did not know Lizzie well enough to trust her completely.

'And what about the funny phone calls you were having, did you do what I suggested and blow a whistle into the phone?' she asked sitting down on a nearby bench in the park and pulling out her sandwich pack of ham and cheese.

'Well not exactly, and besides I am still not sure if they are menace calls or just someone dialing the wrong number' she told her.

'Do you have any children Jennifer? I know you were divorced recently.'

'No we never had any, and I have been divorced for almost nine months now.'

'Hope you don't mind me asking, but were you and your ex husband married long?' she continued.

'No I don't mind you asking and we were married for just three short years, how about you Lizzie?'

'Nothing to tell really. I have never been married at all, but I was in a long-term relationship that lasted seven years. I also have a seven year old son Toby.'

'Oh right and do you live alone with your son?' Jennifer asked

'Pretty much so, but my mother looks after Toby while I am working.' she continued finishing off her sandwich.

'I suppose that's handy.'

'Yes very. Can I ask you if Sudbury is your married name or maiden name?'

'It's my married name, and to be honest I was thinking of dropping it and changing back to my maiden name but I have never got around to doing it yet' she told her.

'What's your maiden name then?'

'It's Beaumont'

'Ah, is that a French name?' she asked.

'Yes that's right my father is half French. I have grandparents in France' she told her.

'I suspect you have plenty of free holidays then, how nice for you.'

'I used to spend lots of time in France when I was a child, during the school holidays. It's quite nice where they live and also not far from the sea' she told her.

'Both of my grandparents are long since dead, in fact I never even knew the ones on my father's side. Still my parents were great and I never wanted for anything' she said finishing off her sandwiches, while Jennifer listened to her. It was good to talk to Lizzie and get to know her, and like she had previously thought she seemed a lovely gentle person.

Before leaving work that afternoon Jennifer decided to see how many holidays she had left, since she had decided that after the investigation she would go over to see her grandparents in France and spend some time with them.

DC McKenna had told her that it could take up to ten days or longer for the lab reports to come back so she decided to book two weeks leave in a months time from now, which would make it the middle of July. Except when she had put her request to Mr Stone, he had said it was too short a notice, so instead she reluctantly had made it for the middle of August.

Back in the police station a few days later DC Alex McKenna looked intently at the file that contained the formal complaint of Ms Sudbury. He had long discussed the case with another colleague

Max and Max had thought that maybe she was not telling the complete truth, but Alex just could not make his mind up. He needed to speak with a few people at the club where Jennifer had gone to first. He briefly knew the new manager there and since he had taken over the place it had a fairly good reputation, better than it had been in the hands of the previous owners. Back in those days they were always getting some complaint or another, but if something was going on, then he would certainly find out. He was an expert in sniffing things out. In fact his nickname was Columbo.

He also had to speak with Ms Sudbury's friend that she had gone to the club with, but it was proving difficult to get in touch with her. He had tried the mobile phone number that Ms Sudbury had given him and even left a message, but she had not got back in touch with him. He would leave it a few more days before going around to her address. He also intended to speak to a few of Jennifer's neighbours to see if they had heard or seen anything unusual that night. In fact he would call around to the apartments later. He had to call into the nursing home first and the apartments were only a short distance away, and so he could kill two birds with one stone so to speak.

Before heading out of the station he decided to grab a quick cup of coffee, his afternoon fix. Not that the coffee was any good in the station, it was more often than not lukewarm, and today was no exception, but it would do. He felt a bit peckish too so finished off his sandwich from the pack he had prepared for himself earlier. He usually could not be bothered and would just grab something in the police canteen when he was not too busy. Occasionally he would prepare something himself and this meant he could sit eating at his desk, and working at the same time, which was what he was doing the time.

He was a confirmed bachelor and lived on his own, although this had not always been the case. Ten years ago he had been in a serious relationship and he had loved her dearly. In fact when she had died he had been heartbroken. Amelia had been his life, although he often thought he should have given her far more time when she had been alive, instead of being the workaholic that he was, and had been then. It was too late to change that now though and neither did he want to. He was one of the best DCs in his field and he was only thirty-eight. That's how he wanted it to stay, he loved his work, and although he had been on more than a few dates since then, on the rare times he was not working on a case, he had just never met anyone that could take her place in his affections and neither did he want to. The only other woman in his life was his granny, who had sadly had to go into a nursing home because she had developed dementia. He had been sad at the though of it because Maisie McKenna had been so independent for all of her eighty-eight years. In fact for the last eight she had cooked meals for him when he had visited and he had also taken his shirts for her to iron on her say so. It was strange to now have to go and visit in the nursing home instead and was not an easy thing to do, but he also knew it was the best place for her.

Laurel Fields Nursing Home was in a lovely location overlooking a cricket club and was shaded by trees and shrubs for privacy. It had a long sweeping driveway with spaces for many visitors' cars. Alex looked at his watch. He had half an hour to spare before getting back to work. This could be fairly easy or very hard, he thought to himself as he walked towards the entrance of the home. His grandmother could either be lucid and remember everything, in which case he would stay the thirty minutes or longer or else be in her own little world and ignore him, and if that happened he would stay for less time, for fear of upsetting her. This did sadden him because once she had become so agitated that she had thought he was someone else and one of the staff thought it would be better for him to leave. He actually stayed for nearly an hour because she was her lovely self. They talked about the olden days when she was working as a nurse and how she had helped to bandage the wounded soldiers. Maisie McKenna had met Alex's grandfather while working as a nurse. He had been wounded and she had been the one who cared for him. They had married soon after. She liked to talk about the olden days and how they had been. She also talked about Alex and asked him how he was keeping, and if he had found a nice girl yet. She told him that she was sorry she could not iron his shirts still, but hoped he was eating well and looking after himself. To which Alex smiled and told her he was doing just fine. One of the care assistants asked if he would like a cup of tea, and he shook his head and said he would have to leave soon, to which he thought he saw a tear appear in his granny's eye, so he relented and told the girl yes he would take a cup of tea after all. She bought two cups on a tray with some chocolate biscuits, Maisie's favourites. So all in all it was almost an hour before he hugged his granny goodbye and told her he would be back to see her as soon as he could.

It was almost two pm when he rang the buzzer to Jennifer's neighbour's apartment. Jo Taylor opened the door to the communal hall and he came inside. He was expecting a plumber to see to the leaking pipe under his sink and had been waiting all morning, and so he had his door open when DC McKenna arrived at the door.

'About time I been waiting all morning, thought you would never come' he told then looked him over. 'Where's yer bag?'

'Sorry! I think you are getting me mixed up with someone else sir' he quickly told him and took out his identification card to show him.

'THE POLICE I ain't done nothing.....what do you want?' he said going pale and trying to shut the door. To which Alex put his foot inside and frowned.

'I never said you had sir but we are making some inquiries. Can I ask you your name please?'

'NO YOU BLOOMING WELL CAN'T, and take your foot outta my door' he shouted.

Please sir I only want to ask you a few questions that's all and I will be gone.'

'What sort of questions?'

'About your neighbour Ms Sudbury' he said to him and Jo opened the door wider.

'What about her? I don't have nothing to do with her, she is a snotty bitch, thinks she's above everyone else.'

'What I would like to ask you is did you hear or see anything suspicious last Saturday night or in the early hours of Sunday morning?'

'Not that I know of. But there was a lot of laughing and noise coming from her apartment, woke me up.'

'What sort of noise did you hear?' he continued.

'Like someone was having a right rave up that sort of noise.'

But nothing to make you think something untoward was happening?'

'Such as?' he replied. 'Look it sounded like she had company, nothing to do with me, what she does when she invites folk over is her business, now is that all? I am waiting for a plumber' he told him getting agitated again as he hated the police.

'I have nearly finished sir, but could you by any chance tell me what time you heard the noise?'

'It was late, well after midnight.'

'And you say it did not sound as if anything suspicious was happening?'

'No I told you, just sounded like she was having a bit of fun.'

'And what did you say your name was' he asked him again with a pen and notebook in his hand to jot it down.

'I didn't.'

'Sir may I advise you it's an offence to withhold information.'

'OK, OK it's Joe... Joe Fletcher. Now is that all?'

'Yes for now but if I think of anything else I need to ask then I will be back to talk to you again Mr Fletcher' he told him. He could see the agitation in his face and he was also visibly shaking like he was hiding something. Alex could smell a rat a mile off and just as soon as he got back to the station, he was going to run his address through the computer to see what he could find out. He had never seen any one so agitated by a simple enquiry in a long time, and he wondered if he had a criminal record or something. He certainly intended finding out.

When he got back to the station DC Max Brennan was there drinking a cup of coffee. Alex told him he had just come back from seeing Ms Sudbury's neighbour.

'Well any leads?' he asked to which Alex pulled a face.

'On first approach he did not want to speak to me at all, to be honest Max he looked shit scared like he was hiding something, then told me it sounded like a party was going on in her apartment.'

Max shrugged. 'I did tell you I didn't think she was telling us everything'

'I know that but I think MS Sudbury's neighbour is hiding something too. I just can't put my finger on it yet but I will mark my word. I intend to run his address through the computer to see what it picks up.'

Max frowned 'What's his name?'

'Joe Fletcher.'

'He would not give it to me at first, which make me even more suspicious, and it was only when I insisted that her gave it' he replied getting down to business. He ran a quick check on who the owner of the house was from his computer while Max looked on.

'I certainly don't recognise the name' he said

drinking his last drop of coffee and pulling his face.

'I swear that the coffee here gets worse every day' he said and then he put his cup down.

Alex scanned the computer database and then came up with a name.

'Ah according to this the owner of the apartment is a Mr James Carmichael.'

'Well all that says is that your Joe Fletcher must be the tenant. Why don't you see if Mr Fletcher's name comes up on any of the criminal records.'

'It was just what I was going to do next' he told him. Then he searched for the man's name in the criminal records around Stoke on Trent and surrounding areas but could not come up with anything at all.

'I still smell a rat. That guy was hiding something and I intend to find out what' he said picking up the phone, while Max shook his head and told him that he still felt that Ms Sudbury had not told them the complete truth.

'Well I guess we will just after wait to see if forensics comes up with anything' he replied.

Chapter 9

It was now almost the end of the week, and Jennifer had still not heard from Francesca, not even a text message. It just felt like she had dropped their friendship completely and it hurt like mad. She had been the only friend she had ever confided in for as long as she could remember. She half wished that she had not bothered to go to the police station at all, but it had been Francesca who had instigated it after all, and now it felt like she had turned her back on her. She wondered if DC McKenna had been in touch with her and what she had told him if he had, she just hoped it was in her favour.

Jennifer had still not remembered how she had managed to get home and into her bed, although she was starting to think that maybe she had got herself home in some kind of drunken state, but that still did not account for why she had got the bruises, that was still a mystery. She just felt relieved that nothing else had happened since then, not even another silent phone call. And come to think of it neither had Mr Sleazy been outside his door when she had been coming home from work.

Jennifer was looking forward to seeing her grandparents again in August. She needed a holiday and the visit to see them would be just the thing. She had also struck a sort of friendship up with Lizzie the girl in the other office. They had both taken to having lunch together, sometimes just in the park and the day after they went to a cafe for a change. But although Jennifer liked Lizzie she was still cautious and never mentioned anything about the club or what had happened to her. Lizzie had also asked her if she would like to come to her house for dinner at the weekend to meet her son Toby, telling her it would be nothing special just a simple meal that she would prepare. She seemed a lonely soul and right now Jennifer could sympathise with that and so she readily agreed. She hoped that in time Francesca would come around and phone or text her. She was almost tempted to do it herself but was too stubborn as she still felt betrayed by her.

It was Friday the last day of the week when she received another one of the silent phone calls, just as she was beginning to think that she had heard the last of them. She had convinced herself that perhaps they were just a genuine wrong number after all. This time the person whoever it was remained connected even thought she yelled into the phone asking them what they wanted and why they were doing it, there was still no reply. It was as if they enjoyed listening to her despair. It had been Jennifer that had replaced the receiver to end the call. She felt shaky and upset that they had started again and wondered if she should phone DC McKenna to ask if there was any news from the lab and also to mention that the phone calls had started up again. He had told her to ring him if anything else happened so she got his contact card out of her purse and decided to ring him.

'Hello this is Jennifer Sudbury here, is this DC McKenna?' she asked.

'Speaking. Hello Ms Sudbury as a matter of fact I was just about to ring you' he told her, surprised to hear her voice.

'You were?' she asked sounding even more surprised. Maybe he had news for her, maybe he had spoken to Francesca, she thought.

'Yes I was about to pick the phone up and dial your number, but you beat me to it' he smiled.

'Have you found anything out? Have the lab results come back?' she asked.

'No not yet, as I told you before it could take up to ten days or even longer, and no it's not about the lab results' he told her.

'Right, then what did you want to speak to me about?' she asked feeling curious about what he had found out if anything. He probably wanted to ask again if she had remembered anything else about the night.

'Would it be possible if I could call around to see you in say an hour's time?' he asked her.

'OK that's fine. I will be here' she answered and suddenly felt a little nervous.

'It's just that I think it's best to have this conversation face to face instead of on the telephone' he told her to which she agreed. She wondered what he had got to talk to her about and if he had managed to find anything out. She hoped he had and she also was going to tell him about getting another silent phone call.

Alex McKenna rang the buzzer to her apartment, and waited for Jennifer to let him in.

Jennifer asked him to sit down then he began.

'Well Ms Sudbury it's like this. I have managed to get in touch with your friend Francesca. In fact I spoke to her myself in depth about Saturday night.'

'And did she tell you what happened that night?'

'She told me that you and her had gone out to celebrate a belated birthdays' celebration she called it, and she told me you had gone out to a restaurant together. Then after you had both gone out to the Club. She confirmed the name of the Club you had both gone out to' he said to her and Jennifer smiled.

'That's good and did she say what else happened?' she asked pleased that he had spoken with Francesca, and she hoped that everything she had told him had been in keeping with her statement.

'That's just it Ms Sudbury' he began.

'Please call me Jennifer' she told him. The constant use of the name Ms Sudbury was making her feel old.

'OK that's just it Jennifer, your friend said the last time she saw you, you were chatting and laughing with a guy that she did not recognise but that it seemed like you might have known him because you looked like you were comfortable in his company' he explained which made Jennifer feel like a fool and she frowned.

'I really can't remember this guy that I am supposed to have chatted to, that's just it. All I do remember is talking to a girl named Lucy, and some one else that was with her. Francesca actually introduced me to Lucy, as a friend of a friend. I do remember that' she told him.

'Well I was coming to that. She never mentioned anything about anybody named Lucy at all' he told her then continued. 'I asked if there was anyone else that could shed any light on all of this, anyone else you might have both spoken to while you were there but she said no, no one at all.'

Jennifer's heart sank. Why was her friend doing this to her? Why had she not told him about Lucy? She just did not understand it. It had been her that had told her to contact the police, and now she was refusing to stand by her. She felt utterly betrayed and like a complete fool. This was what she had been afraid might happen.

'I just don't understand why she said that there was no one else that we spoke to, because I assure you we did' she told him feeling quite annoyed.

'I also asked your friend if she could remember what the guy she saw you with had looked like, but she told me she only saw the back of his head really. Which then made me wonder why she had said she did not recognise him, if in fact she had only seen the back of him. So I put this to her and she then said that she had had quite a lot to drink that night, and so had you' he continued.

'Ms Sudbury.....Jennifer would you say you had had a lot to drink that night?' he asked her, and Jennifer again saw the sparkle in his grey eyes. He was a good-looking man she thought, and found herself glancing to see if he were wearing a wedding ring. Not that that made any difference these days. Then she chastised herself. She should not even be thinking like this.

'We were out celebrating our birthdays so yes we were drinking. But I would not say we drank so much that we did not know what was happening. I have drank more than I did that night before now, and still knew my own way home' she told him. To which he raised his eyebrow.

'Did she tell you about the flowers I found the

95

week before?' she asked him, only hoping that she was not going to be made a fool with over that too.

'Ah the flowers yes. Your friend told me that you had rung her in a right state, and because she was worried about you she decided to call to see you. She told me that on arriving to your apartment there was a lovely bunch of roses mixed with some other flowers and she had thought that maybe someone had left them for your birthday. She said you had become very hysterical when she had taken them in to show her.'

'That's true I was very upset, but did she tell you that the flowers I had found thirty minutes or so earlier were not the same flowers at all that she had found, but they had been obviously swapped. The ones I found were dead carnations and had a card with them, with the name Katie written on it. The ones she had bought in did not' she explained.

'No she just said you became hysterical and told her to throw them away. She thought you were probably stressed and maybe imagined that the flowers were dead.'

Jennifer felt like crying but didn't. She was so annoyed with Francesca for telling him all this.

'Can I put something to you Jennifer?' he said gently. He could see she was close to tears, and in a way he wanted to believe her in everything she was saying. She looked a nice girl and at this moment in time he could not see why she would have invented the whole thing up, unless he was wrong and she had just to get some attention, but for now he did not think so.

'Yes of course ask.' she answered him suddenly feeling very fragile.

'OK but don't take this the wrong way. We have to look at all possibilities. So what I want to ask you if it was possible that you just drank too much that night, and drunkenly asked the guy that you were talking to back home. Now I know that would not explain all the bruises, but do you think you may have fallen down and the guy you were with had helped you up maybe pressing a little too hard on your wrists? Could that have happened Jennifer? There is also something else I want to run past you. I spoke with your neighbour a Mr Fletcher earlier this week' he told her, and her eyes grew wide he must have been talking to Mr Sleazy. She did not know his name.

'Your neighbour said that there was quite a bit of noise coming from your apartment that night. In fact he told me it sounded like you were having a party.'

'That's got to be complete rubbish. Why would I have a party? He has got to be lying' she told him angrily.

'But why would he lie? What reason would he have to lie about hearing noises coming from your apartment that sounded like you were having a party?' he asked to which Jennifer could only shrug that she just did not know.

'Would you say that you got on with your neighbour Mr Fletcher?' he asked.

'Not really, I hardly know the guy except he gives me the creeps.' she told him.

'Why is that?'

'I don't really know except he is usually outside his door when I am going to work or sometimes when I come home and all he does is stare in a horrible way. He looks like a pervert, someone you would avoid. He just gives me the creeps' she explained

'OK but has he ever said anything to you, anything at all to make you feel that way? ' he asked to which Jennifer could only shake her head and say no.

'He mumbles something now and again but I can never make out what he says. All I want to do is get inside my apartment and close the door' she told him.

'How long have you lived here Jennifer?'

'It's got to be at least six months. I have been divorced about nine months' she told him sadly.

'Sorry to hear that. So you have not really lived here that long then?'

'No we...David my ex husband sold the house we had bought together and I decided to rent this place although the rent is quite expensive.

'It must have been hard for you when you split up?'

'Yes it was. I never thought we would ever get divorced.' she answered.

'Can I ask you how long you were married for?'

'Just three years.'

'So short, I am sorry to hear that' he felt sorry for her and wondered who had instigated the divorce.

'And can I ask if there is someone else or has been since. I know it's none of my business but a pretty girl like you.....' he hoped he had not overstepped his mark, but something was making him ask. Maybe it was because it might help in the inquiry or perhaps he felt genuinely interested in her. Jennifer smiled.

'No I don't mind you asking, and no there is no one else' she told him and for one strange moment wanted to ask him the same question. She suddenly wanted to ask if he was seeing anyone or had been, and the funny thing was she had no reason too. He was just a DC dealing with her report nothing more, and just doing his job. But she had definitely felt some kind of attraction for one moment and then it was gone. He continued to jot things down in his notebook then out of the blue and quite cheekily asked if he could perhaps have a cup of coffee, to which she smiled and went to put the kettle on. She needed to tell him about the silent call she had had, and so when she had brought the coffee into him along with some biscuits she mentioned it. Alex frowned and asked how many in total had she received so far, and after she told him he said that she should perhaps report it to BT or who her provider was. They had ways to block the calls if they were becoming a nuisance to her. He also asked if she knew anyone that might want to frighten her, but she could only nod and say no. Then she decided to tell him about the Internet and the online dating website that she had put her profile on under the pseudonym of Katie, omitting to mention the chat rooms that she had also used. She did not want him to think that she was completely gullible.

'Can I ask if you ever met anyone on the dating site?' he asked her and she thought then about Luke, she would have to tell him she knew that, but was there really anything to tell. She had not even met him. All that had had happened was some emails and then she had given him her mobile number and he had texted her only the once. His profile had vanished and so apart from the emails she had no proof he existed. What would he think of her if she told him? So instead she told him it was early days and there was no one. She did not feel wrong in saying this because Luke and her had never met. She didn't think what happened on Saturday night would be anything to do with him, how could it be? When all she had given him was her mobile number, and hadn't even texted him back. After Alex McKenna had finished his coffee he left telling her he would be in touch, just as soon as he heard anything else from forensics.

Chapter 10

When DC McKenna got back to the station he decided to look at Jennifer's file again. It appeared that there were some things that were just not adding up. He had spoken to Jennifer's friend face to face, when she had reluctantly agreed to come down to the station on her way home from work. It had taken ages to get hold of her, and when he eventually spoke to her she had been vague, as if she hadn't known what was going on.

He still smelt a rat with Joe Fletcher too, and even though he had done traces himself on his name, it had not shown anything up. He had also asked a colleague to look on the criminal register for other areas and still nothing had come up. So it would appear that Joe Fletcher was squeaky clean. Yet somehow he did not think so and still thought he was hiding something. He had been so agitated when he had spoken to him. Then out of the blue a thought had occurred to him.

'OF COURSE why hadn't I thought about it that, Joe Fletcher may not be his real name' he said to himself out loud to which the PC who had just brought him a cup of coffee just looked at him confused.

'It's OK Steve, ignore me, just a case I am on' he told him and the PC just smiled and put the mug of coffee down onto his desk.

'Ta for the coffee' he told him and then started clicking away on his computer. After half an hour he had found nothing so decided to call it a day. He needed sleep and besides he had other cases he had to deal with tomorrow.

That night Alex's thoughts were on Jennifer and her case. She just did not seem the type of girl to make up a story like it quite looked like. Yet he knew that things were not as they seemed, he just felt that a piece of the jigsaw was missing, something that someone had left out. Whether it was Jennifer herself, or her friend he was not sure. He intended to have another word with Francesca, and he wanted to ask her about the girl named Lucy who Jennifer had mentioned, and then see what she said about her. He also felt that there was definitely something not quite right with her neighbour Mr Fletcher and he decided he would go back and pay him a visit first thing on Monday. He needed to find the missing piece to the jigsaw of the case, and he would do it or else his name was not DC Alex McKenna.

It was Saturday afternoon and Jennifer had logged onto her Facebook account. She still felt very upset that Francesca had not got in touch, it was as if she had cut her off completely. Not that she felt very friendly towards here after the things she had told DC McKenna and in fact she was still mad with her. When he had left yesterday late afternoon she thought about phoning Francesca up and having it out with her, and asking her why she said what she did. However she did not want to hear her excuses and besides she half expected it was really her boyfriend Paul who did not want her getting involved. So she had decided to log onto Francesca's page. Come to think of it she did not really know what Paul looked like, neither had she actually met him. Francesca had asked if she had wanted to meet him a few times, but she had always declined saying that she did not want to be a wallflower.

She scoured the photos she had displayed on her page to see if there were any of Paul or her together but all there were was photos taken from the places they had been. Then she looked for Lucy's profile but could not find it. It looked like she had vanished off her page completely as a friend, which was strange, unless they had argued and Francesca had deleted her. Before she logged off she decided to have another look at the dating website to see if Luke had put his profile up again. She had not heard a thing from him since the Saturday he had texted her his number, and his text message had mysteriously disappeared off her phone. She could not understand because he had seemed so keen, and sounded nice. Never mind she thought to herself, there were plenty more fish in the sea. Speaking of which she had not checked out the emails from the other two guys. In fact she had forgotten all about them She decided she would check out their profiles and if she liked the look of them she would reply. It would not hurt so long as she played safe, and did not give out any information. Jennifer was due to be at Lizzie's house for five o'clock and was really looking forward to it, and to meeting her son Toby. So she had half an hour before she had to get ready.

The first man looked to be in his sixties, far too old she thought for her twenty-eight years, so deleted his message. The second one did not look much better either, but there was a third email from a guy named Phil and he actually looked quite nice. He had lovely blonde hair and blue eyes, was single and worked in IT it read. He liked going to the cinema, most sport and eating out. It would not hurt to reply and she did just that before getting ready and heading out to see Lizzie.

Jennifer was disappointed to see Mr Sleazy outside and doing something to his door as she shut her own behind her. For some reason he had not been there for quite a few days now, and she was beginning to think he was away. She tried to avoid eye contact with him as she hurried past but he mumbled 'l'm watching you' which made Jennifer draw a sharp intake of breath at the thought of it Why would he say that? What had she ever done to him? She just could not make the man out, all she knew was he gave her the creeps.

Lizzie lived just short walk and a bus ride away in a place called Sandfordhill. She answered the door and asked Jennifer in to meet Toby who was doing a jigsaw on a small table in the sitting room.

'Come and say hello to my friend from work Toby' she told him.

Toby looked up from what he was doing and said hello and smiled at Jennifer, then went back to doing the jigsaw.

'He loves doing jigsaws Jennifer, don't you Toby?' Lizzie said. To which Jennifer smiled and went to sit by him to look.

' I also love jigsaws Toby. You are doing well, I see it's a Star Wars one.'

'Yes I love Star Wars. Do you like Star Wars Jennifer?' he asked her.

'Mmh I can't say it's my favourite but what I

have seen I enjoyed' she answered smiling at Lizzie who shook her head.

'He is Star Wars mad.' she told Jennifer.

'Would you like to watch one of my Star Wars videos?' Toby asked.

'No Toby Jennifer did not come to watch videos, she came to have dinner with us and chat with me' Lizzie told him, and Toby pulled a big sad puppy face.

'Pleassse?' he asked again, but Lizzie said no again, to which Jennifer smiled.

'Maybe another time Toby OK' Jennifer told him.

'Yes Toby another time. We will be eating in another 30 minutes or so' Lizzie explained and then asked Jennifer if she would like a drink of anything.

'I am fine for the moment thank you....by the way something smells good' Jennifer told her. She had noticed the lovely aroma coming from the kitchen the moment she had walked in.

'Oh it's only something simple that I prepared earlier. I hope you like fish?' Lizzie replied.

'Yes I love fish' she told her with a smile and noticed Toby looking up and pulling his face.

'I don't like fish yucky' he told his mother, who then explained that he was not having fish but chicken goujons

'Yay my favourite' he told her.

The meal Lizzie prepared was lovely and for afters she had gone to a lot of trouble and made an apple crumble. If it had been Jennifer doing the meal she would have opted to buy a shop bought one, but then cooking was not her forte. She liked her ready meals too much, although she knew they weren't good for you. Too much processed food was bad for your health, she knew that.

When she had been married to David she had vowed to have cookery lessons and had even dabbled with a few dishes, but for some reason she always managed to burn them. So she went back to the ready meals especially when she had split up with David. She just could not be bothered. It felt hard to just cook for one person somehow.

After Toby had gone to bed, the two of them sat down to relax and Lizzie opened a bottle of white wine and asked if Jennifer would like a glass, to which she said yes please. They sat and chatted about work and sipped their wine. It felt nice to sit and unwind after the ordeal she had had these last few weeks.

'Do you like where you live Jennifer?' Lizzie asked taking a long sip of wine.

'Well I would not say living in a apartment was my first choice, but beggars can't be choosers. It's a nice apartment looking over the park' she told her taking another sip of her wine.

'Yes I know where you mean it is nice around there, very private. But it must have been strange for you to downsize to an apartment from a house' she said.

'Yes it was. It was very hard. I loved my little semi and it had a lovely garden and patio. With the apartment there is no garden, well there is a communal garden but that is shared between the block of four' she explained.

'I see. And do you get on with your neighbours?' Jennifer shook her head.

'To be very honest with you I don't really see any of my neighbours, that is except one of them a grubby little man whose name I don't know, just that he seems to hang around when I leave for work and sometimes when I come home. In fact he was there as I was leaving the apartment to come and see you' she told her finishing off her glass of wine.

'Oh right! How strange...that he hangs around I mean.'

'Yes he really does give me the creeps' she replied.

'Has he ever said anything to you?'

' Not really, except just stare....mind you he mumbled something today as I walked past him.'

'He did, what did he say?' she asked with a frown.

'Well it sounded like he said 'I am watching you.'

Lizzie shivered visibly and poured herself another glass of wine.

'No wonder he gives you the creeps. Do you want another glass?' she asked holding up the bottle, but Jennifer said no, and covered her glass with her hand. She did not want to be too late home.

'Oh one more won't hurt, besides it's Sunday tomorrow, you can have a lie in. What time is your last bus?'

'About twenty to eleven but I have a short walk from where I get dropped off, so I want to catch the ten pm' she told her.

'Well there you are then it's only nine o'clock. You have time for one more before you go.'

'OK then just one more' she told her and Lizzie poured her another drink.

'Are you planning to go away this year on holiday Jennifer?' she asked

'I am hoping to go and visit my grandparents in France' she told her then continued

'I had to make it for the middle of August because I left it too late to book' she explained.

'Ah yes I thought I heard Mr Stone say something about that. There is a big case that may go on for weeks so I hear, but don't quote me on it now' she told her and Jennifer nodded.

'Yes it will be the big drugs case. I know a little bit about that as I had to type a few documents out concerning it.'

'Still the middle of August will be a nice time for you to go and see them, plenty of nice weather, lucky you. I have not planned anything yet, but Toby and I will probably go somewhere nice, just for the weekend. Last year we went to Cente Parcs for the week, all-inclusive. It was lovely and Toby really enjoyed himself' she told her.

'Yes I heard there was lots to do at those places especially for kiddies. I can't say that I have ever been myself.'

'Well they cater for children, and there was always something for him to do' she replied.

'Can I ask you something Lizzie. Has there been anyone else since you and Toby's dad split up?'

She asked her wondering why a good-looking woman like her was still on her own. Lizzie went a bit quiet at first then looked tearful.

'To be honest Jennifer I don't think I could ever trust another man, not after Trevor' she told her explaining that he had let her down pretty badly and she had almost had a nervous breakdown.

'Don't get me wrong he was and is still a terrific father, but he just can't keep it in his pants, if you know what I mean. He liked the women and I am afraid I just was not enough for him. He should never be in a serious relationship because of that' she explained, while Jennifer looked on sympathetically. She herself could sympathise with this because of David, but decided to change the subject.

It was actually the twenty to eleven bus that Jennifer caught. She felt so comfortable in Lizzie's company that she decided to stay. They talked about lots of things, and Jennifer felt she could tell her anything. She pondered whether to mention what had happened to her when she had gone to the club with Francesca but decided not to. Instead she told her about the dead flowers she had found and when she told her that there had been a card attached with the name Katie on. Lizzie had said maybe that was who they were really meant for then, to which Jennifer had had to explain that she sometimes called herself Katie. Then Lizzie thought that Katie was her middle name, but Jennifer told her that sometimes she used the name online. She had looked at her with a puzzled expression on her face, probably because she had never been online. In the end Jennifer decided to change the subject, and that it hadn't been such a good idea to confide in Lizzie after all. But nevertheless she had enjoyed her company and liked her a lot. They talked about maybe meeting up again in a few weeks time. Lizzie said that every so often Toby spent the weekend with his dad, and so maybe they could go out to the cinema or something, and Jennifer had agreed.

She thought about Lizzie on the way home. She had not meant to stay so long. She hated the thought of walking the rest of the way home from where the bus dropped her when it was so late. That was why she had intended to get the 10 pm bus. It would not have bothered her in the past, but she had been more wary since the incident in the club.

She let herself into the communal hall and half expected Mr Sleazy to be there outside his door again, and she gave a sigh of relief when he was nowhere in sight. Thank goodness she thought to herself, then as she approached her door she froze. She could not believe her own eyes what she saw and felt her heart beating like mad, her mouth went dry and she felt sick inside.

Someone had written in big red letters over her door the name Katie. She felt scared at first then rage overcome her and she decided it must be Mr Sleazy himself, who else? He had to have either done it after he had said what he did to her, or someone else in the block had. She realised someone had to let whoever did it in, for there was no other way that they could gain access to the hall. And whether it was the wine that had made her feel bolder, or else the fact she had finally snapped she ran to his door and banged on it shouting in a fit of temper and waiting him to come out. But there was no answer at all. She kicked his door angrily and then just burst into tears and went back to her own apartment. She let herself in ignoring the graffiti, locked and bolted the door behind her and slumped to the floor in a flood of tears. She intended to report the incidence to DC McKenna first thing in the morning, and she would leave it there on her door for him to see.

Chapter 11

Jennifer had another terrible night of tossing and turning. She lay awake for ages wondering who could be doing these terrible things to her. It was strange because every time she allowed herself to think that all the things that had happened were perhaps a mistake, such as the flowers were really meant for someone else named Katie, and that it was just a coincidence that she used the same name online, then something else happened. The silent phone calls she could maybe have passed off as a mistake if they had not kept coming. She also wanted to believe that she had somehow got herself home that night because she had drank so much she was out of it completely, although that would not explain why she could not remember drinking quite so much or the bruises. However this latest thing with the graffiti made her realise the things that were happening to her were real enough. Someone had got it in for her but who?

It was after three when Jennifer eventually drifted off only to be wakened by noises outside her door. She turned her bedside lamp on and considered phoning the police. Someone was outside her door and she was really afraid. She crept out of her bed without turning on the light in the hallway between the bedroom and the front door. She had a spy glass that was fitted on her front door so that she could view anyone there before letting them in. Whoever was out there making the noise must have access to the communal hall, because unless any of the adjoining apartments let them in, the front main door remained locked for security reasons. It was a mystery even how the name Katie had come to be written on her door. Thinking about it, it must be either something to do with Mr Sleazy or one of the other neighbours above her. She had never met any of the other two but had only seen Mr Sleazy. She had thought that one of the apartments above had a child, because on rare occasions she had heard a baby crying.

Her heart felt like it would come out of her chest as she pressed her eye close up to the spyglass in the door. It had been a warm night, yet she felt cold inside and could hardly stop shivering as she wrapped her dressing gown around her some more. The hall was in complete darkness and it looked like no one was there at all, then she saw it, a shadow all in black. It looked like someone was standing beside the main door of the communal hall to her right not far from Mr Sleazy's door. They were just standing there watching her and she was frozen to the spot. Then whatever or whoever it was just disappeared.

She had not dared to open her door, instead she checked that it was locked and bolted. In fact she double checked, then went back to her bed. What had she seen out there, she really did not know. Just that it looked like an hooded figure of a man dressed all in black, and he had appeared to be standing straight facing her door, and in the next instance he was gone.

Jennifer did not know how she managed to fall asleep again, but she eventually did. The next time she looked at the clock it was 8am. After she had showered and dressed she decided to check out her door again. She was not quite as afraid because it was light. She needed to see it again to know it had not been all in her imagination. She intended to report it to the police, along with the figure she had seen in the communal hall early hours of this morning. She opened her door bracing herself to see the horrible graffiti and could not believe her eyes. There was nothing, not even a mark where the writing had been. She moved her hand across the door, not believing what she was seeing. How could it have gone? She was sure it had been written in bold red paint. Surely paint would not have come off that easily.

She toyed with the idea to call the police anyway but decided if she did they would wonder just as she had where the graffiti was. If there was nothing there for them to see what could they do, except put it in a file. She had a thought. The noise that she had heard early hours and the figure she had seen in the communal hall must have been someone wiping it off her door, either that or else she was going completely mad, but she did not think so, she knew exactly what she had seen. She decided not to report it though, and instead wait until she heard from forensics and maybe then some light would be shed on all of this.

It was first thing Monday morning that DC McKenna got Jennifer's file out again. He wanted to try and speak to Francesca to ask a few more questions, and also he intended to pay Mr Fletcher another visit. He still felt he smelt a rat with him. He was waiting for forensics to come up with something but there was nothing yet. It had been seven days since the swabs had been sent and the blood and urine samples but it could also take another seven days he knew that because they were swamped with work, plus it was hardly classed as an emergency since no one had died.

He had also been to visit the nursing home over the weekend, because he was contacted about his granny who had apparently been more confused than usual and had wanted to know where her husband was. He had in fact been dead quite a number of years but Maisie was adamant that he was still alive and in her confused state had struck one of the care assistants calling her a liar. So Alex had to be brought in to try and pacify her. On going in he found her sitting in a chair by her bed with her eyes all red and swollen where she had been crying, and when she had seen Alex she had just burst into tears again. He had held her and gently explained, but all she could do was cry. It was an awful thing to have dementia and Maisie was definitely getting worse as the time went by. It had reduced her from a strong minded woman who had been quiet intelligent, to the frail old lady that she had become, hardly knowing who he was. It hurt him immensely to see her that way.

His granny had practically raised him since he was eleven. He was an only child of a professional couple. His father had been a surgeon and his mother a nurse, who then had become a UNICEF charity worker. Both had been killed in a tragic plane crash that had claimed their lives. Before coming to live with his granny he had lived in various places all over the world. His grandfather had been Scottish and had met and married Maisie and settled in Staffordshire. Maisie had been born and bred in Stoke on Trent where she had remained nearly all of her life.

Alex had been a very bright student and had gone on to University and then joined the police force. He had served over four years as a PC before eventually joining the CID department, which had always been his goal. He had been an excellent PC just like he was an Excellent DC and everyone looked up to him. Then he had met and fallen in love with Amelia. She had been his everything or so he thought she had, except when he really did think about it, he had spent more time away from her during the course of their relationship than with her because of work. He had been lucky that she had understood and still stuck by him. She had her own work of course and she too could be away for days at a time if she was on a photo shoot. She worked for a modeling agency, although not as a model herself but she spent her time scheduling other people's lives. She was mostly confined to the office or waiting for phone calls from would be models.

When Alex had first met her, he had thought she was beautiful with her golden blonde hair and her curvy figure, and had commented that she had looked like a model herself, but Amelia had laughed and told him she was not thin enough, that models today had to be a size 0 and a lot younger than she was. In fact the models she was booking were in their early to mid teens. She often felt sorry for them, because they seemed like they were always trying to get that little bit of extra perfection to what they had. They also sometimes looked miserable because they embarked on new some faddish diet. She had wondered why she had stayed in the job, but the fact she enjoyed the fashion industry and the competition, and the rare times she had gone on the photo shoots with the models she had loved. It had been sadly on one of those shoots that she had been killed in a car accident.

Alex had been devastated at the time, but he had thrown himself into his job and that had been his salvation. After she had passed he had left all her clothes and things exactly where they were as he could not bear to get rid of them or take them to a charity shop, although he knew he needed to do it one day.

Eventually his granny had come to his aid and helped him through it. In fact it had been his granny that had come to his aid many times. That was why he could not bear to see her the way she was. She had been like both a mother and father figure to him.

It was lunch time when Francesca had eventually got in touch with him, he had left her a message on her mobile asking her to please get in touch at her earliest convenience.. He was just about to go down to the canteen for a bite of something eat and his fix of coffee when his phone had rung.

'Hello thank you for getting back to me Miss Davis. What I wondered was if you could possibly call in to see me, or alternatively I could come out to see you' he asked.

He could hear a deep sigh from Francesca in the background.

'Can I ask what's it about this time? I have told you all that I know about that night, I don't think that there is anything else I could possibly tell you' she told him sounding fed up.

'I would really appreciate it if you could come in again, there are just one or two details that I need to go over with you. If you like I could come out to see you to save you the journey in' he told her again.

'No that won't be necessary, I will call on my way home from work if you don't mind. But like I have already told you, there is nothing new I can add' she explained sighing deeply.

'Thank you very much Miss Davis, shall we say around 5.30 like last time' he asked her. He wanted a time or to know as near as possible to when she would be there, so he could be in the station to speak with her himself.

'Yes OK that time is fine, I finish work at five, I will be in as soon as I can after that' she told him reluctantly.

After he had been down to the canteen to get a quick bite to eat, he brought his coffee back up to his office, and he decided he would look again on the database for sex offenders and assault but again like last time there was nothing. There was so much to look at that it would most probably take him all day to go through them all, and with no name to go by it was proving very difficult Max had come into the office and was peering over his shoulder.

'Any news on the Sudbury case' he asked. Alex shook his head and turned the database off

'Forensics are not back yet but to tell you the

truth I smell a rat about that case' he told him

'Well I think there is more to it that Ms Sudbury is telling us' he told him smugly

'I have asked her friend Miss Davis to come back into the station, there are a few more details I want clearing up, then I want to go back and see Mr Fletcher the neighbour' he told Max and then he had a thought.

'Max how do you fancy coming along and seeing him with me? You can give me your opinion on the guy. Say in an hour, that's if you are free' he asked

'OK should be free by then, but I have to interview Jerry again concerning the O'Connor case' he told him.

'Thanks Max. I just think two heads are better than one' he smiled and finished his coffee.

He got on well with Max and although he was a few years older than him, Alex looked the younger of the two. Max was overweight and needed to lose more than a few pounds. He was also losing his hair, although he kept it cropped short, so you could hardly tell. Max was also married, and had been for at least eight years and they had five-year-old twin boys. He had been invited to his house on a couple of occasions for a meal and had met them. His wife was pretty but not beautiful. Just plain looking but she had that fresh look and lovely smile. He sometimes wondered how she put up with him, but then he could have said the same about himself. Amelia had also put up with his working long hours. Long hours and marriage did not mix, maybe that had been why he had never fully committed to her and married her, although he had loved her deeply and she him.

It was two hours later that they were pressing Mr Fletcher's buzzer. It took a while before he responded and then answered.

'Yes who is it?' he said with sharpness to his voice. Alex looked at Max then spoke into the intercom.

'It's DC Alex McKenna again Mr Fletcher and I am here with my colleague to ask you a few more questions if you don't mind' he told him.

'Well I do mind, what do you want with me? I done nothing' he answered.

'We never said you had Mr Fletcher, now can we please come through, ask a few questions and then we will be gone again' he reassured him. There was silence for a few more minutes then there was the sound from the lock on the communal door unlocking, and the DCs went through.

Mr Fletcher was waiting by his door.

'Look I told ya what I know so why are you back? ' he said to them.

'Can we come in Mr Fletcher' Alex asked

'No you blooming well can't unless you have a warrant' he answered crossly and went to close his door again, but Max held it back to which Mr Fletcher got agitated.

'Mr Fletcher why would we need a warrant? Are you hiding something in there?' Alex asked trying to peer in through the gap.

'No of course not.'

'Then why won't you let us in? Just a few questions and we will go, and by the way it would not take us too long to get a warrant if we feel you are behaving suspiciously which at this moment in time we do.'

Joe Fletcher moved away from the door and let them both through. Max looked at Alex and pulled his face, there was a nasty smell coming from the place that he could not quite think what it could be except maybe food that had gone off and not just for a few days either or else something had died. The place was a complete tip and needed a good clean, like he did himself. He was unshaven and smelt strongly of BO. Max took out a handkerchief and held it to his mouth covering his nose, while Alex coughed out loudly.

'Well what questions to you want to ask me, I have not got all day you know' he told them.

'Can I ask where that smell is coming from first ' Alex asked feeling slightly nauseated how could anyone live like this. Looking around the room he saw a computer in the corner and beer bottles here there and everywhere.

' It's from the drains, I am waiting for a repair man to come have a look' he answered looking slightly more nervous than he should have.

Alex did not know what to think, but because they had only been able to gain access through Mr Fletcher's good will they were not entitled to go looking around to check out the place, neither could they look at his computer. So instead they asked him about Saturday night again and what in fact he remembered hearing. But he only told them both the same thing, that he had heard people laughing and music playing, plus a lot of banging going on. So in the end they decided to leave. They had no reason to believe that he was not telling the truth.

When they were back at the station Alex ran it

past Max again.

'I think that given the state of the place we should involve Social Services, either that or find his Landlord Mr Carmichael and have a quiet word with him.'

'I still think he's hiding something though Max' he told him to which Max smiled and answered 'By the smell of the place a dead body.' Alex could only frown. But he intended to find out one way or another.

Chapter 12

When Jennifer arrived home from work the following day she was dismayed to find Mr Sleazy waiting outside his door. When would he give up, she thought to herself as she tried to ignore his awful stares. But this time he tried to stop her.

'WHY ARE THE BLOOMING POLICE SNIFFING AROUND' he shouted waving his fist in the air. Jennifer refused to answer and hurried on past him.

'I'm watching you, remember that' he growled angrily.

'GO AWAY YOU NASTY LITTLE MAN' she called back hurrying inside and locking the door.

She breathed a sigh of relief. She hated the confrontations she had with him, and now it just seemed to be getting worse, why couldn't he leave her alone she thought putting the kettle on. She wondered then if the police had any news for her. They had obviously been around again or Mr Sleazy would not have reacted the way he did. Oh when will all of this stop? She was beginning to wish she had not involved the police at all, but then it would not have altered the things that had happened or were happening. For the life of her she just could not understand it. At least there had been no more graffiti over her door.

She made herself a cup of coffee and a quick sandwich thinking she would prepare something for dinner later. She glanced at the mail she had picked up in the mail box. Not much there just circulars and bills which she put to one side.

Then she logged on to check her emails. There was a message from Phil the IT man from the dating web site.

'Hello Jennifer, thank you for your response. As I said in my message it would be lovely if we could get to know each other. If you have checked out my profile, which I am pretty sure you have, or you would not have replied to me, then you will know I work in IT. My interests are mainly football, swimming and I just love to chill out with a beer or glass of wine over dinner. I love dining out and travel, especially with that special someone.

Maybe you can tell me a bit more about yourself, or if you want to ask any more questions about me, then I will be glad to answer you, but there is no pressure. All good things come to those that wait, well that's my motto anyway. I will write more later and look forward to hearing from you soon Phil.'

Jennifer smiled to herself when she read it, he seemed really nice. She would answer it after dinner, as she did not want to seem to be too keen.

Looking in the freezer she pulled out a shepherds pie. She thought about Lizzie and the lovely dinner she had prepared on Saturday and she had even gone to the trouble of making an apple crumble. And here she was just pulling out a ready meal of shepherds pie. But there just did not seem any point in going to all that trouble preparing and cooking a meal for one.

The day had been busy again and Jennifer had to do a lot of preparing for the upcoming court case.

Also there was another affidavit, which she had to prepare and witness.

She and Lizzie had popped out to the cafe for a bite to eat at lunch time, and Jennifer had insisted on paying the bill, even though Lizzie kept saying that it wasn't necessary, but she wanted to say thank you for Saturday and the meal she had prepared for her. It was the least she could do. Lizzie had asked her if she was still up for going out together to the cinema in a couple of weeks time. She told her that Toby would be going to stay with his dad for the weekend, and Jennifer smiled and said she would look forward to it. There was a new film that Lizzie wanted to see and the first showing was going to be around that time. Jennifer had told her that maybe they could grab a pizza afterwards or something.

She had also given Lizzie her mobile number and she had given Jennifer hers. They seemed to be striking up a good friendship, which was nice since it looked like Francesca's and her friendship was over. She had still not got in touch with her, and Jennifer was hurt, simply because they had history together and she would not have guessed that she would have acted in the way she had done. It just went to prove that you sometimes really don't know a person fully, and it was in the time of trouble that you really knew who your true friends were.

After Jennifer had eaten her dinner she decided to turn the TV on as there were a few soap programmes that she wanted to catch up with, and maybe a documentary on later, but for some reason Jennifer could not get into them. So she ended up turning the TV off and just curling up on the sofa with a book. It was one that she had bought a few months back and had never really got around to reading it. She had started to read the first chapter when the landline phone began to ring. She hesitated at first wondering if it was another silent call and just could not face it if it were, so she let it ring, but it went on for a while so she reluctantly got up and answered warily.

'Hello' she said cautiously.

'Hello Jenny love its nan here.' Her nan sounded strained and Jennifer felt instantly worried.

'Nan what's wrong....is everything OK?'

'No love your grandpa has had an accident' she began.

'When....how?' she asked.

'He was out for his usual cycle and when he did not come back after a few hours I began to get worried. It appears that he was knocked off his bicycle by a hit and run driver' she told her trying her best not to cry.

'How terrible! Did anyone see it happen?'

'Well someone saw him lying in the road and they saw a sports car speeding off but it went far too fast for them to take its number plates I'm afraid. But he is alive and conscious but very poorly love' she continued.

'Oh Nan I am so, so sorry. I will try my best to see if I can get some time off and fly over. I was hoping to come in the middle of August, in fact I was going to book something this week for then, but if you need me I will see what I can do' she told her.

'I will be fine love, just worried about your grandpa you know, and I have tried to get in touch with your father but to no avail I am afraid.'

'Oh dear shall I try to get in touch with him? I know how busy he always is. Have you told Nicole yet? she asked her to which there was a long silence on the other end, and Jennifer thought she had gone, or else they had been cut off.

'I don't know how to tell you this love, but we have not heard from Nicole for ages since....since'

'What is it nan? What happened' she asked her feeling confused.

'Well nothing really happened as such except we had a bit of a tiff.'

'What sort of tiff?'

'Well I would rather not go over it now on the phone, maybe I will explain when we see you. But the bottom line is we no longer have a contact number for her' she explained.

'Oh dear, but you are not to worry, you have enough on your plate to contend with, besides I am sure she will come around, you know Nicole.'

'I am not so sure love, anyhow my main worry is your Grandpa now.....oh Jenny I just want him home, I feel so lost without him' she sobbed and Jennifer felt so helpless being so far away. She was going to have to sort something out at work whether Mr Stone liked it or not. Depending on the condition of her grandpa she needed to get compassionate leave.

'Look Nan I am going to try and get hold of my dad. He should be over there with you, and at the same time, he should know where Nicole is too' she told her.

'OK love but please don't mention Nicole to him and the tiff we had, just tell him about your grandpa' she asked.

'I will.....when are you going to go back up to see him?'

'I will be going back just as soon as I finish speaking with you love.' She told her then that she had had a lift to the hospital from a neighbour and that they had also dropped her back home, so she could have a rest and something to eat, but was restless and although she had made herself a drink of tea and a sandwich she intended to go back up and be with her husband. She actually still drove and had a very small car that she used occasionally, so she was going to drive herself up.

'OK Nan but you drive carefully won't you. I will keep trying to get in touch with my dad for you, and will ring you again before I go to bed. What hospital is he in?'

'I will love and he is in Hospital Pasteur in Nice.'

Jennifer rang off after saying her goodbyes and picked the phone up again to ring her dad but there was no answer and it just kept ringing out. This was not unusual because she always did have trouble getting him. She felt angry that more often than not this was the case. After trying a few more times she decided she would leave it for a while and try again later.

Her father was a workaholic He was a rep for a very busy company in Birmingham and by now he should have probably retired, since he was nearing his sixty fourth birthday but like he had told her before, work was everything to him. She had often wished that he had remarried, but he hadn't and she did not think he was likely to now since as far as she knew he was not seeing anyone.

She wondered then about Nicole and what the tiff had been about. She could not see it had been about anything too serious because her grandparents were not like that. In fact she could not remember having a row with them, they were gentle good-natured people, although they still never took any nonsense from anyone either. So if they had lost contact with Nicole, it had to be something bad she had said or done.

She knew there was no love lost between her and her sister. It had been quite a few years since she had spoken to her and she never even received a Christmas card from her. She wondered what she was doing with her life, or if she was with anyone. Why oh why couldn't things be different, she thought. She would have loved to have had a sister that she was really close to.

Jennifer decided she could not be bothered to go back to the book she was reading, she felt too churned up inside. She was really worried about her grandpa and hoped he was going to be all right. It was impossible to know how bad his injuries really were since she was not there. She would ring her nan before she went to sleep. He just hoped she managed to be able to contact her dad. Half an hour later she dialed his number again and this time after a short time he answered.

'Hello Dad.'

'Oh Hello Jenny how nice to hear from you. Did you have a nice birthday?....I' he began but Jennifer continued.

'Dad its Grandpa, he has had an accident, someone knocked him off his bike. I have been trying to get you for ages and so has nan' she told him.

'Oh no! When did it happen? Is it serious?' he asked

'I don't really know, just that she says he is very poorly. He is in the Hospital Pasteur and nan is with him' she explained.

'Right. I had better phone the hospital then and find out what's happening. Sorry you could not get me. I have been working late and it's been manic this week. Better go and ring' he told her and before she could say anything else, or ask about Nicole he had put the phone down.

Oh well at least he knows. She wondered if he would fly out to be with his parents. If not she was going to ask if she could get compassionate leave first thing in the morning.

Fifteen minutes later the phone rang again and this time Jennifer hurried to answer it, thinking it was news about her grandpa and it was her dad ringing her back to update her.

'Hello Jenny love just updating you. I have spoken to the hospital in Nice and they say he has sustained very serious injuries but not life threatening. For now they say he is stable' he explained.

'Oh thank goodness. Can I ask if you will be flying out to see him' she asked feeling a little relieved.

'I doubt if I will be able to get away for at least a week, I wish it was that simple, but I have a lot on that I can't get out of '

'Dad, nan may need you, don't you think it's more important, surely if you explain they will understand, compassionate leave and all that' she replied feeling a little annoyed with him. He just never changed. For him work always did come first.

'Jenny it's not as simple as that, and you don't understand. Of course if dad was critically ill I would be there like a shot, you know that. I will ring the hospital or my mother tomorrow to see what the situation is and then decide. OK now I need to get a bit of shut eye.'

'Dad...Dad don't go. I want to ask.......' she continued but he had already put the phone down. She was totally gob smacked. She had wanted to ask him if he knew anything about Nicole or where she was, omitting to tell him about nan and the tiff they had had, but it was too late as he had put the phone down. She had been tempted to phone him back up again, but she was so angry with him she did not bother.

She would ring her nan later to see if she was back home, and ask how everything was. It was so typical of her dad to think of work first, but to be fair he had phoned the hospital straight up and asked how he was. She was sure that if they had said her grandpa was critical he would have flown out to see him, at least she had hoped he would have done.

It was almost eleven o clock when Jennifer picked the phone up to ring her Nan again but there was no answer this time, only the answerphone, so she just left her a message saying that she would ring again in the morning, and telling her not to worry too much, and to get some rest.

She was just about to get into bed when she remembered Phil the guy from the dating site. So she logged on and wrote him a brief email telling him a little bit more about herself, but not too much. He knew her as Katherine and she left it at that for now.

After she wrote the email she was tempted to log onto the chat line, but was feeling tired from her lack of sleep the previous night so decided not to. It was now nearly eleven twenty and time for bed.

Tomorrow sometime she would maybe phone DC McKenna to find out if forensics had been in touch. She hoped they had, and she also hoped she had a better night, without being disturbed by noises outside her door.

Chapter 13

Miss Davis called in to see DC McKenna like she promised after work, and he had taken her into one of the interview rooms, and had asked Max to sit in with them. When he had asked her again to tell them what had happened that night, right up to the time they had gone to the club, she complained that she had already made a statement to that effect and told them what had happened. She said there was nothing more to add.

'Miss Davis can I ask if you know a girl name Lucy and if she was in the club the same time as you and Miss Sudbury?' he asked her.

'She may have been' Francesca replied.

'Well either she was there or she wasn't, which one was it? he asked her.

Francesca rolled her eyes. It was easy to see that she was getting fed up with all of this.

'You have to understand that that night we both had so much to drink, that even I had trouble remembering who was there. The last time I saw Jennifer she was with this guy talking and laughing. I only really saw the back of him but it looked like they were having a good time, so I left them to it' she continued Then when it got late, I thought it was time to go home and went to look for Jennifer but could not find her.'

'What happened next?' he asked.

'I rang her mobile a few times but there was no answer, and so in the end I left her a message asking her to ring me just as soon as she got home.'

'I see. And did she ring you back?' he asked.

'No not until the following day' she replied.

'Were you not worried that she had not phoned you?'

'Not really no because I just presumed she had gone off with the guy she was having fun with. She's a big girl you know, quite able to look after herself' she told him with a big frown.

'That's just it though, Miss Davis. Jennifer can't remember what happened that night, or how she got home which is worrying, especially as she has some unexplained bruises.'

'Look I have told you everything that I remember. I have no idea how Jennifer got home, or how she got her bruises, maybe she invited the guy she was with around to her apartment and they had rough sex or something.....I just don't know.'

'Maybe, or maybe something else happened to her and that's what we are trying to find out' he told her to which she looked down and shrugged.

'Can I ask how you got home yourself that night?'

'My boyfriend called into the club and gave me a lift' she answered.

'Oh right and what is your boyfriend's name?'

'Paul, Paul Blake, but he never saw Jennifer. She was gone before he picked me up' she told him.

'OK Miss Davis that is all for now. Thank you for coming into see us' he told her getting up from his chair.

'She is OK.....Jennifer I mean?' she asked him standing up.

'Why do you ask? I mean have you not been in contact with your friend? he answered looking at her strangely.

'I......I have been busy and I........' she told him suddenly feeling guilty that she had not in fact contacted her friend at all since she last spoke to her. But Paul her boyfriend had told her that she should not get involved, and that it was best she kept out of it.

'Right Miss we will be in touch if we need to ask anything else. In the meantime if you remember anything, anything at all give us a ring' he told her before she left.

After the interview he asked Max what he thought, and Max had told him that it was hard to say and that she seemed genuine enough. But Alex felt pensive about the whole thing, there was just something that was not adding up. He was going to have to go back and see Ms Sudbury again but wanted to find out what forensics said first. And so first thing Monday he had rung them up and they had told him that the results should be in the station within the next few days, so he decided he would wait until then before contacting her again.

DC McKenna had managed to get hold of Mr Fletcher's Landlord and explained the situation with the apartment He had thought long and hard about bringing in the Social Services, but he wanted to see what Mr Carmichael said first. He had left a recorded message for him on his answerphone, and he had phoned him back soon after sounding worried. When he had explained about the situation there, he had said he would go around and check the place out when he had time, but he was far too busy at the moment. Alex had thought this strange, because if he were a landlord to a property and someone contacted him about it, he would be there as quick as lightning. Yet he did not seem too bothered. He told Alex that because he was always on time with the rent he left him alone. The last time he had visited was six months or so ago, and apart from being a bit untidy everything looked fine with the place. But Alex McKenna then told him that it looked like it had been neglected for a longer period than just six months, to which Mr Carmichael had told him just as long as he was not destroying the property or causing a nuisance, and paying his rent on time, it was fine. He had a right to do what he wanted in his own space. Alex was not happy about this, but for now he decided to leave it at that. He also asked if he knew any of the other neighbours in the block, and he had told him that he owned one of the other apartments beside the one that Mr Fletcher lived in, but it it had been empty for a while and not rented out. He was in process of having work done to it. As for the other one he was not sure who lived there, or in fact who owned it. Alex still felt there was something going on and he intended to find out what.

He had also contacted the new owner of the club to see if he had seen anything untoward happening that night. But apparently he had not even been there that Saturday, instead his manager had been on duty and he had said he had not mentioned anything to him, or reported anything. Usually if anything had happened they had an incident book that they had to write in. He had gone into his office to see if there was anything written down, but there wasn't.

Jennifer rang her nan first thing in the morning. She knew that she would be awake, because they were both early birds and got up at six o'clock every morning. Usually her Nan would potter around in their house or garden, she had very green fingers and loved looking after it, and while she did that her grandpa always took their dog for a good long walk, before going for his cycle. She answered after the first two rings.

'Hello Nan it's only me. How's Grandpa?'

'Hello Jenny love it's early' she said to her and Jennifer thought she sounded very tired.

'I hope I did not wake you?'

'No of course not. I have been awake for ages. In fact I was up at five am. Your dad rang last night while I was at the hospital. Grandpa is still stable but very poorly. He took a right battering from that car' she told her to which Jennifer closed her eyes. She could only imagine the state he would be in. His bike must also be a write off. Poor grandpa, she thought.

'You need to look after yourself too for when grandpa gets home. Don't forget to get plenty of rest and eat. We don't want you landing up in hospital as well with grandpa. Did you manage to drive yourself there and back OK?' she asked her, feeling concerned. It was at times like these she had wished her grandparents had been living in England instead of France.

'Yes there is nothing wrong with my driving love' she told her.

'I know that but you know how I worry, especially since I know your mind is on grandpa.'

'You are a good girl Jenny and we love you dearly' she said to her.

Jennifer smiled to herself. She loved them too and told her so.

'I will ring you later just as soon as I get home from work'

'How is work Jenny?' she asked

'It's fine Nan everything is fine here' she lied. She really wished that that was the case but until the lab reports came back she would worry. At least when they came back she would know if she had been sexually assaulted. She told her Nan again that she would ring when she got home then put the phone down, took a shower and got ready for work. She decided that today she would make a packed lunch to eat in the park. And when she left this time she was pleased to see Mr Sleazy was not outside waiting for here.

At lunchtime she and Lizzie went to the park as usual to eat their sandwiches. It was a fairly warm day and Jennifer thought Lizzie looked stressed and pale.

'Are you OK Lizzie you look a bit pale looking?' she asked her sitting down on a bench and unwrapping a sandwich.

'Do I? To be honest I am just a bit worried about Toby' she told her.

'Oh why is he ill?'

'No nothing like that, but last night I told him that he would be going to visit his dad again in a few weeks time for the weekend, and he just said he did not want to go' she explained to which Jennifer looked puzzled.

'I just can't understand it; he loves going to stay with him. In fact he has never said he did not want to go in the past' she continued. 'That is why I am worried.'

'And did you ask him why he said he did not want to go?'

'Yes but all he did was run up to his room. I went up to talk to him and he shouted go away and turned away from me.'

'Strange! Maybe you should ask his dad if everything was OK the last time he was there'

'Yes maybe....oh well it's probably something or nothing you know what kids are like?' Lizzie said without thinking and Jennifer only shook her head and thought to herself I wish.

She decided to change the subject and then told her about her grandpa being in hospital.

'Oh No, what will you do? Will you have to fly out to see him?'

'I am waiting to see how he is first when I phone up later today. I am sure Mr Stone will not be very impressed if I tell him I need some time off' she replied.

Lizzie rolled her eyes.

'It's just too bad Jennifer, he would have to get a temp in. You are allowed leave on compassionate grounds you know.'

'Yes I know that, and if he took a turn for the worse I would be there in a flash. I will know more by tonight and I just hope he is OK' she told her finishing off her sandwiches.

'What happened to your grandpa?'

'Apparently he was out cycling and got knocked off his bicycle by a hit and run driver' she explained.

'How terrible I hope they catch the person that did it' she said to Jennifer who nodded in agreement.

'Yes me too it was just terrible that whoever it was left him in the road like that. An old man in his nineties, shocking'

Lizzie could only shake her head in sympathy and agree and there was a moment of quietness with them.

It was always nice in the park at this time of year, and she would often go there to eat her lunch. A young mother walked past them pushing her baby in a pram, looking as proud as punch as she suddenly stopped to check on him, cooing sweet noises. The baby was obviously a boy because there was so much blue in the pram, even the rattle that hung down from the canopy had been blue, and Lizzie turned and smiled.

'Would you like to have children one day Jennifer?' she asked her.

'Gosh yes. I always wanted children when I was married to David and I thought we would have them one day' she replied

'Well it's not too late, you are still young enough. How old are you twenty-five?' To which Jennifer could only smile. She told her she was twenty-eight and that to have children you first have to find a man.

'Ah yes there is that of course, but twenty eight is still very young, you will find someone else one day' she told her with a smile.

'I hope so, but there has been no one so far that's taken my eye. What about you? Do you think you will ever have any more children? A little brother or sister for Toby?' Jennifer asked her. But she just shrugged and looked away with a look of sadness in her eyes.

'I don't think so. Oh don't get me wrong I do love children. But I had an awful time with Toby, it was a long labour twenty-four hours in fact, and I nearly died. So I don't think I want to take that risk again' she told her. It hit a raw spot for Jennifer when she had told her that she had nearly died, especially since her own mother had died during childbirth with her, but she did not say anything. After lunch they both got up and walked the short distance back to work.

After work Jennifer caught her usual bus to take her back home and then it was just a short walk to her apartment. She hoped Mr Sleazy would not be there, she had been relieved to see he had not been anywhere in sight when she had left this morning. She just could not make her mind up about him.

Her friend Francesca had said that perhaps she should try talking to him, but she shivered at the thought of it. Knowing him, talking to him would only give him the wrong impression. Then she mulled about Francesca. She really did miss her, even though she had wronged her by not supporting her, and making her look a fool at the same time. Yes Lizzie was nice and they had struck up a good friendship together, but Francesca was her oldest friend, someone who she had been able to confide in. She just wished she would get in touch and ask how she was doing, but she would not hold her breath.

She was relieved to see all was quiet in the communal hall, no Mr Sleazy, and definitely no more graffiti on her door. She let herself into her apartment and closed her door. She had picked up the mail outside first. There were separate post boxes outside for each apartment. She put the mail down and went to press the kettle on in the kitchen, but something just did not feel right. Before she had left that morning she was sure she had closed the room between the kitchen and the sitting area that led to the hall. It was something she always did by habit, yet it was open, and also the book she had left on the coffee table was on the floor. She frowned picking it up again and putting it back on the coffee table. No one could have been in because she had had the locks changed and only she had the key. Maybe she had been mistaken. She had been so upset about her grandpa that she might have forgotten to close the door. It was easily done and she was just being paranoid now.

She made herself a cup of coffee and took a ready meal out of the fridge for later. Then she picked the phone up to call her nan, wondering if there was any improvement with her grandpa and hoped there was. She dialed out the long number to France and waited. It rang out for ages and no answerphone clicked on, so she put the phone down, and she thought she would try again later. Maybe her Nan was still at the hospital.

She then decided to turn on her computer and check to see if Phil the guy from the dating website had replied. Sure enough there was a message from him.

'Hello Katherine, so glad you decided to reply and that you want to get to know me better. Thank you for telling me a little more about yourself. You seem a really nice girl. I am away for the next few days on another course to do with IT. How are you and how is your work going? I hope you don't think this is too soon saying we have only exchanged just a few emails, but how would you fancy meeting up some night - somewhere of your choosing of course, maybe we could arrange it when I get back.

Yours Phil.'

Jennifer sighed deeply. She knew she would have to tell him her name was not Katherine but Jennifer, especially if there was a chance of them both meeting. It was only right. Besides she was getting fed up with the pretense of the name Katherine or Katie. It was fine in the chat rooms where she knew she would never meet any of the people she spoke to, but she felt she now wanted to tell Phil her real name, and would reply later.

She glanced through the mail that she had put to the side, the usual circulars and junk mail, plus a red-letter reminder for the gas bill, which she had forgotten to pay. Then she looked at the last letter type written and froze. It said the name Katie on it nothing else, no surname no address just Katie. In fact it had been hand delivered because there was no postage stamp.

Jennifer felt afraid to even look inside and put it down again. Sitting on the sofa she felt suddenly sick with nerves. What could be inside it?

She toyed with the idea of phoning DC McKenna and telling him she had received an anonymous letter, but what could he say? Even she did not know what was inside it. After fifteen minutes she plucked up the courage to open it. Inside was no letter of explanation, and there was in fact nothing at all just a photograph.

Chapter 14

Whether it was the shock of seeing the photo, combined with stress about her grandpa she did not know, she just felt physically ill and only just made it to the toilet before she was violently sick. Wiping her mouth with a piece of toilet paper she went back into the sitting room and picked up the photo again and pushed it into the back of a drawer

Jennifer knew she could never show the photo to anyone never mind DC McKenna. If she did where would that leave her? Her reputation would be in shreds, that's for sure. She felt scared, very scared. Who on earth could have sent the photo, except someone that knew her past? But even that did not explain why the name on the envelope said Katie.

She had never called herself Katie except online, nothing made sense anymore. It felt like she was living a nightmare. It was all too much for her and she was beginning to think she should go and stay with her nan and grandpa. Tomorrow she would speak to Mr Stone about compassionate leave. She knew that there was a chance he could still say no but nevertheless she would try.

She decided to open a bottle of wine to have with her ready meal of spaghetti bolognese and then she would try to ring her nan again. After she had eaten she poured herself a glass of wine. Then she decided to log onto her computer again to try and relax. She had had a shock when she had received the photo and needed to relax, and usually the computer helped. On logging into the chat room she noticed that Prince of Mystery appeared to be online, but ignoring him she clicked on another name Tarzan and she smiled to herself when he instantly flashed a message to her.

'Hello Katie I am Tarzan will you be my Jane?'

'It depends' she typed back.

'Do you like Jungles?' he asked and Jennifer screwed her eyes.

'Not really I am afraid of bugs' she typed.

'Ah but I will keep you safe if you become my Jane' he replied.

And then Jennifer got a message from Prince of Mystery asking if she would chat with him. When she totally ignored him he then send a crying face icon, immediately followed by another and then a broken heart icon. Jennifer knew she shouldn't be but she was intrigued and decided to send him an angry face icon, to which he then sent a sad icon. This went on for a while until he sent another message asking her to chat with him. In the meantime Tarzan had gone off to find another willing person to play his Jane.

'OK Prince of Mystery but no funny business' she told him finishing off her wine.

'What do you mean funny business? Don't you like my games?' he typed back.

'It depends, sometimes they get a bit weird.'

'Weird in what way, all I am interesting in is getting into the truth, the truth of all things of course' he said to her.

'What do you mean getting into the truth?'

'Just what I said. I ask questions, you answer and I get to the truth' he typed and Jennifer rolled her eyes. This guy is one weird person she thought.

'So will you play the game with me?'

'OK what do you want to know now?'

'Good, first question if you could call yourself by any other name rather than Katie what would it be?' he typed. That's easy she thought.

'I would call myself Jane' she thought that Jane had been random enough.

'Jane are you really sure and not Katherine?' he typed back. Jennifer looked at where he had written the name Katherine, and wondered why he had said that. On her dating website she had used the name Katherine in her profile, but he could not possibly know that, so she typed back.

'Why did you say that?'

'Say what.'

'Why did you ask if I was sure that I would not want to call myself Katherine.'

'Simple, because isn't Katie short for Katherine? he typed back.

Jennifer breathed a sigh of relief, she had not thought of that. She was really getting paranoid now because of everything that had happened. She decided to pour herself one more glass of wine. She told herself that all this was was a game nothing else. The person on the other end did not know her from Adam. She needed to try and relax or else she would drive herself mad.

'Oh right OK, no my choice would still be Jane' she told him.

'That tells me that Katie is not your real name am I right?' he typed and then sent a icon face winking. Jennifer decided to ignore this.

'My next question is who am I really Katie or should I say Jennifer' he typed which made Jennifer so shocked she logged straight off the computer.

147

This was more than weird and also not even possible. Who on earth was this guy and how did he know her real name?

She was still shaking when her telephone started to ring. She quickly got up to answer it and was relieved to here her nan on the other end.

'Hello Jenny love I just thought I would let you know that your grandpa is still very poorly but is conscious and although he is in a lot of pain he managed to say a few words to me' she told her.

Jennifer was close to tears but did not want her nan to know that. She felt relieved that her grandpa was not any worse but the shock of what had just happened had been too much for her. She decided that it was the very last time she would log onto any chat rooms.

'I am so glad nan, what do the doctors say about him?' she asked trying to forget about what just happened and focus on what was happening with her grandpa.

'Well he has got a few serious injuries, broken ribs and a broken leg. They are doing more tests love, but he is in a bad way, and of course his age goes against him too' she explained.

'Oh dear nan, I am so sorry. I really do wish I could be there with you, I feel so helpless you know'

'Now, now Jenny I don't expect you to dash over here at a drop of a hat. So long as I know I have you to talk to, that's all that matters, and you know I will keep you updated as much as I can don't you?'

'Yes nan and thank you. Has my dad been in touch again?' she asked.

'Not yet Jenny he will probably ring later. I did try to ring him before I rang you but there was no answer' she told her. Jennifer thought to herself why did that not surprise her. She felt annoyed with her father.

'Have the police found out who the hit and run driver was yet?'

'No, but they were in to see us while I was there today, to see if he remembered anything. But all your grandpa could do was moan in pain. The one person that vaguely saw the accident told the police in his statement that they thought the car looked like a black sports car, but it was going far too fast for them to read the number plate'

'Oh nan. Are you at home to stay tonight?' she asked her, suddenly not wanting her to go out again to the hospital; she just did not think it was wise. She was not fifty and really at ninety she should be taking things easy or else she too could become ill.

'Yes I think so love. I feel so tired tonight and think I will have an early night. It was late before I got home last night, and I have been at the hospital nearly all day. One of our neighbours had to feed the dog and take her for a walk. She is getting old now poor dog she is at least twelve' she continued, and in spite of having the shock she had just had, Jennifer could not help laughing at what her nan had said about the dog getting old at twelve. Yes it was getting old but so was her nan. In fact not all ninety year olds could do what she did. She was still as bright as a button, and would easily pass for a lady in her seventies.

'Okay Nan I will let you go, try and get a good night's sleep, you will need all your strength for when grandpa comes home' she told her, and then they ended the call.

Jennifer too decided to go to bed, she just did not feel in the mood even to answer Phil the guy from the dating website. What had happened in the chat room with Prince of Mystery had shaken her to the very core. For the life of her she could not understand it. How was it possible for him to even know her real name? She had never given any details away. She felt uneasy at the thought of it that there was someone out there that had it in for her.

The photo had disturbed her too. It had been a right blast from the past and something she would rather forget about. There was no way she would be able to show it to the police, unless she wanted other people to know, which she didn't. It was a part of her she wanted to keep hidden and for eleven years she had done that.

That night her dreams were strangely around DC McKenna. He was looking at her accusingly and calling her a liar. She was in this small room sitting in a chair and appeared to be unable to move, as if she was tied up, and Francesca was there too, dressed as a policewoman. She then started to say nasty things about her, that no one knew what she was really like, only she did and always had. It was so vivid that Jennifer woke up in a sweat, and looked at her alarm clock beside her bed. The red luminous dials told her it was just three thirty.

She decided to get up and make herself a warm drink of Horlicks. While she was making it she thought that she could hear noises like shuffling and creaks that seemed to be coming from the apartment above.

She had often wondered who had lived there, she had never seen any other neighbours apart from Mr Sleazy since she had moved in, although she often heard doors opening and closing and on rare occasion she had heard a baby cry. But that could have easily come from a TV. Sometimes it disturbed her to think that Mr Sleazy was her only neighbour, so she liked to imagine other people living in the block above for her own sanity.

When she had first enquired about renting a apartment, she had seen it advertised in the Evening Sentinel. It had read 'downstairs luxury apartment in a block of four, available for long lease. Owner now living abroad.' She had loved it the first time the woman at the Estate Agents had shown her around. The added bonus was that it was facing a lovely big park. She had asked at the time who owned the rest of the apartments in the block, and been told that they were most probably let out by a different landlord. Her landlord who she had never met now lived abroad and left the estate agent to deal with everything.

The noises seemed to have stopped and as Jennifer finished her drink her thoughts turned to her grandpa. She really hoped that the accident he had had would not be the beginning of the end for him. She also hoped that her dad had been in touch again with them. She still felt he should be flying over to see them, instead of putting work first. But she was not altogether surprised by this. His work had always taken first place for as long as she remembered, or at least since she had been about ten years old. It was then that he had got the rep job that had places based between the Potteries and Birmingham. At first he had worked from one of their firms in the Potteries. This suited him since that was where he was living. But later when Nicole moved out and then at a early age so did Jennifer, he had up-sticks and gone to live near Birmingham.

Jennifer went back to bed and it was not long before sleep overcame her and this time she only awoke with the sound of her alarm clock going off. It was 7am.

Chapter 15

DC McKenna had a busy day ahead of him. He had been asked to sit in on another interview with Max. It was concerning a shop lifting offence that could have turned nasty. Apparently a man was being accused of stealing designer clothes from a major store, and when approached he had apparently pulled out a gun and frightened the security guard who in turn had suddenly clutched his chest and fell to the floor in pain. The guy ran away in fright dropping the gun on the floor, but someone else in the store had recognised him, and consequently he had been later arrested. The gun had turned out to be a fake gun, and the security guard was alive but had suffered a mild heart attack. The interview was with one of the witnesses.

He thought that the Sudbury case could be pretty much sorted before the end of the week, depending on the forensics reports, which were due in today or tomorrow. Also Alex wanted to look at the HOLMES database again as he was still not convinced that Mr Fletcher was squeaky clean. There was just something about him that just didn't ring true, and he kept seeing that big computer in the corner of the living room. The place had been a complete tip and the smell had been something else, although his explanation of it being due to the drains could still be true. How anyone could live like that he just could not visualise. He was a bachelor himself and sometimes a little untidy around the house, but he had still prided himself on cleanliness.

He had telephoned the nursing home where his gran was first thing, and had asked how she was. One of the care assistants he presumed that was new had left him hanging on then had put him onto someone else, and when the other person spoke he recognised her voice as Margaret one of the senior care assistants.

She had told him that his gran was in her dementia state at the moment but was OK and happy enough. He in turn decided not to visit, thinking that she would not remember him anyway. Then he felt a bit guilty and knew whatever state she was in, she was still his gran. She had given him the best part of her life. He really needed to be there for her, and so he told Margaret he would call in later to see her.

The interview with the witness went well which meant the case was practically cut and dried, and afterwards Alex and Max went down to the canteen for a quick bite to eat.

'Have forensics got back yet with any results?' he asked tucking into pie and mash that was the canteen specialty. They sold a lot of the meat and potato pies.

'They are due back anytime now' he told him. He had decided to have the same. Usually he just grabbed a sandwich or an oatcake or something, but today he couldn't resist, especially as Max had ordered it too.

'Do you think there will be any proof of sexual assault?' Max asked between mouthfuls.

'I have not got a clue. I think she is genuine enough though, although I think like you there is more to it than she is saying. I hope I am proved wrong, because I quite like her' he told him and Max smiled.

'Best not get too involved, remember work and pleasure don't mix.'

'You don't need to tell me that, I already know. Besides I don't intend to get too involved with her or anyone else for that matter,' he told him and Max could only smile again.

'They all say that mate' he told him.

'I mean it' he replied.

'By the way thanks for sitting in on the Brentwood witness. It was just as I thought, mostly cut and dried' and Alex could only nod in agreement.

As usual he took a mug of coffee back up to his desk. Taking a sip of it he then turned his attention to the computer and going through the database, which proved both painstaking and time consuming

It was well into the afternoon when one of his colleagues dropped a file on his desk that read Lab results for the Sudbury case. 'Bingo!' he said out loud as he turned his attention to the report.

After carefully reading through all of the results he closed the file and sighed deeply. He needed to go to see Jennifer and give her the results.

Jennifer had just finished work and was on the way home when her mobile had rang. Taking it out of her bag she was pleased to see that it was DC Alex McKenna.

'Hello is that Ms Sudbury....Jennifer?'

'Yes speaking' she replied.

'It's DC McKenna here. I wonder if I could call to see you later this evening, say around seven?' he asked her. Jennifer wondered if he had any news for her, or whether he just wanted to ask more questions.

'Yes that's fine I will be at home' she told him.

'OK see you then or just after' he replied ending the call.

She wanted to ask if the lab results had come back but didn't, she would know soon enough she thought. It had seemed a long workday for Jennifer and she was glad it had finally come to an end.

The only consolation had been that her boss Mr Stone had seemed in a much better mood than of late, and she was able to explain the situation concerning her grandpa. He seemed very sympathetic towards her and told her that if things worsened to tell him and he would organise compassionate leave for her, it was the least he could do he had told her.

The bus dropped her off and she then started on the short walk to her apartment. Like always she hoped that Mr Sleazy was not around. She also thought about the noises she had heard in the night that seemed to be coming from the apartment directly above her. Maybe someone had moved in without her knowing. Then her thoughts turned to the chat rooms and Prince of Mystery. She had promised herself that she would never log on to that chat room ever again, not after that. She was also not going to use the name Katie ever again either. And when she got home she was going to write a email to Phil telling him her real name, thus abandoning any connection to the name at all. She also could not wait to find out how her grandpa was doing, and hoped he was OK. She would ring her nan later.

She neared her apartment and for a brief moment Jennifer looked up at the one directly above hers to see if she could see anything. The noises she had heard in the early hours had definitely been coming from there. Yet on looking up at it the place seemed empty. There were no curtains up just windolene on all the windows as if the place was being decorated. Before letting herself into the communal hall she collected her post from her mailbox, and gave a big sigh of relief when there was nothing there but circulars. She had half expected to find another envelope with the name Katie written on it, and was glad when there had been nothing She braced herself when she let herself into the communal hall in case Mr Sleazy was there. She was certainly not in any mood for him today, not that she was in a mood for him any other day either. In fact she had even been considering trying to find another place and to give her notice in for the apartment. Since all the strange things had been happening she had felt ill at ease there. She was pleased to see Mr Sleazy had not been waiting, in fact he was nowhere in sight. Good, she thought opening the door to her apartment. She put on the kettle and picked the phone up to ring her nan. But there was no answer, except this time the answerphone kicked in and so Jennifer was able to leave her a message asking how her grandpa was and telling her nan that she would ring her back later before she went to bed.

She then looked into her fridge to see what she could take out for her dinner. She would need to do some shopping soon she thought, to stock up on ready meals. Jennifer decided to take a shower before dinner as she felt hot and sticky from the day. The office where she worked had air conditioning, but more often than not it was not working correctly and Lizzie had said the same about the office she was in. They had both shared sandwiches in the park again, and Jennifer had asked how Toby was and she had replied that he was still insisting he did not want to go to visit his dad, which was very puzzling to her. She was going to take Jennifer's advice and ask her ex if anything happened when he was last there. She did not want him to stop going to visit his father because she knew he needed this contact.

After she had her shower she got changed into something more casual, jeans and a t-shirt and brushed her hair into a ponytail. It was still very warm as she ate her dinner, which was chilli con carne and a baked potato. She was out of salad or else she might have had that. She really needed to make a mental note to go shopping tomorrow, either that or get a pizza bought in. She was also running short of milk for her night drink and coffee, and if she made DC McKenna a cup of tea or coffee then she would have to forget her night drink. She hoped he would want one, as she quite liked him, although liking him was not an option, as or a start he was out of bounds to her. He would probably never look twice at her either. She needed to alter her ideas. Just as she finished eating her dinner her phone rang and she got up to answer it.

'Hello Jenny it's me nan. I hope I am not disturbing your dinner love?' she asked.

Jennifer was relieved to hear her voice, she had intended to ring her back later if she had not phoned.

'No nan I have had my dinner, how is grandpa?'

'Not well Jenny, I have been there practically all day. He is in so much pain and I hate to see him like that, I am at my wits end. The neighbour has been good again walking Bella, but I am worried about your grandpa, he is on all kind of drips' she explained. Jennifer felt awful. All she wanted to do was to be able to give her nan a big hug and be there for her. She just wished that her dad would pull his socks up and go over to see them.

'Does my dad know grandpa is no better?' she asked

'I have not spoken to him today. I tried to ring him yesterday but could not get hold of him, maybe he has phoned the hospital, I just don't know' she told her, which made Jennifer think she was going to have to try and ring him again herself. He should be planning to go out there and stay with his mother, not messing around with work. Which also brought Jennifer to the conclusion that she herself needed to go over. Depending what the results were with forensics she would have another word with Mr Stone tomorrow and arrange something, but she was not going to mention it to her nan until she could book.

'I am sure he will OK nan. I suppose he is going to have a lot of pain with all the injuries he has had' she told her.

'I'm just scared Jenny, he is no young chicken you know, and I am beginning to feel my age too. I am so tired from all the visits to the hospital, I doubt if I would have enough energy to walk Bella myself, it's a good job I have the neighbour. They both come in and feed her then later they take her for a walk' she continued. And Jennifer felt so sorry she was not there with her, and at the same time felt angry with her dad. It was totally wrong of him she thought. She intended to ring him herself and tell him just that.

'Enough of me now love, how are you?' she asked changing the subject.

'I am just fine nan, my only concern is you and granddad. I want you to promise me you will have another early night and don't forget to eat' she told her.

'I will love. I am going to do myself a sandwich and a nice cup of tea, then its off to bed for me.'

'Good nan and in the meantime I will ring my dad and speak with you tomorrow OK.' Then she put the phone down.

Immediately after that she rang her dad but again there was no answer and no answerphone this time so she was unable to leave a message. Now she was fuming. What was wrong with her dad? Yes she knew he had his work but surely his parents were more important. She looked at the clock and it was nearly half past six. DC McKenna would be here in half an hour. Jennifer decided to write an email to Phil to tell him her real name was Jennifer and not Katie. She decided to explain that while online she preferred to use a Pseudonym and Katie was what she had picked. She tried to word it as best she could, and at the end she told him that she would be happy to arrange a meeting sometime in the near future when he had got back from his course, provided he was still interested. Then she signed of with her real name.

DC McKenna had decided to call at the nursing home before going to see Jennifer. He had also arranged for a female colleague to meet him outside the apartment at 7 o'clock. He had thought it best that he took someone else preferably a female, so that she could be present when he told Jennifer the news.

He had bought a bunch of his grans favourite flowers from the florist on the way. She always did like alstroemerias. They were her favourite for as long as he could remember. So he hoped it would trigger off a memory with her if she were still in her dementia state. He remembered his grandfather buying them for her every anniversary and sometimes on her birthday. She had always loved them. He parked his car in the grounds of the nursing home. There were already a lot of cars there, probably people visiting their relatives and maybe some cars that belonged to staff members. It was still a warm but muggy kind of night and he only hoped that he would find his gran more her usual self. Maybe the flowers would help.

Margaret greeted him as he made his way to the large communal sitting room that had a large picture window overlooking the well-kept gardens, of shrubs and flowers that were in bloom.

He had often sat and looked out of the window talking to his gran. He thought that whoever managed the gardens did a wonderful job. Gardening had never been his forte, although he liked to see a well kept one, but doing it was another thing.

Margaret smiled when she saw the flowers he was carrying, as she knew straight away their meaning. Maisie had told her that her favourite flowers were alstroemerias, and she had also told her on the many times she had been lucid, that her late husband had always bought them for her.

'Hello Mr McKenna your gran is over there taking a nap in her chair, I will go and get a vase for those beautiful flowers. I am sure your gran will be happy to see you' she told him.

'How is she Margaret, is she any better than earlier when we spoke?' he asked.

'She picked up a little but then she got very tired after dinner and when we brought her into the sitting room with the others she dozed off, so it's hard to say' she replied and then went off to find a vase.

Alex looked around him. There were a few more old people just dozing in chairs and a few sitting in their wheelchairs unable to walk. There was a old lady cradling a doll in her arms like a baby, and when she saw Alex she smiled and went to him to show him her baby. Alex smiled back and made a pretense of looking at the doll and saying how lovely her baby was. She then asked Alex if he wanted to hold her, but before he could answer Margaret was back again with a vase for the flowers filled with water and she also had scissors just in case the stems were too long. She smiled at the old lady who she called Alice and told her that it was time for her to feed her baby and get it ready for bed, which seemed to satisfy Alice and she pottered away cradling her doll.

Just as soon as Alex sat down besides his gran, she opened her eyes and seemed to recognise him. Her eyes filled with tears and she held out her arms for a hug. Alex gave his gran a big hug and then showed her the flowers he had bought for her. She loved them so much she did not want them put down anywhere. Instead she insisted she held them in the vase all the while he was there. It was so lovely to see his gran like this, she seemed more content than the last time he had been there, and he ended up staying longer than he meant to. Margaret went away to make some tea and brought it on a tray for them, along with some chocolate biscuits. By the time Alex left it was ten past seven. He had told Jennifer he would see her at 7pm or just after. It was only a short journey away from the home to where Jennifer lived so by quarter past he drew up outside the apartments and saw that his colleague was waiting outside in her car. When she saw him she got out to meet him, and Alex pressed the buzzer to Jennifer's apartment.

Chapter 16

Jennifer unlocked the communal door as soon as she heard the buzzer sound. She knew it was DC McKenna because she had been expecting him any minute. In fact she was getting nervous at what he had got to tell her, she just hoped he had the results of the tests she had had done.

She opened the door of her apartment to let him in, and was surprised to see that he was not alone, but had a female colleague with him disappointed even, which she could not explain why. She asked them both to come through to the sitting room.

'Hello Ms Sudbury I hope you don't mind but I have brought my Colleague DC Isabelle Flack with me as well. We have had all the results back from the lab and we are able to tell you them' he said to her.

'Oh right. Please take a seat' she told them.

'First of all you will be pleased to know that there is no evidence at all to suggest that you were sexually assaulted' he said to which Jennifer breathed a sigh of relief.

'Thank God for that, but what about the rest of the things that happened such as my bruises?' she asked him.

'I was coming to that. What the lab was testing for among other things was the date rape drug GHB otherwise know as cherry meth. It takes only fifteen to thirty minutes to become effective, but only stays inside the body for twelve hours. In your case it was longer than that by the time you came to the police station and were examined. Also the fact that you must have gone to the toilet before hand does not help' he told her.

'But the lab must have picked something up, surely?

'I am sorry Ms Sudbury but the only thing it did pick up was the large amount of alcohol that was in your blood, actually a very considerable amount. In fact it was a wonder you did not get alcohol poisoning. They also checked for other drugs beside GHB but I have to tell you nothing was found, nothing at all.'

'But what about the bruises on my thighs and wrists?' she told him clutching at straws. It looked like this was not going to be solved after all, and she felt scared.

'The thing is there just do not seem to be any witnesses to say a crime has been committed. Yes you had bruises and we have photographic evidence to support this, but as you cannot remember how you got them, and the fact that there were no witnesses I am afraid there is just nothing more we can do.'

'So all of this has been for nothing?' she asked feeling upset.

'I would not say that, the fact that we have now got it all on record, if something else does happen it will help. Of course if you remember anything else please don't hesitate to call us' he explained.

'Would it help if you talked to my colleague here?' he gently asked her. He could see that she was close to tears but Jennifer nodded her head no. The female DC looked on sympathetically. After a few more minutes they both got up to leave.

'Remember if anything else untoward happens give us a call OK?' Alex told her and she closed the door to her apartment.

Outside he turned to his colleague Isabelle and asked what she thought, to which she replied 'it's hard to say. Maybe the bruises were due to a date gone wrong, it does happen' she told him.

'I am not so sure, I still think there is more to it than meets the eye, but our hands are tied now because there is not a spot of evidence to suggest anything else.' Then he said goodbye and they each got into their separate cars and drove away.

After she closed the door Jennifer just burst into tears. I can't believe they have found nothing. All that trouble going to the police station to report it, and the humiliation of being examined and for what, she thought to herself. It had been a complete waste of time, and in the process it had also looked like she had lost her friendship with Francesca. Yet there were still things happening, so someone must have it in for her. But how could she have shown the DC the photo that she had received. She knew that deep down she should have reported it and the strange things that had been said to her via the chat lines, but she could not bring herself to tell him. She felt so ashamed. The photo had been apart of her life that almost no one knew about only Francesca, and now she could not even confide in her, since she had not phoned or texted since. She felt utterly alone in all of this.

She had also been disappointed that DC McKenna had brought someone with him to tell her the news, and that had been sad in itself, because she had thought perhaps there had been just a hint of something with him. She could not explain it, except it has all been going around in her head. Why would a man like him look twice at her anyhow? She must be really lonely and clutching at straws to even think so.

So unless anything else happened this was the end of the case she had filed, and she hoped that nothing else would happen. She would have a word with Mr Stone tomorrow about getting leave, even if it were just for a week. Maybe a week or two away from the apartment might do her good.

Jennifer had just settled herself down when her mobile bleeped that a message had come through. She picked it up to see who it was and she felt a sudden jolt. It was from Francesca, just as she had been thinking of her, she had written the message.

'Jen just to ask if you are OK I am sorry how things went between us, maybe we could meet up tomorrow for coffee or something after work, Fran x.'

Well that's a turn up for the books, she thought with a smile and instantly send her back a text.

'Hi yes OK meet you tomorrow after work say around five where?' she said.

'Good! Meet you in the corner cafe at five, see you there Fran x.'

Well at least she wanted to see her again, Jennifer thought to herself. She then huffed a little bit, and just hoped that she would have a good explanation on why she had not supported her. But secretly she felt happy and knew that she could not be cross with her friend for long. That night she managed to get hold of her father too.

'Hello Dad it's me Jenny. I have been trying to contact you and so has nan.'

'I am sorry love but I have not long got in, I was just about to ring your nan before you rang. How is grandpa?'

'Dad he is not well, nan says he has broken ribs and one leg' she told him.

'He won't be well will he love after what he has been through, it's going to take time' he told her and Jennifer felt cross.

'I know that but don't you think you should be over there with them to support them?' she told him.

'Jennifer we have been through this before. I can't just up and go, I wish it were that simple you know, I really do but it isn't.'

'It's because you make it not simple'.

'And what's that supposed to mean....please explain?'

'Well your work always does and always has come first' she explained then continued 'it should be the other way around. Family should come first, your dad has been in a dreadful accident and your mother needs you as simple as that!' she told him. To which there was silence at the other end. Then he spoke again

'You just don't understand do you? I think you are being a tad unfair on me. If it were a matter of life and death I would drop everything just like that and go, but I phoned the hospital myself and they told me that although he was quite poorly he was stable' he continued to which Jennifer lost it.

'DAD JUST FORGET IT, I will go over there myself, you just do what you normally do' she half shouted at him.

'And what's that supposed to mean? And please don't shout at me, I have perfectly good hearing young lady!'

'What you always do is bury your head in the sand. Grandpa is ninety four for goodness sake!'

'Jennifer I am quite aware of how old my father is. What you don't understand is things are not quite that simple.'

'Easy dad you just book a plane ticket and go over, which I intend to do within the next few days.'

'OK OK .....I see it's no use talking to you while you are in this mood. I suggest you phone back when you are much calmer' he told her and then he put the phone down.

Jennifer screamed out loud with frustration. Tomorrow she was going to speak to her boss about getting some time off. She felt both disappointed and fatigued and decided to just go to bed and try to sleep. She was just about to turn the lights off when the phone rang. Thinking it might be her father ringing back she decided to ignore it at first, but then she thought it could be her nan so hurried to answer.

'Hello' she said then froze. She was having another silent call. Whoever had rung was clearly there but not saying a word.

'Hello who is this? What do you want?' but not a sound until she heard the familiar click of the receiver going down.

Jennifer was going to have to get these silent calls sorted, she was getting far too many now for it to be just a mistaken number, and it was starting to peeve her. She turned the sitting room light off and went to bed.

During the night the noises that seemed to be coming from the apartment above started again and woke Jennifer up. She ignored them at first until they got louder and louder. It was a strange kind of noise like a distant knocking that seemed to gradually increase in sound. At first when Jennifer was half asleep she had thought she was dreaming and that someone was knocking on her apartment door with the knocking gradually getting louder. She turned the bedside light on and just lay there until they eventually stopped. The rest of the night was spent tossing and turning again, and by the time morning came and the alarm sounded telling her it was time to get up, she had been practically awake. She could not have had more than three hours sleep all night, and she was feeling wretched.

She caught sight of herself in the mirror when she went to the bathroom and could hardly recognise herself. Her face was so pale with dark circles under her eyes from lack of sleep and she looked and felt stressed. She had a quick shower and then got dressed for work. Before she left she made herself a round of toast but could hardly eat it, so threw it in the bin. She had been too tired to eat, and too tired to even do herself a packed lunch for the park.

On leaving the apartment Jennifer just missed Mr Sleazy. He had come out of his door as she closed the communal hall door behind her. Jennifer could not help looking up at the apartment above her. She had been puzzled where all the banging had come from, because like before it looked to be empty. She walked the short distance to the bus stop. The bus was due in another ten minutes if it arrived on time. She had loved her apartment when she had first moved in, loved the thought of living right across from the park, but now she was beginning to hate the place. All the silent phone calls plus Mr Sleazy.

The bus was crowded as usual with people on their way to work, and this morning smelt slightly stuffy. She sat down on the only seat available next to a very large woman somewhere in her fifties. After numerous stops she finally came to hers and got off. It was not a bad day but looking at the dark clouds in the sky there was a hint of rain.

It was another busy day in the office and during her lunch break Jennifer had a word with Mr Stone.

'Hello Jennifer what can I do for you?' he asked looking up from his desk. He had a pile of papers that he had gone through and looked like he was still busy. Maybe this was not such a good time, she thought to herself, but it was her break time and she wanted to get it over and done with.

'It's about my grandfather sir' she began.

'Ah your grandfather, how is he Jennifer?' he asked looking over his glasses at her.

'Not good, in fact he is quite poorly and remember when you said that if he got any worse you would consider letting me bring my holiday forward? Well I was wondering if you would consider it Mr Stone' she asked him.

'When would you want to go Jennifer?' he asked her then continued. 'I would need to get a temp in, would you need to go before next week?'

'No Mr Stone next week would be fine' she told him feeling relieved. She could now book a ticket.

'OK leave it with me, I will get onto the agency. How long do you think you would need, a few weeks?' he asked. To which Jennifer nodded and thanked him. At least she would now be able to tell her nan she was planning to come over sooner than later.

The rest of the day went fairly quickly and at last it was time to walk the short journey to the cafe to meet Francesca. Jennifer had been looking forward to seeing her again, although she still felt that her friend had let her down by not supporting her, but it was hardly worth bothering about now, since they had found nothing in forensics.

When she walked into the cafe Jennifer was surprised to see Francesca already there waiting for her. She was sitting at a table by the window, so that she could see people walking past and as soon as she saw Jennifer she waved. She already had a drink so Jennifer ordered herself one and sat down facing her. It was a nice cafe that had tables for two or four people with lovely blue gingham tablecloths and little vases of delicate forget-me-not flowers in the centre.

'Hello Fran,' she smiled at her sheepishly and Jennifer could not help noticing she did not look herself.

'Fran are you OK?' she asked suddenly feeling concerned and any hind of annoyance she had felt for her was forgotten.

'No not really' she told her looking down as if she could not look her straight in the eye.

'What's wrong, what has happened?' she asked, at which Francesca unexpectedly burst into tears. Jennifer reached over and touched her hand. Then Francesca took a tissue out of her bag and blew her nose.

'I am sorry Jen, sorry for everything, I really mean that. It was just awkward for me. I think Paul is going to finish with me' she told her.

'Why do you say that? What's happened with you and Paul?'

'Well, these last few weeks he has been acting strangely, and to be honest making excuses why we can't meet. I just don't know what to do or think' she told her.

'When did you last see him?'

'A few days ago, but he is always preoccupied when we are together. Why I ever thought he wanted to ask me to marry him that time I have no idea. You probably won't believe me when I tell you this but we have never actually made love, maybe came close to it a few times. But he always made some excuse or other. At first I just thought he was being the gentleman and it was lovely for a while, and I felt respected. But he seems to have a side to him that I never saw before and it's getting to me' she told Jennifer.

'What kind of side, what do you mean?' she asked looking puzzled.

'Well sometimes the way he looks at me it's as if he hates me, then a few minutes later he is lovey dovey again. Anyhow Jen enough about me how are you and like I said I am sorry.'

Jennifer looked at her and knew she needed to ask.

'Can I ask why you never told the police about that girl you know in the club, the one you called Lucy?' There she had said it as she had felt she really needed to ask.

'Oh Jen it was hard for me you know. Lucy and Billy are Paul's friends, and he did not want them getting involved. Paul said they would not know anything anyhow so why involve them. I am sorry Jen' she told her again and Jennifer had somehow known that had been the case. Then Jennifer decided to change the subject and told her about her grandpa, and then it was Francesca's turn to squeeze her hand.

'Will you fly out there to see them Jen?' she asked looking sympathetically at her.

'Yes I have already asked for compassionate leave and will be going at the week end all being well' she said.

'So soon? Jen do you think we could meet up before you go?' she asked her.

'Yes I can't see why not. What about Friday night?' she asked and Jennifer nodded. 'We will text each other tomorrow and decide where and what time to meet.'

Then they chatted about other things to lighten the mood. Jennifer decided not to mention that she was still having silent phone calls, or about receiving the photo. She also did not tell her that the forensics had found nothing.

Chapter 17

That night just as soon as Jennifer got back home she booked a plane ticket online to fly to Nice airport from Manchester. She was planning to fly in the afternoon on Saturday and the flight would take her two and a half hours. She needed to catch a train from Stoke station and arrive at the airport two hours beforehand. Suddenly she felt both excited and relieved that she was finally going to see her grandparents. She had felt troubled that her dad had not gone out, and also a little bit guilty that she herself was not there either. Family was family, and her nan needed someone there with her. It would also get her away from the apartment for a while. She had decided to just book a one way ticket and that way she could decide later whether to stay the two weeks or not, depending on how her grandpa was doing. After she had booked the ticket she decided to check to see if Phil had sent a reply. She knew he was on his course, but he could still probably get access to a computer or he could have taken his own. Anyhow on checking there was nothing from him, and so she logged onto her Facebook page, which she hadn't done for a few days. There were two friend requests one from a guy she did not know from Adam and another from Lizzie her friend from work. Lizzie had asked her if she was on Facebook, and when Jennifer had said yes she had said she would add her as a friend. She deleted the one from the guy. After the trouble she had had from the Prince of Mystery she could not face anything else, and besides his profile looked weird. She then accepted the other one from Lizzie and then put an update on her status saying that she was flying out to France at the weekend to visit her grandparents, and that her grandpa was in hospital after having a accident, omitting to say that he had been knocked off his bike by a hit and run driver. Then she decided to go and look on Lizzie's page.

It gave her status as single and said she was not interested in men. She must have been really hurt with her ex, Jennifer thought. Her profile picture was of her with her son. There was not a hint that she had ever been in any relationship at all, the few photographs that were on were only of her or her son. She then decided to see if there was anything new on Francesca's page, but there wasn't anything at all to see, and so she then logged off.

She wondered if she should let her dad know that she was flying out to France at the weekend, but decided not to. If he could not be bothered to ring her back after he had put the phone down on her, why should she bother? But the truth was she was bothered. She loved her dad even though she had been annoyed with him over not going over to see his parents. She also wanted to ask about Nicole, because even though she and her grandparents had had a tiff, she still should be told about her grandpa's accident. Instead she rang her Nan who answered the phone almost immediately.

'Hello nan' she said when she heard her voice and continued 'how is grandpa doing?'

Her nan sounded very tired when she spoke.

'Nothing has changed love, he is still very sick and is being given antibiotics intravenously' she told her.

'And how are you nan? Are you looking after yourself, you sound very tired.'

'I am OK just worried about your grandpa, you know what a worrier I am Jenny' she told her.

'Well I have some news for you nan.'

'Oh what's that love, you aren't pregnant are you?' she asked sounding even more worried.

Jennifer could not help but laugh out loud.

'Nan whatever made you think of that! For a start I am not with anyone, and another thing I am not that stupid not without being in a serious relationship' she told her.

'No I know you are not love, it's just that when you said you had some news of your own for me, I just thought.....well never mind, what's your news Jenny?'

'I have booked a flight ticket and I will be flying over at the weekend, so you won't be on your own' she told her.

'Oh Jenny that's lovely, but what about work are they all right about it? I don't want you getting into any trouble' she replied.

'Nan don't you worry, I have spoken to Mr Stone and he has given me compassionate leave, so the ticket is booked. I should arrive in Nice Airport by four thirty on Saturday' she explained.

'I will get Jacques to pick you up. What time did you say the plane lands in Nice?'

'About four thirty nan but I can get a taxi to Agay so don't worry.'

'Jenny I don't want you spending your money on a taxi. My neighbour Jacques will be pleased to do it. I will ask him tonight. Oh I really can't wait to see you again, and I am sure your grandpa will love seeing you too.' She sounded so excited and no longer seemed as tired. It had done her good to hear that she was coming out to see them.

'OK nan I will look out for him on Saturday and thank you' she told her.

'It's a pleasure love and to be honest Jacques would not have it any other way, you know how fond he and his wife are of you' she said, and Jennifer could only smile. She had known Jacques and his wife Fleur since as far back as she could remember. They were both lovely gentle people in their mid fifties and they had always been very good to her grandparents. They had no children of their own and so when ever Jennifer and her sister Nicole had been to stay in the school holidays they had always made a big fuss of them, although Nicola had been Nicola her usual ungrateful self and told Jennifer she did not like them, and that they treated them like babies bringing sweets for them. But Jennifer had liked them and she was really looking forward to seeing them again.

She decided she would try to ring her dad to let him know her plans but as usual there was no answer to his phone. He was most probably working again. Well at least she had tried, she thought to herself and then her mobile phone bleeped with a message. It was from Francesca.

'Hi Jen it was great to see you again have you managed to book a flight yet?' she wrote. Jennifer texted back that she had and that she was going to fly over on Saturday and her flight was at 2pm, so she would still be able to meet her on Friday after work. Then Jennifer asked her how everything with her was.

'Oh you know so so. Paul is still being a bit distant, although I am supposed to see him tomorrow' she told her. Then they arranged a time for meeting on Friday.

The following day Jennifer told Mr Stone that she had booked a flight ticket for the weekend, and she would not be in to work on Monday. He asked her how long she wanted off, and she told him that it was hard to say until she had seen her grandpa and knew what the situation was at the hospital in Nice. He understood and told her to keep him informed. He then phoned the agency to arrange to get a temp worker in for the following Monday.

When Jennifer and Lizzie were eating their sandwiches in the park Jennifer told her what the situation was with her grandpa.

'So you see according to my nan he is still very poorly. I feel so helpless not being able to do anything' she told her.

'Well that's good that Mr Stone is giving you compassionate leave anyhow, I knew he had to. Did you tell your nan you will be flying over?' she asked.

'Yes and you could tell she was relieved. She really needs someone over there with her, I am just sorry that it could not have been any sooner' she told Lizzie.

'Well you are going and that's all that matters, she will be glad to see you I am sure.'

'Yes, of course but that also means we can't have our girly night out now yet either, but I am sure we can catch up when I get back if you like' she explained.

'I would love to Jennifer' she smiled.

'By the way how is Toby now, did you find out why he did not want to go to his dads?' she asked and Lizzie went a bit quiet.

'Yes, it was because he didn't like his new girlfriend apparently Miss Snooty Pants' she told her.

'Oh right! Is that what Toby told you or did you hear it from your ex?' Jennifer asked.

'No, Toby told me that. I had said that I would ring his dad to get to the bottom of it if he would not tell me the reason' she explained. Then she continued 'apparently when he was there before this new girlfriend was also there and was not very nice to Toby.'

'In what way?' Jennifer asked, as she could not understand why anyone would not like Toby. He was a character and very polite even though she had only seen him the once.

'Apparently he dropped something on the floor by accident while they were eating their dinners together and she yelled at Toby to be more careful. Anyhow to cut a long story short he does not like her, hence he does not want to go again to stay, not while she is there' she told Jennifer.

'I see.'

'Which does not help me of course, as it now means it will be difficult to get him to go and stay there, and no more weekends for me without him' she explained.

'Oh I am sure he will come around. You are going to have to explain all of this to his dad, or else he will wonder why he is not going to stay with him anymore' she told her.

'I know, I am going to have to tell him the reason and then let him sort it all out, but if I know my ex this new girlfriend won't last long anyhow because he goes through his women like hot dinners.'

'That sort of guy is he?' she asked.

'You could say that. Put it this way, there is always someone new' she told her and Jennifer thought he must be even worse than David. At least David had still been with the same girl he had cheated on her with, not that it made it right.

'What about all your silent phone calls, are you still getting them?'

Jennifer nodded and sighed.

'Yes worse luck. I really have no idea who it could be, except some sicko that gets off doing them maybe' she told her.

'You should try blowing a whistle down the phone like I told you. That would soon stop them I am sure.'

'I was meaning to phone BT up and get something done about them, but with having all this worry about my grandpa I have just left it, hoping they will stop on their own' she told her.

'People like that should be locked up, going around scaring people' she replied and Jennifer thought to herself that Lizzie did not know half of what she had had to put up with.

'So you go to Nice at the weekend?' Lizzie asked changing the subject.

'Yes I fly out this Saturday at two pm' she told her then continued ' I am looking forward to it now. I not only get to see my grandparents but there is the added bonus of a holiday, just what I need' she smiled.

'It will most probably be really hot over there at this time of year. Do they live in a nice house, your grandparents?' she asked.

'Yes it's a fairly big villa, too big for the pair of them really, but they will never move. They love the place where they are and the neighbours are good to them, I don't know where she would have been without Jacques and his wife, it does not bear thinking about. They have a dog named Bella, a golden retriever and she is getting old now, but still needs walking. Grandpa used to walk her every morning before breakfast. They apparently go in and feed and walk her a few times a day while my nan is at the hospital with grandpa' she explained.

'That's lovely of them, no wonder they don't want to move then'

'I remember Jacques and his wife Fleur from way back and you could not get kinder neighbours she told her.

'Well I hope your grandpa improves Jennifer, you will have to text me and let me know how he is won't you?' she asked.

'Of course Lizzie. I have your mobile number and I will definitely keep in touch' she told her and then they both walked the short journey back to work.

The rest of the afternoon passed by quickly and it was soon time for Jennifer to go home. In her excitement about going to France Jennifer forgot all about if Mr Sleazy would be waiting in the communal hall. She felt happier in herself just knowing by the weekend she would be away. So when she saw him doing his usual pretense of doing something to his door it startled her, especially since when he saw her he seemed to just stand there. Then he walked close to her and looked with a horrible expression on his face. At first Jennifer had thought that he was actually going to approach her this time, but instead as she approached he stepped out of her way and sneered loudly as she passed him and told her to watch herself. She was certainly not going to miss that, she thought to herself as she closed her apartment door and bolted it.

The following day passed in a blur. Jennifer had packing and other things to do in preparation for the weekend. She had also kept in touch with her nan and according to her there had been no change at all with her grandpa's condition. Neither had the police had any information about the hit and run. Since he or she had been going far too fast the only witness that there was had been unable to take the car registration number plate, but they had definitely said that the car had looked like a black sports car. It was so unsettling for her nan that no one could be bought to justice without more evidence or witnesses.

His bicycle had been a complete right off, and in fact according to what she had heard it was a mangled wreck. Anyone would have wondered how he had still been alive.

It was Thursday night, and tomorrow was her last day at work before Jennifer went to France and she was so looking forward to it. She had even packed her all of her case. She was taking lots of light clothes with her plus a few cardigans and a light jacket just in case it got cool at night, but she did not think it would. June in the South of France was very hot.

Jennifer had finished her dinner and was sitting down relaxing with a class of wine when her phone rang. She had half expected it to be her dad as she had not spoken to him since he had put the phone down on her, telling her to ring back when she was in a better mood. She had tried to ring him herself too, but like always there had been no answer, and so she had given up. Instead she had intended to phone him when she got to France.

Jennifer picked the receiver up to answer but this time even before she spoke she could hear the same eerie silence. Eventually she did speak because whoever was on the other end of phone seemed to whisper something that she could not quite pick up but it sounded a bit like 'whore.'

'Hello.....is there anybody there?' she asked. But there was nothing else just the one gentle whisper and then the eerie silence. So this time Jennifer put the phone down. Jennifer felt a shiver run down her spine at the thought of it. When would it all stop she thought, as she went back to sit down. The only consolation was that she was going away in a few days time, and she would at least have respite from it. But she knew that when she came back she was going to have to contact BT, and if she had to get her phone number changed then she would.

Before she went to bed she checked her emails to see if Phil had written back and was pleased to see there was a reply from him. He told her that he did not really care that she had used a pseudonym in the dating website and he said that he preferred the name Jennifer to Katie, which made Jennifer smile. He also told her that he still wanted to meet her at a place of her choosing, maybe sometime next week.

Jennifer frowned, she would have to reply and let him know that she would be away for a few weeks in France. She decided to send a quick email back and then she went to bed.

Chapter 18

After another long and restless night of tossing and turning, and checking the alarm clock for the time Jennifer decided to get up and make herself a drink. It was barely light outside and as she drew her curtains back she could see the eeriness of the park across the road in the kitchen window. It was strange how when she had first moved into the apartment she had been really pleased with its position, but now after all that had happened she felt differently. She suddenly longed to be opposite somewhere with a bit more life about it. Instead all she could see were dark shadows from the trees and bushes, and as she pressed the kettle on she thought she saw a figure moving about. She stared at it for a few seconds. It definitely looked like a figure dressed in black and it looked as if they were standing straight in front watching her apartment. She drew a sharp intake of breath and closed her eyes and when she opened them again the figure had gone. Had she imagined it? She did not know, except that it felt very real to her and she was instantly spooked by it all. She was just glad that she was going to France tomorrow. What with the silent phone calls and everything else, it was all getting too much for her.

She thought about her friend Francesca and how she was looking forward to seeing her. She was glad that they had made up, and she thought that she might confide in her about the photo she had received in the post. In fact she knew that there was only her friend she could tell, because only she knew about that time in her life. She would also tell her about the silent phone calls continuing and see what she thought. She wondered how she was getting along with her boyfriend Paul. It had been funny that her friend had at one time thought he would ask her to marry him and now she felt almost certain he was going to split with her. Relationships were strange sometimes.

She remembered her relationship with David and how she had thought that they would have been together forever, until they had eventually split. It had not been her doing but Davids. She had been more than devastated. Why hadn't she realised that something had been wrong? All the late nights home and the fact that they had not been as close as they used to be. At night he would give her a peck on the cheek and then turn over to go to sleep. So why didn't she read the signs? Was it because she had thought that all marriages were like that after a few years. Also he had been very stressed out with work and she put a lot of it down to that.

Jennifer showered and dressed and made herself some toast. Even after that it was still too early to go to work, so she decided she would double-check her suit case. Underwear, nightclothes, three pairs of shorts, tops, one pair of jeans a few sundresses, day dresses, sunglasses, flip flops, a couple of cardigans, walking shoes and she would definitely take a few swimming costumes. Her grandparents had a pool in the garden of the villa. It was not massive but big enough for a swim to cool off in the hot sun. Her grandpa Jean-Paul was always taking a dip after walking the dog. She must not forget her camera either, not that she would be taking many photos unless her grandpa improved. She also checked that she had her passport safe. She opened it and looked at the photo in the back of herself. It was due for renewal in another year or so. Her hair was lighter in the photo than it was now, a lot lighter come to think of it. She would probably dye it back that colour as she rather liked her hair that way.

She put her passport along with the boarding pass she had printed out, into the handbag she was taking with her. Then she decided to make a few sandwiches to eat in the park at lunch time. Then she made another drink of coffee hoping that it would pick her up and make her feel more awake. She had had a terrible night again, but hopefully by tomorrow late afternoon she would be either at the hospital with her grandpa or else sitting with her nan in her Villa in Agay and she couldn't wait.

After work she made her way to the cafe to meet Francesca, and like last time she was waiting for her, seated by the window, and Jennifer saw her instantly and waved.

'Hi how was work?' Francesca asked. She had ordered a latte and asked Jennifer if she wanted the same.

'Yes please, and I think I will have a raspberry and white chocolate scone too. Work was busy but OK' she told her.

'Well are you all packed for tomorrow? What time did you say you had to be at the airport?

'I need to be there for about twelve as the plane leaves at two and I like to be there at least two hours beforehand' she told her.

'What airport is that?'

'Manchester why?'

'Well I am free tomorrow so I could drop you off if you like' she suggested.

'That would be fantastic Fran if you are sure? It beats getting the train any day.'

'Well that's settled then, I will pick you up say around ten?' she told her.

'Now can I ask how are you really? I mean what about the police, what are they going to do about what happened to you?' she asked and Jennifer could only shrug.

'Nothing the case has been dropped. The forensic report came through and they found out nothing....nothing at all' she explained and then continued' which is a big disappointment to me.'

'Well Jen all I can say is thank God that you were not sexually assaulted.'

'There is that I suppose, but you know Fran it's not over?'

'What do you mean it's not over?' she asked looking puzzled.

'What I said, I am still having a lot of strange things happening to me Fran, like silent phone calls, and not just one or two, quite a lot really for them to be just mistaken numbers. Plus strange noises in the night, and one day I came home and there was graffiti dabbed over my door spelling the name Katie.'

'I hope you reported it.'

'Well I was going to, but the very next day it had gone, so whoever did it must have come back in the early hours and wiped it off, so it was no use logging a complaint was there?' she told her taking a bite of her scone. Francesca looked puzzled by it all.

'Have you not got a clue to who it could be?'

'If I had I could do something about it?' she replied.

'And that's not all that's happened Fran. Now you remember when I was just seventeen and I went through that bad patch?' she said to her and Francesca could only nod that she did remember. It was something that they had not discussed for a long time, and she knew that Jennifer preferred to forget about it.

'What about it Jen?'

'Well put it this way, I received a nasty surprise in the post, no message nothing only a photograph' she told her.

'You are joking? not of..........'

'Yes exactly, and you know Fran there are not many people if any that know about those times, except you of course.'

'Jen I hope you don't think that I would or have ever told anyone, because I haven't' she told her suddenly looking on the defensive.

'I am not saying that. It's just that it's strange who could be doing all this and why? And another thing on the front of the envelope it said Katie. The thing is back then I never called myself Katie at all' she explained to her.

'Don't you think you should have reported that to the police, I mean it would have added strength to the fact someone had it in for you surely?'

'NO NO how could I, how would it make me look? It's a part of my past that I never want to remember' she told her then continued 'you of all people should know that Fran! Those were dark days for me' she told her then continued 'not even David knew.'

'Maybe things will settle down when you get back. How long do you think you will be away for?'

'That depends on how my grandpa is of course, but maybe two weeks.'

'At least you will have a break from work. I envy you. I am hating work at the minute' she told her

'Why what's happened?' she asked.

'Nothing really just the new boss he is a slave driver' she laughed.

'Aren't they all!' she said and then she asked how she and Paul were getting on, and Francesca went a bit quiet.

'We are fine' she told her.

'Well I can't say you look fine, in fact when I asked you that you looked pretty miserable.'

Francesca sighed deeply and played around with her coffee cup not saying anything at first.

'You can tell me Fran, sure don't we tell each other everything, or we used to do' she said to her.

'There is nothing really to tell, except sometimes he scares me' she began to explain.

'What do you mean Fran scares you? He does not hit you does he?' she asked suddenly feeling concerned.

'No nothing like that, just his moods. He gets angry with me and tells me I am stupid and how lucky I am to have him' she explained then continued 'but he does not hit me' she told her and Jennifer looked at her very concerned.

'Do you think you will stay together I mean.....'

'I do love him so much Jen, but he messes with my head. One day he is very loving, and the next day he is in a black mood. He goes away a lot too' she told her.

'Where does he go to do you know?' she asked.

'Not really he never tells me......oh he's OK really, it's just sometimes he's like Jekyll and Hyde and it confuses me' she told her and Jennifer looked shocked. Maybe it was for the best that he never asked her to marry him if he was like that.

'He just messes with my head, one minute I know he loves me then the next he really looks at me with this look of pure hatred. I just can't make him out.'

Jennifer squeezed her hand and said nothing.

'So tomorrow you fly out to France. I will be at your apartment at ten o'clock or just before' she told her.

'OK but are you sure Paul won't mind' she asked.

'No it's fine I mentioned it to him and he was OK about it. I think he is away tomorrow anyhow' she told her and Jennifer told her that ten o'clock would be OK.

'Don't forget to text me when you get to your nan's'

'Oh don't worry Fran I intend to keep in touch with you. I will let you know how he is.'

'Good. Will you get a taxi to their house?' she asked.

'No Jacques their neighbour is picking me up.'

'Jacques a sexy Frenchman?' she laughed and Jennifer rolled her eyes.

'He is fifty three and also married.' she explained.

'Right.....sorry! I will be thinking about you while you are away, all that sun and sand.'

Jennifer smiled, yes she was looking forward to that too she thought to herself. Before they went their separate ways Francesca gave Jennifer a big hug and told her that she would see her in the morning.

Back at the apartment she first telephoned her nan as she planned to have a nice soak in the bath after that and then go to bed early, so she would be refreshed for her journey. She dialed the number and her nan answered after just a few rings.

'Hello nan.'

'Hello Jenny love I was expecting you to ring. Well this time tomorrow you will be here' she told her.

'Yes I can't wait to see you and grandpa. I am all packed and will arrive around four thirty. How is grandpa?'

'Good! Jacques will be waiting for you. I saw him a few hours ago when he took Bella for her walk and he asked me the time the plane lands and I told him four thirty. There isn't much change in grandpa love, I hate to see him in so much pain.'

'I know it must be hard for you' she told her and that after tonight she would no longer be alone, and that she would be there with her. Then Jennifer said goodnight and that she would see her tomorrow.

'OK love and look out for Jacques, he will be waiting.....goodnight Jenny.' Jennifer sighed as she put the phone down, and went to run the bath water.

She was just about to get into the bath when her mobile bleeped loudly telling her she had received a text message. She quickly put her bathrobe on and went to answer it. She frowned when she saw it was from her friend Francesca.

'Jennifer I need to talk to you, is it possible to meet me?' it said and Jennifer felt confused. She had met her earlier so why would she need to meet her again- it just did not make any sense. She quickly sent a text back.

'Why what's wrong, can I ring?' she asked.

'No don't ring. I need to talk to you face to face' she told her to which Jennifer texted back again.

'It's late, nearly 9.30, I was just about to get into the bath then bed, can't you tell me what it is tomorrow when you pick me up?' she asked.

'Please Jen. I have to talk to you face to face, not on the phone....please?'

Jennifer thought about what she was asking then decided she would get back dressed again, and meet her. She sent a text that she would meet her and Francesca told her where.

Jennifer could not understand what was wrong, and she wondered if something had happened with Paul. She quickly dressed and grabbed her keys and phone. She would find out soon, enough she thought to herself as she closed her apartment door behind her. Her bath would have to wait.

Chapter 19

It was just after 10.15am when Francesca finally pressed Jennifer's buzzer. She had been running a bit late because she had been looking for her mobile phone. She had searched high and low for it nearly all morning. It was strange why she could not find it. She had tried to remember when she last had it and had even rung it from her parent's house phone but to no avail. Last night when she had briefly met Paul she had definitely had it because he had texted her. It was really getting to her why she could not find it. There was no answer to Jennifer's apartment and so she pressed the buzzer again.

'Come on Jen or else you will be late' she said out loud to herself, pressing the buzzer a third time.

Still there was no answer and she looked at her watch that showed it was almost 10.20. If they didn't get a move on they would definitely be late. She just wished she had her mobile and then she would be able to ring her. Francesca waited until 10.30 continuously pressing the buzzer to Jennifer's apartment but there was still no answer.

After a while she got so fed up she decided to leave. Maybe Jennifer was annoyed because she had been fifteen minutes late and just gone. Knowing her friend she was more likely to do that. Jennifer never did have any patience, she thought to herself as she got back into her car more than a little annoyed. She would go back home, try to find her phone and when she did she would leave Jennifer a right message.

She pondered on the way home how she had first met Jennifer. They had both been five and Jennifer had been the new girl in the class. She was as shy as Francesca was outgoing, yet they had got on like a house on fire when they had got to know each other. She remembered how sorry she had felt for her because her sister was horrible to her, always pushing her away. And Jennifer would burst into tears and still follow her, like a lost puppy. It had been around about that time that they had both become firm friends and friends they had stayed.

She had felt a bit guilty when she had not supported her over what had happened, although Francesca had genuinely thought she had left the club with someone that night. It had been Paul's friend Lucy that had said she had seen her leaving with a guy. Then when Jennifer had phoned her to tell her she could not remember anything, she had just thought that she had just been too drunk. It had been what Paul had suggested too, as sometimes Jennifer did dramatise about things, she knew that from the past. Francesca had wished she had not told Jennifer to go to the police, because all it had done was cause a rift between them. Paul had got annoyed with her and even called her a silly bitch because she had told him that Jennifer wanted to tell the police about Lucy. She had asked him if he knew where she lived, and he had flown off the handle in a right rage and told her not to get involved. He did not think Lucy or Billy would know anything, and besides they hated the police. And then when she had been curious and asked why they hated the police, he had just made excuses. Then when she had got upset, he told her he was sorry and put his arms around her and held her tight, and everything was OK again. That night he had stayed with her holding her close, stroking her hair and kissing her on top of her head. They had never made love though, even though she had on rare occasions stayed overnight at his place, which he shared with another guy, although she had never met this other guy. Maybe he did not fancy her in that way, she had often thought, but when she had mentioned it to Paul he had got annoyed again and told her that it would happen when the time was right. He had asked her to promise him that she would not get involved with the police, and because she loved him she had promised that. She knew that by doing that she would hurt her friend, but because she loved Paul she couldn't do anything else. It was as if Paul could ask her to do almost anything, he only had to snap his fingers and she came running. He was like a drug to her and she was totally addicted to him even though he messed with her head sometimes with his coolness towards her.

It had even been Paul's idea for Francesca to make up with Jennifer again. She had actually been too embarrassed to contact her after what she had done, and had told him so, but he had told her that she was nothing but a selfish bitch and that she should value friendships. She had been literally gob smacked and in the end for a bit of peace and quiet she had texted her. Afterwards she had been glad that she had, because she had missed her.

When she arrived home there was no one in. Her parents must have gone out. Saturday was usually the day they either went visiting or out for a drive. She hated living at home now. When she had left home the first time around to share accommodation with a work friend, she had been really happy and had felt so independent, until the final blow had come when she had lost her job and could no longer afford to pay her share of the rent. Consequently she had to move back in with her parents.

Not that she did not have good parents, she did, in fact her father had loaned her some money when she had moved in with her friend from work. He had also given her some money to buy her little car. But it had always been awkward bringing anyone back to the house, and only rarely did they allow anyone to stay the night. She had thought that Paul had been going to ask her to marry him, and that they could get a place together, but how wrong she had been about that.

She let herself into the house and was surprised to see her mobile phone lying on the hall floor just inside the front door. She frowned and thought that it was strange. It was certainly not there when she had left, that was for sure. She picked it up to switch it on but it was dead, out of charge she thought finding her charger and plugging it in. She would ring Jennifer later and ask her why she left instead of waiting for her to give her a lift to the airport.

Paul had told Francesca that he would be away for a few days, and that he would contact her when he got back. When she had met him last night, he had seemed in a better mood, and even showed an interest in Jennifer, asking if everything was alright now between them, and when she had told her that she had offered to drop Jennifer off at the airport he had told her it was a good idea, since he would not be back until Monday, so it would give her something to do. He had taken her briefly to a pub and bought her a drink and then, while she was away to the toilets he had put her drink on the table and told her he had an urgent phone message from his boss and was sorry but had to go, but would see her after the weekend. It was because of times like this his attitude got to her. All she knew was that he was a courier and had to sometimes go off at the drop of a hat. She had asked what sort of things he delivered and he had told her that they were just parcels, and he did not know what was inside them.

When her phone had enough charge she checked to see if there had been any messages from Francesca but there were none. She decided she would send her a message herself. She knew by now she would probably be boarding the plane, since it was 2pm but at least she would get it when she arrived in France. She was confused why she had just gone and not waited for her, but she decided to send a simple text.

'Hi Jen I called at your apartment like I promised, sorry I was a bit late. Can you text when you arrive in France Fran x' Then she pressed send.

She also sent a text to Paul to say she was missing him, but she did not expect a quick reply. Paul never did. Sometimes he would reply after an hour or two, or not reply at all, which really hurt Francesca, because when they were together he seemed to be nearly always on his phone or else receiving text messages. So she knew that he had always had his phone on him. It just made her feel that she was not as important to him as he was to her. Sometimes she thought it would be best if they did finish the relationship. She was finding it hard.

Jacques and his wife saw the planes descend into Nice airport. It was exactly 4.30pm and the plane had been on time. They had watched from the terminal building, and when they saw it descending they went straight to arrivals in readiness to meet Jennifer and take her to Agay. Her nan Maggie was still at the hospital with Jean-Paul and had been there nearly all day. She had phoned to say that he had taken a turn for the worse, and that they were transferring him to ICU where they could monitor him better. She had been in tears over the phone and was concerned that they did not forget to pick her granddaughter Jennifer up. They had reassured her that they would both be there early just in case, and they had also walked and fed Bella.

Both Jacques and his wife were very fond of the Beaumonts and had known them for a very long time. They were looking forward to seeing Jennifer again, and felt that this was just what Maggie needed to have her there. They were only sorry that their son was not there too. Maggie had been through a awful lot since Jean-Paul had been knocked off his bicycle. She looked like she had aged a lot from all the stress of continually being at the hospital, and knew that seeing Jennifer would do her the world of good. They only wished that Jean -Paul had not got worse.

Jacques remembered the very first time he had met Jennifer and Nicole, they could only have been about four and eight. Initially they came over with their father and then afterwards when they came in the school holidays. Their father would see that they got on the plane, then Jacques and Fleur would meet them at the other end. They had been great children, although they had felt that they had got on better with Jennifer, Nicole had been more sulky and apt to getting her own way. Whereas Jennifer was the more easy going of the two of them, always wanting to please, and both he and his wife had been very fond of her. She had become the daughter that they had never had.

At first when they had moved into the villa in Agay, which was almost the same time as the Beaumonts, they had thought that they would have children at least three, but it was not to be. So the arrival of the Beaumont children had been a great blessing to them.

Chapter 20

Jacques looked at his watch and then looked at his wife. There had been a steady stream of people coming into arrivals, but they could not see Jennifer. It was now nearly five and even if she had difficulty in retrieving her suitcase from baggage reclaim she would have arrived by now. Fleur told him that she would go and get a coffee for them both while he stayed to wait, and he nodded his approval.

It had been a long day and he was feeling tired. He sat down on one of the seats and checked out his mobile phone to see if there were any messages from Maggie Beaumont to say that Jennifer had missed her plane, but there was nothing. He put his mobile back into his pocket and decided to speak to a airport official as he was wondering if there was a problem.

'Bonjour je me demande si vous pourriez m'aider on s'attendait a ce que quelqu'un a partir de la 4.30 vol au depart de Manchester a Nice, mais il semble qu'elle n'est pas ici.'

He asked him if he could help him, he told him that he had been waiting for someone from the 4.30 flight from Manchester to Nice, but that they were not there. The Official asked her name and he told him, and then the official went away to check for him. It seemed ages before he came back. Fleur had brought the coffees and they were both sitting and drinking them when Jacques saw the Official approach. He smiled down at them 'Monsieur

Madame il semble que Mlle Jennifer Sudbury
n'etaient pas a bord du vol.'

Jacques could only look troubled when he had
told him that it appeared she had not been on the
flight. He thanked him and both he and Fleur got
up to go. It just did not make sense to them why
there had been no messages from Maggie if
Jennifer had missed the plane. Now they would
have to get in touch with her to tell her the news,
although they thought that maybe it would be best
to leave it until Maggie got back home to the Villa
or else phoned them again from the hospital. It was
not as if they knew that Jennifer was in any danger.
It just appeared that she had not boarded the plane
at all. Maybe there was a problem at her end, and
she had already phoned her grandmother. They
decided to drive home and wait.

Maggie sat looking at Jean-Paul as he lay there
motionless in the hospital bed, willing him to get
better. She had hated to see him in pain, but this
was even worse, for at least before he had managed
to mumble a few words to her. In fact she had even
told him that their beloved granddaughter was
flying over to see them, and she had thought that
she had caught a glimmer of a smile cross his face.
She had spent every day at the hospital since he
had the accident. When he had been late she knew
something had been wrong. Almost every morning
he would take Bella for her early morning walk,
and then either have a dip in the pool or else go for
a cycle. The longest he had ever been away was an
hour. But this time it was nearer two and Maggie
had an uneasy feeling in the pit of her stomach that

something was wrong, and when she saw the police car draw up outside the villa she knew she had been right.

The ICU was a bustle of activity with nurses busying themselves doing observations. Jean-Paul was coupled up to a few monitors plus a drip.

'Ah Mrs Beaumont - Maggie, why don't you go and get yourself a nice cup of tea or coffee?' one of the nurses said. She spoke to her in English, not that Maggie would not have understood her if she had spoken in French, because living in France for almost twenty years now Maggie had become fluent in the language. But the nurse was actually from the south of England.

'My granddaughter is coming over, she should be here soon' she told her without looking up at her, and ignoring the bit about going to get some tea or coffee. She just could not bear to leave him. The nurse stood by her and put her hand on her shoulder. Maggie looked so frail today and she was concerned.

'That will be just great for you to have her here, but that is even more reason to take a break and get yourself something to drink and maybe a little snack as well' she told her and then continued 'I will come and fetch you if there is any change.'

Maggie looked up at her then with sadness in her eyes. All she wanted was to be left alone with Jean -Paul. She did not feel hungry and neither did she want a drink, all she wanted was for her beloved husband to wake up and everything to be back to normal again. But she knew that was not going to happen. At first she had feared the worst when she had seen the police officers arrive, then later at the hospital she had thought that maybe he would be OK after all. Now she just did not know. Seeing him lying there so very still, not moving, it worried her and she was just glad that Jenny would be here soon. She had tried to ring her son, but again to no avail. He always seemed to be busy. Maggie knew he had his work, but surely she and Jean-Paul mattered to him too. He had had a rough life, Maggie knew that. He had been widowed at a young age with two little girls to bring up and it had been really tough on him. She had sometimes wished that he had remarried but instead her son had thrown himself into his work. When the girls had been very small Maggie and Jean-Paul had helped out until they had eventually moved to France.

Agay was where Jean-Paul had grown up and his goal was always that they would go back to live there one day and they had. It had been a big decision especially for Maggie, because she was English and had lived in Staffordshire nearly all of her life. She had met her husband while he had been working in England. When he had gone back to France they had kept in touch and eventually they married and they set up home in Staffordshire hoping that one day they would both retire and he and Maggie would then move to France and buy a villa which they had done. It had been a happy marriage and when Maggie had found out she had been pregnant with Clive it had been complete. They never did have any more children though, because when Clive had been just three Maggie had a bad miscarriage and consequently had to have a hysterectomy.

She knew that Clive should be there at the hospital too, if only she could get in touch with him she thought. Maybe when Jenny arrived things would feel better. She looked at the clock in ICU and it was nearly five thirty. Jenny would be here now, and maybe she had gone back to Jacques and Fleur's house for a meal before coming over to the hospital. She could not wait to see her.

'You have to at least drink something, I have bought you a nice cup of tea. If you won't go for a rest at least drink this' Lisa the English nurse told her, handing her the cup of tea she had bought.

'Thank you' Maggie said taking a sip of the hot sweet tea. She was surprised that she had indeed been thirsty after all.

'What time is your granddaughter due?' the nurse asked. She could see that Maggie was getting weary and what she really wanted to say to her was that she needed to go home and sleep for a while. She had seen it many times, where visitors of a loved one had eventually made themselves ill by constantly keeping a bedside vigil, and she knew that Maggie was no spring chicken at ninety years old.

'The plane arrived at 4.30pm so Jenny should be here soon I expect' she told her. The nurse gave a sigh of relief, and thought if she could not persuade her to take a rest, maybe her granddaughter would. She had watched Maggie turn from a bright and energetic old lady to a tired and frail one. She knew if she kept this up Maggie would need medical attention herself.

'Well maybe when your granddaughter arrives then she could take over from you, while you get some sleep?' she said with a smile, but Maggie just looked at her and nodded. In reality she had been afraid to go and leave Jean-Paul. It had been different when he had been conscious, even though he had been in so much pain. But now that they had moved him to ICU she was worried.

His consultant Mr Roux had been to see her and given her the news that all the signs had pointed to his heart. It seemed it was failing and along with his other injuries, his broken leg and a few broken ribs he had consequently got pneumonia. All in all it all did not look good. All she could do now was wait, pray and hope. She decided that she would have another go at ringing Clive. He needed to know.

'Clive it's me' she spoke as he answered the phone after a few rings.

'Mum I was just about to ring the hospital, but you beat me to it' he told her and Maggie rolled her eyes but did not comment.

'How is dad?' he asked suddenly feeling guilty that he had not phoned earlier. Work was a complete mess up these days. He just did not seem to have time to eat never mind anything else, and was only getting a maximum of four hours sleep each night.

'Not good love, he is now in heart failure and unconscious. I just think the accident was just too much for him' she told him.

There was a moment of silence the other end then Clive spoke again.

'Oh mum I am so, so sorry, I just don't know what to say. Have you told Jenny?'

'Jenny is here love, she arrived at 4.30 this afternoon, Jacques picked her up at the airport'

'Oh right, can I speak to here then' he told her.

'Well when I said she was here, I meant she flew was arriving at 4.30 and Jacques was picking her up. I have not seen her yet so I imagine Jacques and his wife have taken her to their house for a meal, and then she will be up to see your dad' she explained.

Clive closed his eyes. He knew he should book a plane out too. It was only right he was there. The burden should not rest solely on Jennifer.

'What about Nicole is she there too?" he asked. He felt choked up inside. He decided that he would speak to Jennifer or Nicole first to see what they thought of the situation and then look to book a plane ticket to come over.

Maggie was quiet at the mention of Nicole, and she did not know what to say to him. Maggie had thought that Nicole would have told her dad that she was no longer staying with them, but it seems he did not know.

'Mum are you there?' he asked above the silence.

'Nicole is not here Clive, in fact she has not been here for some time' she thought it best to tell him outright.

'Ah but I thought she was staying with you and dad, does she even know about her grandpa?' he asked suddenly feeling worried. He had not heard from Nicole for a long time.

'To be honest Clive I could not let her know even if I wanted too, I have no forwarding address or phone number' she explained.

'No forwarding address or phone number? What about her mobile number? It does not sound like Nicole, did something happen while she was with you?' he asked. This was what Maggie had been dreading to tell him about his eldest daughter Nicole and the tiff they had that had finally caused her to leave and not have any more contact with them. She just did not want the discussion over the telephone either. She suddenly felt the need to get back to her husband.

'Look Clive I have to go, I don't want to leave your dad for very long while he is like this. When Jenny arrives I will tell her to give you a quick ring, OK?' she told him.

'OK mum and in the meantime I will contact Nicole on her mobile number. I have it in my mobile phone' he told her and Maggie thought to herself but did not say it 'good luck with that.'

After Clive had finished talking with his mother, he scrolled down to Nicole's number on his phone and pressed the number. He would get to the bottom of why Nicole had suddenly left her grandparents house, and even more importantly why she had not even told him.

'That's very strange' he thought aloud to himself when the number appeared to be dead. He had always thought that Nicole had still been at his parents Villa. How could he have got it so wrong?

He felt worried as well as a bit guilty that he had not phoned her before, but it wasn't his fault he told himself. Both his daughters had his number and surely they could have rung him. Then he remembered Jennifer's words 'I can never get in touch with you' he sat down with his head in his hands. Had he really been too busy? What had happened to his family? His youngest daughter was probably not speaking to him because he had put the phone down on her when she had become cheeky and told him off, and his eldest daughter could not think fit to even text him her new number.

So many things went through his head. Maybe Jenny had Nicole's number he told himself, as he then rang Jenny's number. But strangely that too was unobtainable. Maybe she was at the hospital now and she had turned it off, which was understandable especially in ICU. He would try again later, he told himself making a cup of coffee. He felt so tired and work was beginning to be a real struggle for him.

Chapter 21

It was now nearly 6.30pm and after checking her mobile phone numerous times that day Francesca felt very annoyed. Jennifer was either totally ignoring her or else something was wrong. She had sent her a few text messages asking her to ring her when she had arrived in France, but there had been no reply to any of them, which she could not understand. Apart from being about fifteen minutes late, she had done nothing to upset her that she could think of. It was all very strange. Perhaps something bad had happened to her grandfather, maybe that was it, she told herself.

There was not even a message from Paul telling her he missed her, but that no longer surprised her either. She was never sure where she was with him. As she had confided to her friend Jennifer he had a Jekyll and Hyde personality, and she was not sure how long she could put up with it for, even though she loved him very much, as it was just messing with her head.

It was exactly 8pm when a text message came through from Paul.

'Hi Babe I won't be able to meet you on Tuesday like I thought. I have to stay over. Will contact you when I get home Paul x'

Francesca's heart sank. She was really fed up with this. It had happened before and so she should not have been too surprised when it happened again, but she was. She had known Paul for over nine months now and nothing had changed. Francesca thought back to when she had first met him. She had actually been in the same club as she and Jennifer had gone to for their birthday celebrations and that time she had been sitting by the bar with her friend from work, when a guy had approached them. At first they had not thought much of it, but the next minute the guy slipped a piece of paper with his mobile number on it, and handed it to Francesca. He did not say a thing, just gave her the piece of paper and smiled the loveliest smile she had ever seen and then left. Her friend had nudged her and smiled as if to say she had coped off. Then Francesca had quickly put the piece of paper into her handbag. When she had got home she had taken it out to look at and there was his name and number. It took about two days before she had plucked up enough nerve to ring him and when she did he had pretended he did not know what she was talking about. He had sounded so serious she had believed him and was just going to put the phone down feeling humiliated that she had even bothered, when he suddenly burst out laughing and said something like. 'Oh yes you are the cute little chick that was in Martinez.' She had not known what to think, but afterwards they had arranged to meet up again the following day. After about a week she had been smitten. She just wished she knew where she stood with him.

That night Francesca decided to wash her hair for something to do and as she checked her mobile phone for any word from Jennifer she felt worried. It was not like her friend to totally ignore her. She had wished that she had asked for her grandparents home number now, at least that way she could find out what was going on. She thought about her own grandparents and how sick her grandpa was. The last time she had been to visit with her mother and father he had been very confused. Her Nan looked stressed out too. On the drive home from Manchester her father had been very quiet and so had her mother. It was sad to see him the way he was. She knew she should make more of an effort to go and visit and in fact her parents had asked if she wanted to go with them only last weekend. She had told them that she had already made arrangements to go out with Paul, which her father had not been happy about. They had met Paul a few times but had found him quiet and not wanting to enter into any conversation, totally different than any of their daughter's previous boyfriends, which bothered them. They also did not like to see their daughter upset at the times he had let her down when he was supposed to have picked her up. For what seemed to be a dozen times that day Francesca checked to see if there was a reply from Jennifer, but there was nothing.

It was now nearly 8pm and Jacques was wondering what was going on at the hospital with Jean -Paul. They had not heard from Maggie since early that morning when she had told them that Jean-Paul had taken a turn for the worse and had been moved to ICU. They were supposed to have picked Jennifer up at 4.30, but when she had not shown up they had presumed that there had been a problem at Jennifer's end and she had let her grandmother know. Jacques decided to go and give Bella her last feed, and then take her for her night walk. Maybe by then Maggie would be back home again and they would find out what had happened with Jennifer. They had both been worried about Maggie, and had thought she spent far too long at the hospital. Once Fleur had sat with her there to keep her company. Then another time Fleur had gone up to take some sandwiches for her, and she could see that it was taking a toll on her as she looked pale and weary.

Jacques had always thought that the Beaumonts were quite healthy for their ages. He knew that Jean-Paul loved to swim and keep fit, and had often seen him in his pool very early in the mornings. It had amazed them both. In fact Jean-Paul had looked more like a seventy four year old than a ninety four year old. This accident had shocked them both, especially since it had been caused by a hit and run driver. All they knew about that was it had been a black sports car that had been going miles too fast. The witness that had seen it all, had said they did not have time to take down the registration number because it had sped off like a whirlwind, not even stopping to see if Jean-Paul had been alright. In fact according to the witness it looked almost as if they had intended to knock him off his bike. The police had been around to the villa only today and at first Fleur had thought that they had some news for Maggie about the hit and run, but it had only been because they had wanted an update on Mr Beaumont's condition.

Jacques let himself into the Villa and he could hear Bella instantly getting out of her basket to greet him, maybe expecting also to see Maggie. 'Bonjour jeune fille' he told her as she come towards him wagging her tail. He reached down to stroke her and then went he filled her bowl up with water and fed her. Afterwards he got out her lead and took her for her nightly walk. He could see she was missing her owners, the way she just looked up at him with her sad eyes. He told her that her mistress would soon be home.

Jacques wondered what would happen with Maggie if Jean-Paul never recovered. Would she stay at the Villa or decide to go back to England to be with her son and granddaughters, although he was not even sure if Maggie's eldest granddaughter was living in France or England now. In fact neither he nor Fleur had seen her for quite some time, and when they had asked Maggie about her, she had always seemed to change the subject and so they had eventually stopped asking. There had always been something about Nicole that Jacques never quite liked. She had a vicious side to her, that's for sure. He remembered one day seeing her pushing her little sister towards the pool and screaming at her at the top of her voice to go away and that she should just fall into the water and drown. It had taken Maggie to come out and separate them both and poor little Jennifer had been reduced to a flood of tears. Why Nicole disliked her so much they never knew, except on the times that Clive had been over it was as clear as day that Jennifer had been his favourite, so maybe it was just plain sibling rivalry. Eventually when they had grown up they had both spent separate holidays at the villa, and rarely had both been there together. It was as if Nicole could not stand the sight of Jennifer at all. In fact it was a miracle that she had even gone to Jennifer's wedding when she had married David. When Maggie had told him that she had gone with her father he had been quite surprised. It had been a very low-key kind of wedding and not even Maggie and Jean-Paul had gone. It was not that they had not been invited, but at the time Maggie had fractured her leg and it had been very painful and besides the wedding preparations had all come along too quickly. Jennifer had promised that she and David would go over to stay as soon as they could.

Maggie looked at the clock and frowned. It was now nearly 9.30pm and still no sign of Jenny. She had been so worried about her husband all day that she had not think to ring her mobile to see how she was getting on. She had expected her to have at least come on up to the hospital by now, but there was still no sign of her. She ought to give her a ring and see what the delay was. She also needed to go home soon, but was afraid to in case Jean-Paul got even worse. Lisa the English nurse had gone off duty and the other two nurses that took over had no idea that she had been at the hospital since early this morning. She would wait a little while longer then ring Jenny. Maggie's back was aching just sitting in the chair. She had gone for frequent walks up and down the corridor to try and relieve it.

'Well Jean-Paul' she said to him although she was not even sure he could hear her. But she had heard that speaking with people that were in a coma helped. She continued hoping he could hear her.

'I wonder if our Jenny will come up tonight or tomorrow now. She is here my love, all the way from England, and I know you can't wait to see her, or her you. Please get better my love. I want you back home with me where you belong' she told him gripping his hand.

Then she tried to ring Jenny, but got nothing. It looked like her mobile was dead. She just could not understand it. Jennifer should surely be here by now, how strange. She decided that she had better ring her neighbours Jacques and Fleur to find out what was happening, and why Jenny was not at the hospital. Then a thought occurred to her that maybe Jenny was ill. She started to worry as she rang her neighbour's number.

'Hello Fleur its Maggie 'she spoke to her in French 'is Jenny there?'

'Jenny? Non, she is not here' she explained and Maggie became confused.

'But didn't Jacques pick her up? I don't understand' she said panicking.

'Well we both went to the airport to wait for her, but apparently she didn't board the plane, or so an official told us. We thought she may have phoned or texted you' Fleur explained.

'No she neither phoned nor texted. I just thought you had taken her back to your house maybe for dinner' Maggie continued. 'Do you think something's happened to her......oh please God I hope not. I could not stand anything else happening.'

Fleur was beginning to think that they should have contacted Maggie when Jennifer had not turned up at the airport, but at the time they had thought that she would have definitely contacted her grandmother to explain.

'Try to calm yourself Maggie, there is most probably a good explanation why Jennifer did not catch the plane' Fleur told her. But Maggie was clearly upset.

'Before you go how is Jean-Paul?' she asked looking at Jacques who was looking at her.

'Jean-Paul is not good. He is still in a coma' she replied then burst into tears. It was all too much for her to bear. Oh why had she not phoned Jacques sooner, but she had thought that they had taken her granddaughter to their house for dinner, and likewise Jacques and Fleur had thought that when Jennifer had not turned up she would have rung or texted her grandmother. Everything was a mess, she thought to herself as she ended the call with her neighbours and then rang Clive her son. Surely he would know something. He was her father, she thought dialing his number, but as usual there was no reply. She swore to herself as she turned the phone off. Why oh why was Clive always difficult to get in touch with? It should have been him getting onto that plane, not Jennifer. It was his father who was lying unconscious in the hospital, his father that might not even wake up. Where was his responsibility? She felt a sudden anger for him, their only child.

Chapter 22

It was almost 10pm when Maggie eventually got hold of her son Clive. She had decided that she needed to go home to get a shower and some sleep. She had felt sticky with perspiration both from the heat of the hospital and the temperature outside. She was also sick with worry about both Jean-Paul and now her granddaughter Jennifer. She felt sure that she was either ill, or else she had had an accident on the way to the airport and that was why she had not boarded the plane. It was just not in Jennifer's character to let her nan down like this and not be in touch. Of course Nicole had been a different kettle of fish, but not Jennifer.

'Clive at last I have been trying to get you' she told him. When Clive heard his mother's voice for a second time today he froze.

'What's wrong mum is it dad?' he asked suddenly anxious at what she wanted to tell him.

'No Clive your dad is exactly the same. Still in a coma, no it's about Jenny' she told him.

'What about Jenny?' he asked.

'Clive Jenny is not here, she just didn't get onto the 2 o'clock flight to Nice.'

'What do you mean she didn't get onto the flight. Are you sure?' he asked sounding confused.

'Of course I am sure. Jacques and Fleur were at the airport to meet her and when she didn't arrive they asked an official to find out if Jenny was on the plane, but it seems she never boarded' she told him.

'But I thought you said she was there in France when we spoke earlier.'

'I know I said that, because I thought she was with Jacques and Fleur at their house and they had taken her for dinner before she came up to the hospital. I was wrong' she continued.

'Good grief where on earth can she be then?'

'I thought maybe you would know, that maybe she had sent you a text' she replied. Then she thought to herself that even if she had have done she most probably wouldn't have been able to get hold of him.

'No she has not contacted me at all' he told her.

'Well apparently not or you would know what had caused her to not board the plane. I am really worried Clive in case she has had an accident or something on the way to the airport. It's just not like Jenny at all, especially since she knows her grandpa is really ill' she told him and her son could only agree that it was a complete mystery.

'Look I will ring her mobile and if there is no answer I will go down to see what's happened to her. It might take me an hour or so, but I will go down. Why don't you go and get some sleep, and when I hear something I will let you know, I promise' he told her.

'OK love but please do ring me when you find out what has happened, I am worried sick, it's just not like Jenny at all'

'I know and just as soon as I find out something I will ring you, promise' and then he put the phone down and straight away rang Jennifer's phone, but it only said this number is unobtainable. It was now his turn to be worried. He just could not work out what was going on. First Nicole and now his youngest daughter Jennifer. He tried one more time then picked up his car keys. As tired as he was he was going to have to drive the fifty miles to Stoke on Trent to his daughter's apartment to see what was wrong. His mother had been right, this was totally out of character for Jennifer. He was both worried and stressed. He just hoped when he arrived at her apartment it would be something simple that had gone wrong to prevent her boarding the plane, and yet in his heart of hearts he had a nasty feeling about it all. He also blamed himself. If he had gone over in the first place then Jennifer would not have had to go. Halfway there tiredness overcame him and he felt his eyes closing. He pulled up into a service station and bought himself a cup of strong black coffee to keep awake.

Maggie got into bed. She was so tired she felt she could easily sleep for a month. Every bone in her body ached and was crying out for sleep, yet sleep just would not come. Her mind was racing on ahead of her. She was worried about her husband and worried about her granddaughter. She was just glad that she had been able to get in touch of her son. He had not rung her straight back, and so that meant he had not been able to get hold of Jennifer. So she knew that he most probably was on his way to the apartment where she lived. It would take him at least an hour maybe longer and she just hoped everything was all right there and that Jennifer had just missed the plane. She could not stand it if her granddaughter had been in an accident too.

Clive had asked about Nicole, and why it had hurt Maggie not to have a forwarding address or phone number for her. Part of her was glad that she had left. She became totally unbearable to live with. She had no respect for them or their property, and was rude. It had finally come to the crunch when she had abused their trust yet again.

Why she was like that Maggie and Jean-Paul couldn't fathom. The two girls were as different as chalk and cheese. She also knew that there was no love lost between them, although it was not Jennifer's doing, it was as if Nicole just could not stand the sight of her. It had been a relief when they had both got older and were able to spend separate holidays at the villa and less arguments.

She thought of her beloved husband then, Jean-Paul. Would this be the end of him, or could he still recover from the accident even though his injuries were quite serious. Now he was in a coma, Maggie just did not know. She could only hope and pray that he would. She also hoped that her son would decide to fly out. She wanted him here. It had been strange but she had never liked to tell him that he was needed, as she did not like to sound too pushy. She knew he had his own life, and that mostly his life was his work. Maggie had never liked to portray herself as being needy, and neither had Jean-Paul. It had been the opposite away around, they liked to feel that they were always on hand for others.

When Clive's beloved wife had died in childbirth, they had been there, and from as long as she could remember it was they that had been there for Clive, then for Nicole and Jennifer. Never did they ask for anything back. Maybe that was her fault, maybe she should have shown Clive as they were getting older that they needed him, and even asked advice from him occasionally. But instead they had never let him know that they required anything.

She felt weary and was feeling her age, as if she had suddenly woken up and realised that she was not young anymore but was in fact in the waiting room of her life, the very last chapter so to speak, and she wondered if Jean-Paul was nearing the end of his. She had had a good life so couldn't complain, and had never really been seriously ill in her life. Maybe that was because she had taken care of herself. She had never abused drink, only drinking occasionally and had never smoked or taken drugs. Maggie contributed her almost flawless skin to her good lifestyle. People were amazed when she told them that she was ninety. But now she thought that she looked her age. This thing with Jean-Paul had knocked her for six.

Eventually sleep overcame her and she drifted off into a deep but unsettled sleep. She dreamed that she and her husband were both young again and were running together along a seashore, her long hair flowing in the wind. Then it changed to both her granddaughters when they were small and Nicole was trying to bury little Jennifer in the sand with her spade even covering up her head until she had totally disappeared from view. Maggie panicked and was down on her hands and knees in the sand trying to get her out, but when she had removed all the sand that Nicole had covered her up with, she just was not there at all. She had

223

totally gone. She woke up in a cold sweat and could hear her phone ringing.

Clive Beaumont drank the rest of his black coffee that he had bought at the service station. He had been feeling so tired and his eyes had been shutting, but the coffee was doing the trick and making him alert again. It had been a long and tiring day for him at work, but then every day was long and tiring. And just lately the job he was doing had become something of a hassle to him. Jeff his boss was nothing but a pain in the ass. No matter what he did for him, it just was not enough. In fact since Jeff had taken over the partnership it had not been the same. It was not that he could afford to retire either, he could. But his job had been his life especially since the girls had flown the nest. There was a time when he really had enjoyed what he was doing, but since Jeff had taken over it had all gone pear shaped.

Just another few miles to go he thought to himself, and he would be at Jennifer's apartment. He just wished that the last time they had spoken he had not put the phone down She had annoyed him though. She just did not know what his boss Jeff was like, he was a slave driver and it would have proved hard to get even a week off. He intended to keep working as long as he could, even though he did not need the money. His retirement plan and pension he had set up for when he eventually retired was a good one. He had no mortgage to pay either, and did not owe anything to anyone.

At last he had arrived and drew up outside the block of apartments. He had only been here the once and that was when Jennifer had moved in. He came to check it out with her. He had thought that it was in a good area and very private, overlooking the big park. He had even offered to give Jennifer some of the deposit but she would not hear of it, and had refused. Not like his eldest Nicole who would have taken his money without a second thought. Not that he minded, what else could he spend his money on. He rarely went on holiday and the times he did travel was with work. Jennifer was a good girl and he only hoped there was a good enough reason why she had not caught that plane to Nice. He got out of his car and locked it. Everywhere looked in complete darkness but he rang the buzzer anyway. There was no answer as he looked around wondering where she was. There was still no answer from her mobile either, all very strange he thought. He decided to ring the buzzer again, but still there was no answer, just silence. In fact coming to think of it it was a pretty lonely place his daughter was living in. It had not looked the same in daylight. He rang for a third time, just in case Jennifer had been in bed, but still there was no answer. He could not understand why but he felt very uneasy. Clive was not the sort of man to panic but he felt something was definitely wrong. Jennifer would never arrange to fly out to see her nan and not turn up, not without telling her that something had happened.

He decided he would call in at the local police station and report his daughter missing. He knew they probably would not do a thing yet, only keep it on report, but he felt he needed to do that. He wished he knew Francesca's number so he could check if she knew anything at all, but he didn't have it. He pressed the buzzer one last time and then walked to his car and drove away.

The police station was well lit up and he was wondering if he was doing the right thing at first reporting Jennifer missing like this, but he saw no other solution. Besides they would probably check to see if there had been any accidents. It was now getting late and would be even later by the time he got back home again. Then he would probably only have a few hours sleep before he went to work, but this had to be done. He also had to ring his mother to let her know what was happening. He wondered if he should ring her first before going into the police station. He hated waking her up if she was sleeping, but at least it was better to ring now than later still and so he dialed her number before he got out of his car.

'Hello mum it's Clive here' he told her as she picked the telephone up. She had been having a bad dream when she had suddenly been awakened by the ringing of the phone.

'Oh Clive thank goodness it's you. Have you spoken with Jenny? Is she all right?' she asked him glad to hear his voice.

'Mum now I don't want you worrying because it's probably just something simple, but I have been to Jenny's apartment and there is just no answer' he explained. He was almost frightened to have to tell her just in case she jumped to the wrong conclusions, but knew she would be waiting to hear something, so it was now or later.

'Oh good heavens where can she be? I hope she is OK, it's just not like Jenny. Have you phoned the police and reported her missing?' she asked sounding worried.

'That's what I am about to do now mum, but don't you worry too much, it could be just that she missed the plane or something happened to prevent her catching it' he told her, but she was not convinced and neither was he. Something just did not feel right and he was about to get to the bottom of it.

Chapter 23

Clive Beaumont walked into the police station and spoke to the desk Sargent on duty.

'Hello I want to report my daughter missing please' he told him and he was then told to take a seat until someone could see him. He sat down and sighed heavily.

'Where are you Jenny?' he thought to himself as he looked around at the posters up on various parts of the wall. He was the only one that was sitting in the small waiting area, and it seemed like ages before anyone came out to see him. After about fifteen minutes someone was sent out to him.

'You want to report someone missing?' the police officer said as he approached him, and then continued 'please follow me.'

Clive got up and followed him into another room that had a table and a couple of chairs. The police officer told him to sit down, and Clive noticed then that his name badge said PC George Jones.

'The first question I want to ask you, what is your name and address Sir?'

'Clive Beaumont 55 Hill View Gardens Birmingham.

'And who is it that's missing sir?' he asked taking the details down.

'My daughter. She should have caught the 2pm plane to Nice yesterday and according to my mother's neighbours she never boarded it' he began.

'Can you give me her name please?'

'Jennifer Sudbury'

'What age is she sir?

'She is twenty-eight. In fact her birthday was recently' he told him.

'And does your daughter live alone or with someone?'

'She lives alone. She was divorced about nine months ago' he told him.

'And is it possible that her ex would know where she is?' he asked.

'I doubt it, he left her for another woman' he told him and the policeman nodded sympathetically.

'What's your daughters address?' he asked and Clive told him. He then asked when Clive had last seen her or spoken to her.

'Quite a few days ago now, we spoke over the phone' he replied and the policeman asked him if everything was all right when they last spoke.

'Before I answer that question I think I need to explain about my father who was recently injured and knocked off his bicycle in a hit and run accident. Jenny was concerned that I should fly out at once to see him. I told her that it was not possible to just up and go at the drop of a hat, and she became annoyed. So we did have words, but it was nothing serious.

The policeman then put his pen down and asked if he usually got on with his daughter.

'Of course she's my daughter; she just caught me at a time when I had been driving virtually all day. I was so tired and stressed out with work, and so was she that night. She was very worried about her grandpa. She still arranged to fly over to stay with them though. My mother was expecting her. In fact my mother told me that Jenny had rung her the night before and let her know when to expect her' he said as he continued to explain.

'She was to be picked up by a neighbour of theirs in Nice airport.'

'What is your mother's address in France?' he asked to which Clive gave him both the address and also his parent's phone number.

'I don't suppose you carry a recent photo her?' he asked.

'No I am afraid not' he answered and then proceeded to give a description of Jennifer that the police officer took down.

'Does your daughter suffer with any illness at all, like diabetes, epilepsy or asthma?'

'No nothing at all'

'What about the state of your daughters mind' he asked him.

He then elaborated 'can I ask you if your daughter Jennifer ever suffers from bouts of depression? Clive shook his head and said 'no not that I am aware of.'

'And has your daughter ever gone missing before?'

'No certainly not. In fact this is totally out of character for Jenny. If she could not have caught that plane she would have certainly let my mother know' he told him and the police officer wrote it down and then explained to him that he needed to ask all these questions so that he could determine what level of risk he needed to put her in. Clive looked puzzled. So he continued to explain that when someone is reported missing, each person is filed into either a low medium or high risk. Clive nodded then he told him that he was very worried about her.

'Try not to worry sir, we will be putting Jennifer in the medium to high risk, simply because it's something she has not done before and it's totally out of character for her' he told him and Clive could only breathe a sigh of relief.

'What will happen now Officer? I need to go back to Birmingham, I have to work tomorrow' he told him.

'Well we now have your daughter on file as a missing person, and this report will go out to all our officers. Just one more question Sir, do you happen to have a key for her apartment?'

'No sorry I don't'

'Does your daughter own her apartment or is it rented?'

'It's rented but I don't know who her landlord is I am afraid' he told him.

'Not to worry we can soon find that out on our computer database.'

'OK I think that is all we need to know for now, but any further questions we will be in touch'

He then handed him a card for Clive to contact if he himself heard from his daughter.

'I hope everything is sorted soon and your daughter gets in contact, but like I said try not to worry, these things mostly turn out OK. It could just be something quite simple you know, like staying with a boyfriend or maybe she just missed the plane' he told Clive.

'As far as I know Jennifer is not seeing anyone, so I doubt she has a boyfriend, and as I explained she would have let my mother know' he replied taking the card from the officer and thanking him.

Then he left the station and went back to his car. It had started to rain quite heavily by this time and was a dismal night, as he headed for the motorway. He only wished now that he had asked his daughter for a spare key when he had last been down to visit her. Then he could have at least gone inside the apartment and had a look around, but that was all in hindsight. He still felt uneasy even though he had reported Jennifer missing. He wondered if they would send somebody out tonight or leave it until the morning.

It was Monday morning and DC McKenna had gone back into work earlier than usual after his weekend break, which he rarely got. He had just taken a cup of coffee up to his desk when Max came walking into the office.

'I see your Ms Sudbury has been reported missing then?' he told him learning by his desk with his arms folded. Alex frowned and took a sip of his coffee, and pulled his usual face and thought the coffee did not get any better.

'What's that about Ms Sudbury? You say she's gone missing?'

'Yes apparently she's now on the missing persons register. Her dad came in late Saturday night and reported it'

'I wonder what the story is behind it?' Then he saw the information he had been left about it in a file lying on his desk waiting for him.

'So she didn't board the plane to Nice?' he told Max reading the information and picking up the telephone, making a quick phone call. He decided he needed to get a key from her landlord to take a look around in her apartment. Someone from the station had already contacted the Estate Agent and they had given permission for a key to be released.

'I knew there was more than met the eye about this case. It does not mention her friend Francesca Davis and I think it might be worth giving her a ring too, just in case she knows something, but first I think we need to take a look inside her apartment. In fact I am surprised no one has already done it' he told Max.

'I think two PC s went around in the early hours of Sunday morning, but everything was secure from what they could see, so they thought it would be best to wait for a key instead of breaking in. There was no suggestion that she might have harmed herself or anything, it was just that she did not board the plane.'

'Yes I can understand that' he answered then asked if Max would be free to accompany him to the apartment.

Two hours later they were letting themselves into the communal hall, and then opening the door to Jennifer's apartment.

'Well here goes, let's see what we can find out' he told Max as they entered shouting 'Police here,' just in case anybody was there. They looked around separately in each of the rooms. Max called Alex to come into the bathroom.

'It looks like she was about to take a bath and then decided not to, look it's still full with water?' Alex frowned.

'Her suitcase is also in the bedroom packed, and her handbag is on top of it' he said and checking the contents he found that her passport was there.

'I am not happy about this. It does not make sense. Why would you pack a suitcase and get everything ready to go on your trip then just disappear?'

Max nodded and agreed. They continued to look around to see if they had missed anything.

'Alex come here, take a look at this, he told him. It's to someone named Katie, whoever she is. Alex opened the envelope containing the photo and rolled his eyes and replaced it.

'Do you think the girl in the photo is Jennifer Sudbury?' he asked.

'It looks like her albeit a good many years younger maybe. What do you think is going on here?'

'Not sure but I intend to find out' he told him replacing the photo inside the envelope back into the drawer.

'There is no evidence that there has been a struggle or anything, which you would expect if she had been taken without her consent.' he told Max then continued ' I think I will pay our Mr Fletcher a visit to see if he heard anything'

Alex McKenna banged on his door but there was no answer, so he banged again. Eventually an unshaven Joe Fletcher popped his head around the door.

'What do you want?' he told them angrily. I've done nothing'

'We didn't say you had, now can we come in? Alex asked him impatiently.

'Do you have a search warrant?' he replied trying to close the door on him.

'No we don't, but as I told you before we can easily get one and then we will be back in a flash. It might go in your favour if you cooperate with the police' he told him. Mr Fletcher opened his door reluctantly to let them in.

The place was the same as it was before a complete tip, but did not smell as bad.

'What's happened? What do you want?' he asked them, aware of Alex and Max looking around the room. Empty beer bottles and cans were everywhere.

'What do you know about your neighbour Ms Sudbury? Alex asked him.

'Nothin. I know Nothin' he insisted.

'Well it appears she may have gone missing, I don't suppose you know anything about it, or if you heard or saw anything strange happening, in the last few days or so?' Max continued.

'I told you I know nothin, and if she's missing it's nought to do with me' he replied.

'What do you use the computer for? ' Max asked walking over to it.

'What do you blooming well think I use it for? It's a computer isn't it' he answered angrily.

'Less of the funny remarks, you know what I mean' Max told him.

'Look I think you had better go now, and before I let you in again you will need a search warrant' he told them getting agitated.

Alex looked at Max and they both went to leave.

'We'll be back.....and with a search warrant if necessary ' Alex told him. Then they both left his apartment.

Before they left the building altogether they decided to take Jennifer's computer as a precaution just in case it showed anything in her history that would shed any light on her whereabouts.

Chapter 24

Maggie Beaumont had spent a terrible weekend worrying about her husband, and now her precious granddaughter had gone missing too, it had just been too much for her. She had spent most of the weekend at the hospital with him, and now they had told her that the only thing that was keeping Jean-Paul alive was the life support machine. They had still been hoping for him to recover enough so he would not need it and could breath on his own, but it was all looking doubtful now. When the consultant had told her earlier today she had broke down in tears, and Lisa had held her hand.

How she wished he had not gone cycling that day. But Jean-Paul was a health fanatic, and if he was not riding his bike he was either swimming or taking Bella for long walks. The police had been to see her to ask her if there was any improvement with him, and when she had told them what the consultant had said they realised the situation was grave. The hit and run driver if found could face a murder charge, since the witness had said in his statement that it looked as if it might have been done on purpose.

Clive had been keeping in touch over the weekend and told his mother that if there was any news about Jennifer he would ring her straight away. He was going to book a plane ticket to fly over within the next two or three days. He had told Jeff that he needed to have some time off to be with his family. He was just hoping that the police would find out what had happened to Jennifer before he came, and although Maggie was fearful that he would not make it in time before something happened to Jean-Paul, she understood that he also needed to stay over in England in case Jennifer was found.

She just could not bear thinking about what could have happened to her. Usually people that went missing were either never found at all, or else worse almost worse all sorts of horrible things had been done to them. This was going through her mind as she sat there talking softly to her husband, and willing him to open his eyes hoping be alright even though there was no longer much hope for him.

'Maggie I have bought you a nice cup of tea and a sandwich to keep your strength up' Lisa told her.

She felt so sorry for what Maggie and what she was going through. It was one thing for her husband to be on life support, but now the added burden of her granddaughter going missing.

'Thank you Lisa but I am not hungry' Maggie told her shaking her head sadly.

'But you have to have something, just drink the tea then' she told her. She looked so pale and her eyes were puffy and red where she had been crying. Maggie took the tea with shaking hands and took a small sip. She was far too pent up to eat or drink. She felt sick to the stomach at what had happened, and as she sat there she felt so lifeless. She did not think she could go on if anything happened to Jean-Paul let alone her Jenny, nether would she want to.

She thought about Bella their dog. She could imagine her fretting for Jean-Paul. Every time she had gone back home the dog was so glad to see her and she would come running with her tail wagging. Then after a while when she knew that Jean-Paul was not with her, she would go back to her basket with a sad eye, as if she knew that something was wrong.

Fleur and Jacques had also been up to the hospital to sit for a while with her. They were both devastated about Jean-Paul, and now with the news that Jennifer was missing too, they blamed themselves because that they had not told Maggie straight away when she had not turned up at the airport. How could they have stupidly thought that Jennifer would be OK, and that she had probably phoned her grandmother to say she had missed the plane. Instead they should have gone to the hospital to tell Maggie. But Maggie had insisted that it wasn't their fault. She had told them that the police were doing everything they could to try and find out what had happened to Jennifer, but so far it was all a complete mystery.

It was now Tuesday morning and Jennifer had been missing for the fourth day. DC Alex McKenna had still been searching the database for any information he could find on Joe Fletcher, but it was all proving tiresome. He had arranged for Francesca to come in again. When he had phoned her mobile she had wondered what he could want with her, since Jennifer had told her that the case had been dropped, but he was not saying a thing over the telephone, instead he wanted to talk face to face. All he could tell her was that it would help him with his enquiries, and so she had agreed to go in later after work. He had still been studying all the database two hours later when he suddenly called out 'Got ya!" His voice was so loud that Max stopped what he was doing and went to look over his shoulder.

'Look at this Max' he said grinning from ear to ear.

Max looked at the computer screen and smiled down at him.

'It's definitely him, albeit a slightly younger version of him.'

'Just as I thought Joe Fletcher is not his real name. It says here his name is Walter Smyth.'

'How long ago is this then' Max asked.

'At least seven years ago. It says he was cautioned for stalking some lady around the same age as Ms Sudbury. Also one or two other minor sexual discrepancies' he told him. Max shook his head.

'Maybe we should bring him in for questioning?' he suggested and Max agreed.

'I knew I smelt a rat with him, yes we will definitely bring him in.'

Francesca walked the short distance to the police station after she finished work. She was wondering how she would be able to help the DC with his inquires as he had told her on the phone, unless they were reopening the case, but she did not think so since Jennifer was now in France.

'Ah Miss Davis, thank you for coming in' DC McKenna said to her as he led her through to a interview room and asked her to sit down.

'Can I ask what all this is about? I thought the case was dropped, at least that was what Jennifer told me' she told him looking confused.

'You have spoken to Jennifer then?' Alex asked her looking surprised. The last time he had talked to her, she had told him that she her and Ms Sudbury had not spoken.

'Yes of course just before she left for France' Francesca replied.

'I see. So when was the last time you saw or spoke with Ms Sudbury?' he asked.

'It was Friday after work, we arranged to meet up for coffee, and then I told her that I would give her a lift to the airport' she explained.

'And did you? Give her a lift to the airport'

'Well I was supposed to pick her up at her apartment around 10am, but I was a bit late, almost fifteen minutes late to be exact and so when I got there she had already left' Francesca explained looking puzzled then continued 'Why all the questions? ' But Alex asked another question.

'What made you think she had already left? Did she phone or text you to say this?' he continued.

'No, but then I did not have my mobile with me so if she had have done I would not have known. The reason I was late picking her up was because I spent ages searching for it. I just presumed she had left when there was no answer from her buzzer. Look can you tell me what all of this is about?' she asked.

Alex sighed loudly. 'It appears your friend Ms Sudbury has gone missing' he told her.

'What.....but why? How? I mean I thought she was in France?' Francesca said looking worried.

'No it appears she never boarded the plane to Nice, and consequently she was later reported missing by her father Mr Beaumont' he explained, and Francesca realised that it was the reason she had not heard from her friend. At first she had thought that Jennifer was just giving her the cold shoulder because she had been late, but at least this explained it. She now had to think about whether or not to tell the DC about the photo that Jennifer had been sent anonymously. She knew that Jennifer had said she did not want to report it because it would make her look bad, but surely it was different now that she was missing, any information at all would be welcome by the police, especially if it led to her where about.

'Can I ask if Jennifer told you about something that was sent to her?' she asked him, knowing that she had not reported it; at least that was what she had said.

'And what may that be? If there is anything, anything at all that you know about that may help us, then I think you owe it to your friend to tell us, anything at all?' he asked and Francesca decided he needed to know just in case it helped. She would risk Jennifer getting annoyed with her later.

'OK well when we met on Friday before she disappeared, she told me a few things. One that she was still getting the strange silent phone calls, and also that she received an envelope which had the name Katie written on it' she started to explain.

'Katie? Who is Katie? Alex asked with a frown.

'Katie was the name she called herself when she was online, either in the chat rooms or whatever else, a sort of pseudonym instead of her real name' she told him.

'I see, and did she tell you what was in the envelope?' he asked.

'Yes she did. It was a photo'

'And what was the photo of?' he asked suddenly realising it would be the photo he had put back in the drawer.

Francesca suddenly looked embarrassed and said a quiet (sorry Jen) in her mind then explained.

'Well when Jennifer was about seventeen she got mixed up with the wrong crowd and was involved in a few things' she began.

'What sort of things? Can you explain?' he asked her.

'Well for a very short time she worked in this club.'

'Go on.'

'It was a sort of lap dancing club and the photo she received was of her when she was doing the lap dancing' she explained.

'OK but did she call herself Katie while she was working there?'

'No that was the weird thing about it all. No one knew about her working there except me, and she never used the name Katie, not back then. Katie is the name she has only used recently.'

'How recently?' he asked her.

'Very recent....say within the last nine months, since she started to go online in the chat rooms.'

'Did she tell you what chat rooms she went into?'

'Just that they were chat rooms and also she set up a profile on a dating web page' she explained.

'And did she also call herself Katie on the dating website?'

'I think so. No wait, she used the name Katherine'

'Right.....well Katherine or Katie, is pretty much the same name really don't you think?' he said to her and she nodded.

'You say she worked in a lap dancing club? For how long?'

'Oh it was only for a very short time, maybe about six months or less' she told him.

'And you say nobody knew about this? Not even her father? What about the ex did he know?'

'Nobody knew, and certainly not her father. She was just seventeen and it was a dark time in her life that she preferred not to talk about any more. It was not something that she was proud of' Francesca explained.

' Okay so she was seventeen and you say she was at the club for about six months?

'Yes that's correct'

'And while she was working at the club, was she ever hassled by anyone, or did anything sinister ever happen there?'

'Not that I know of, although most men that go to that kind of club are, are not the sort of men you want to get to know if you know what I mean' she told him, all of which Alex continued to write everything.

'And you say she never used the name Katie there while she worked at the club, only online?'

'Yes that's right'

'What was the name of the club? Do you remember?'

'It was the Gentlemens Private Club.'

'And where was that? '

'In Manchester.'

'Okay I think that is all for now Miss Davis' he told her.

'But what about the pervert that lives next door to her?' she asked.

'Pervert? Are you talking about her neighbour? Did Jennifer say anything to you about him?'

'Yes she was always going on about him giving her the creeps, waiting around for her when she went to work, or coming home' she told him. 'She wondered if her disappearance had something to do with him.'

'Did she ever say he did anything to her or said anything?'

'I don't think he did anything, not that he wouldn't have liked to. I mean he was always there watching her, and I think he may have said one or two obscene things. She was just afraid of him.'

'Rest assured that we will be questioning him' he told her, and then he got up.

'OK as I said that is all we need to know for now, and thank you for coming in Miss Davis. If we need to know anything else we will contact you. Or if you remember anything else that you may. have forgotten please let us know' he told her. And Francesca got up to leave.

DC McKenna picked up his phone.

'Hello Steve, DC McKenna here. I think it's time we bought Walter Smyth in for questioning.'

Chapter 25

Francesca was in deep thought as she made her way to the pub where she had agreed to meet Paul. Where on earth could Jennifer be? It just did not make any sense. She had been absolutely sure that she had gone to France, and now she was worried that something awful had happened to her. She just hoped that she was wrong.

Paul had texted her earlier to arrange to meet her, since he was now back home again from his travels. She had mentioned that she had to stop off at the police station after work first, and he had texted back why, and when she had said she hadn't a clue but it was something about her friend Jennifer. Then he texted that he thought she had taken Jennifer to the airport on Saturday.

Paul was in the pub already when she walked in. Francesca saw him sitting at the bar talking to another guy, and when he saw her he got up, said something else to the guy and then led Francesca to a table at the far side of the room.

'What do you want to drink babe?' he asked with a smile and giving her a peck on the lips.

'Just a lemon and lime' she told him sitting down and putting her bag under the table.

'Don't you want something stronger than that? 'he asked pulling a face.

'No a lemon and lime will do, it's not yet seven and I have not been home yet' she told him.

'OK lemon and lime it is then. I won't be long' he told her and went back to the bar, and she saw him say something to the guy again.

Francesca was not in the mood to drink tonight, and in fact all she really wanted to do was go home. Not that she was not glad to see Paul, as she was. It was just that his constant questions were beginning to annoy her. It was as if he was always asking this and that.

'So what's all this about your friend then?' he asked handing Francesca her drink, and sitting down with his pint. Francesca rolled her eyes and thought here we go again, then looked at him sadly.

'She has gone missing' she told him.

'No, you are kidding. I thought you had arranged to take her to the airport? At least that was what you told me'

'I should have; only when I called for her she was not there. I rang her buzzer and there was just no answer so I presumed she had left earlier. I was a bit late, because I could not find my mobile. Speaking of mobiles, you did not find it did you, and then push it through my front door?' she asked him, and she saw his face change suddenly and he looked really angry.

'Now why would I do that? What are you saying?' he asked taking a big drink of his pint.

'Nothing, I just wondered if it was you. My parents said that they didn't do it, so I don't know who it could have been, that's all.'

'Well it wasn't me OK. Maybe it was that loony friend of yours, what do you call her Jennifer? Maybe she did it.'

'Why would she do that? Besides she has gone missing remember?' she said to him and Paul had a horrible smirk across his face.

'If you say so' he replied.

'Paul do you know anything about where Jennifer is?' she asked him because something about the way he looked scared her.

'Look let's get this straight. I will tell you once and only once, right. I have no idea where that loony friend of yours is, why should I? And if you think that then we are totally finished, is that clear you stupid bitch' he told her angrily.

Francesca was taken aback by his outburst so just nodded. It was at times like this she wondered if she really knew him at all. After a few more minutes he got up to go telling Francesca that he had to see someone.

'When will we see each other again' she asked him in a softer note. She hated to see him angry.

'I am not sure. I will text you' he said downing the rest of his pint and placing it back on the table.

Francesca felt close to tears. He was playing mind games with her again and she did not like it, but knew unless she ended it with him, she had to go along with what he said and so just nodded OK and Paul left.

She was hurt and angry and close to tears. Why did she allow him to play with her feelings like this she thought picking up her bag? It was all making her ill, but she knew that she was not strong enough to end it. She really did love him, all of him, warts and all. She left the pub soon after without finishing the lemon and lime, and headed home. It had been a long day and she was really worried about Jennifer.

As she was walking a text message came through to her phone. Taking it out of her handbag to look who it was from, she saw that it was from Paul.

'Hello Babe. Sorry I got annoyed see you soon, Paul x.'

Francesca had tears in her eyes when she read it, then replacing the phone back into her bag again she felt a lot lighter in her mood. This was the Paul that she loved, the Paul that she would do anything for if he asked her.

Lisa the English nurse held Maggie's hand. The Consultant who was looking after Jean-Paul had just been to see her again, to explain that in the next few hours or so they were going to turn off the life support machine which was keeping Jean-Paul alive with her permission. There had been a meeting to discuss what was happening the day before and it was decided that it was not in his best interest to keep it going. All his organs had virtually shut down, he had heart and kidney failure plus his liver was not working properly. He had told Maggie gently that it was time to let him go peacefully. She had sobbed and asked him to reconsider as all she wanted was for him to wake up, and she had spent days willing him to do just that.

Her son Clive was flying out later that afternoon, and would be there at the hospital just as soon as he could. He had been in touch with her and told her that he had booked a plane ticket and would be with her later that day. And when she had then offered to get Jacques to pick him up at the airport, he had refused point blank, saying he would prefer to get a taxi straight from the airport to the hospital, and so she had not said anything else. He had left it for a few days before coming over to see if there was any news from the police about Jennifer, but although he had phoned the police station virtually every day there was nothing. Her disappearance still remained a mystery. Maggie just hoped that her granddaughter was OK and that the police would get to the bottom of it. Her son knew he could not leave it much longer to fly out to see his parents, because she had needed him, and from what she had told him about his fathers condition, if he left it a day or two longer it might be too late. And so Clive made his way to the airport and checked in. He was only taking hand luggage so after he went straight to security and once through he sat in the lounge awaiting the plane that would fly him to Nice.

Max came into the office to tell Alex that they had just picked up Walter Smyth alias Joe Fletcher. At first he had not answered the buzzer to his apartment and the arresting police officers had thought he was out, then one of them spotted him peeking out of the blinds and had pressed the buzzer again.

Walter Smyth was brought to the police station read his rights by the custody officer, and then asked if he wanted to ring his solicitor or anyone else. He declined this, so was then shown into the interview room and told to sit down, which he reluctantly and sat with his arms folded.

'Well, well if it's not Mr Fletcher, or should I say Mr Smyth. We meet again' Alex said sitting down opposite him. He then turned the voice recorder on.

'Can you please state your name and address aloud for the sake of the recorder' he told him, but he refused to say anything.

'For the purpose of the recording I am DC Alex McKenna in interview room 4 along with DC Max Brennan and suspect Mr Walter Smyth Apartment 1a Parkside Road'.

'Mr Smyth can I ask you when you last saw your neighbour Ms Sudbury?' Alex asked looking him straight in the eye.

'No comment' he replied looking down to avoid eye contact with Alex.

'OK Mr Smyth did you or did you not ever say anything untoward to Ms Sudbury or wait for her at times you knew she was going to or coming out of her apartment?'

'No comment.'

'Did you at anytime between Friday last to Saturday or even later have any contact at all with Ms Sudbury? he continued.

'No comment.'

'Come on Mr Smyth admit it. Do you realise you could be in some serious trouble.'

'No comment'

DC McKenna then spoke into the recorder that the interview was over for now and turned it off.

'Right Mr Smyth we are holding you in police custody for 24 hours while we continue with our enquiries.

'I bleeding well done nothing' he told Alex who ignored him and beckoned another officer to take him down to the cells

'We have applied for a search warrant and mark my words we intend to be back at your apartment before the day is out. So if I were you I would spend your time thinking about what you want to say when you are brought back up here again. It might be in your interest to talk to us' he told him as he was led away.

Alex then picked up his phone and rang his superior officer to ask if the search warrant had been granted.

'Max, YES we can go' he grinned from ear to ear and picked up his jacket and slung it over his shoulder.

Chapter 26

The smell from Walter Smyth's apartment was worse if anything than it had been that first day when they had visited him, the DC's thought as they entered.

'Crikey the smell is terrible in here, what can it be?' Max said covering his mouth with his handkerchief and trying not to gag.

'You would wonder how anyone could live like this' Alex replied looking around and shaking his head. The usual beer cans and bottles were strewn everywhere with half eaten food left out on a plate on the floor.

'I would like to see what he has on this computer for a starters' Alex told him and turned the power on. 'I wonder if he has a password?' It started up immediately and then a box came up on the screen saying 'enter password.'

'OK it might be a good idea to take it in and let the team look at it anyway.'

'Alex come here and take a look at this?' Max said from another room.

There were two or three photographs up on the wall in the bedroom, and when Alex looked closely they were clearly pornographic and one had Jennifer's face pasted on to someone else's body.

'The dirty little bastard' Alex said taking a picture of them as evidence.

'I knew I smelt a rat with him' he told Max

'I wonder who the other two girls are?' Max said taking a closer look.

They searched through drawers and looked in cupboards, and found more pornographic material.

The smell seemed a lot worse in the bathroom, and when Max lifted up part of the carpet he could see that someone had put bleach down to mask the odour. They both looked at each other.

'We had better take a look under there I suppose, but I think I had better report back first to the station, I don't think I like the look of this at all' he told him taking out his portable radio.

Maggie Beaumont had managed to persuade the Consultant to leave the life support machine on until her son arrived from England. It was the least they could do, so that he too could say his goodbyes to his father. She had been down to get a cup of sweet tea, even though she did not feel like eating or drinking, but she knew that when Clive arrived she needed her strength. She looked at the stillness of Jean-Paul and listened to the life support machine keeping his heart beating with every bleep.

Thoughts of happier times went through her mind. She remembered back to the earlier days when she had first met Jean-Paul. Then she thought of her wedding day, when she had never been happier, except perhaps the time that she had found out that she was pregnant with Clive. There were so many happy memories. Of course there had been sad times too. The deaths of both their parents and also the miscarriage that Maggie had which was so bad that she had to have a hysterectomy. Then came the death of Clive's lovely wife, leaving him a widower with two little girls. They had been through thick and thin together. She just could not see the future beyond Jean-Paul.

She had always hoped that she would have been the first to go, but maybe that had been a selfish thought, after all everyone knew that normally the woman lived longer than the man. She wondered then why that was? She thought women went through more stress than a man, childbirth for one thing? Then she thought of poor Clive's wife, and how she had actually died through childbirth and Jennifer had been her last gift to Clive.

'Oh Jenny, dear dear Jenny' she sobbed thinking of her granddaughter 'Where are you?' she said aloud.

Maggie just could not fathom what had happened to her, one minute she was coming over to see them and the next she had just disappeared. Clive had told her that the police were doing all they could to try and find her. He had told her to try and not worry, but how could she not worry? People just don't disappear do they? Good kind people like Jenny don't just disappear unless something bad happens. Unless someone takes them! A shiver ran up Maggie's spine at the thought of it, at the very thought of someone hurting her lovely Jenny. She started to cry again and the English Nurse Lisa came to sit with her.

'There there love, maybe your son will be here soon' she told her gently squeezing her hand.

Maggie could only sniff and wipe her eyes with her handkerchief.

'Is there any news about your granddaughter?' Lisa asked gently almost afraid to ask. Yet if there was good news it might comfort Maggie.

'No, nothing at all, it's a complete mystery' she told her and Lisa could only shake her head and sympathise.

Just then Clive arrived at the hospital carrying a small holdall. He asked directions in French to where the ICU was and within minutes he was hugging his mother. They both clung to each other like they would never let go

'Clive....oh Clive thank God you are here.' she told him and they both went to stand at Jean-Paul's bed. He looked ghostly pale as Clive took his hand, and gently whispered to him 'I am here now Dad.'

The Consultant was giving them a bit of time with him before he switched the life support machine off. Clive broke down as he looked at his father and was lost for words. He regretted leaving it so long before flying out. He knew that he should have come earlier. If only Jennifer had been here too to say goodbye.

Fifteen minutes later the machine was finally turned off, and they both whispered their goodbyes to a loving husband and father, and before they turned to go Maggie thought she saw a lovely change appear over Jean-Paul's face. He was now at peace.

DC Alex McKenna along with his partner Max peered into the hole they had made when they lifted the floorboards up. The smell was so overpowering that Max had to run to the toilet where he was violently sick and then he opened the windows to let some much needed air in.

'Are you OK mate?' Alex asked him. He knew it smelt awful in there, and even more so since they had lifted the floorboards.

'I think we had better get forensics in here' he told him looking at something that was wrapped up in a sort of white sheet.

Max looked as pale as the white sheet that was down there, as he peered inside the hole.

'I am sorry about that mate, the smell just got to me' he told him wiping his mouth.

'What do you think it is' Max asked.

'Dunno but we will soon find out' he replied.

Within twenty minutes a couple of guys from forensics had lifted whatever it was out from under the floorboards while the DCs waited in another room. In less than five minutes they were back out again to give them the news.

'Emergency over. It's just the body of a rotting dead cat!' one of the men said removing his facemask.

'Ah thank goodness, we were worried it was something more sinister' Alex told him with a sigh of relief.

'Still what stupid bugger would put an animal under the floorboards anyhow. It was bound to smell' Max said screwing up his face and remembering.

'Somebody like Smyth that's who' Alex replied with a wry smile and Max could only nod.

'I think we are pretty much finished here don't you? Although I would like to take a look in the apartment above the one that Mr Carmichael owns. I had better let him know about Mr Smyth too.

The last time I spoke to him over the phone he did not seem too bothered when I told him that the place was a complete tip. Maybe when we tell him that he kept a dead cat underneath the floorboards in his bathroom he will take notice' he told Max. Then they left and went back to the station taking Mr Smyth's computer with them.

'Well it's been quite a day Max' he told him then continued 'glad it was just a dead cat under those floorboards' and Max pulled a face.

When he got back to his desk there were a few documents on it with Jennifer's name on them.

'Ah the results from the computer' he thought to himself, opening them. The examination had been completed and showed that she had frequented a few chat rooms in the last few months, and also it showed her Facebook page and another website that she had set a profile up calling herself Katherine. There were a few emails from a guy called Luke and also someone named Philip, which were both traced to two different IP addresses.

An hour later he had got in touch with Mr Smyth's landlord again and this time on mentioning the cat he had agreed to go down and take a look. Alex was sending someone around at the same time to look inside the top apartment that also belonged to him, and Mr Carmichael had said he would be there.

He had telephoned Francesca earlier to ask if she could come back into the station after work. There were just a few other things that were troubling him that he wanted to clear up with her, and she had agreed. She was eager to know if they had found out anything else about   her friend.

Francesca was really worried about Jennifer now. It had been nearly a week since she had gone missing. She hoped that the police would have some leads as to where she had vanished to.

DC McKenna had not said much over the phone when he had rang her, just that he wanted to go over a few things. She had not mentioned it this time to Paul when he had phoned her earlier asking what she was doing later, because she did not want an inquisition. Also she thought it best not to mention Jennifer in case it changed his mood. This had been the first time she had heard from him since he had texted her saying sorry.

Alex led Francesca into the waiting room and thanked her for coming. She sat down and Alex sat down opposite her.

'Can I ask if there is any news about Jennifer yet?' she asked him eagerly.

'No news as yet I am sorry to say' he told her, and Francesca's face fell. This was not looking good, she thought.

'Now Ms Davis the reason I asked you to come in again was because I want to go through a few things with you about the time in the club' he told her and Francesca looked puzzled.

'OK but I told you everything I knew about that time, even before my friend went missing' she replied.

'Can I ask you again about a girl named Lucy? I remember you saying that you were unsure whether she was there at the club or not. Didn't you say it was because you had had too much to drink?' he asked.

'Yes that's right. I did say that, because both Jennifer and me did drink too much that night. Lucy may have been there' she told him swallowing hard because she also knew that if she said too much Paul would go mad with her.

'Can you think back to when you were there at the club. Try to remember if you can. Yes I know you said you had too much to drink, but this is really important. You see Miss Davis, Ms Sudbury made a statement to say that the girl Lucy was indeed in the club that Friday night, and she said you would vouch for that' he explained to which Francesca swallowed hard again. She knew she had to say something.

'I think Lucy was there, but if she was it was only briefly' she told him relaxing now she had finally said it, and wishing she had mentioned it before.

'Okay. What about your boyfriend? What did you say his name was?'

'What about him? He only came to collect me after I could not find Jennifer, he does not know anything about this' she replied.

'How long have you known him? What's his name?' he continued to ask.

'Paul, his name is Paul Blake, and we have known each other for over nine months' she told him and again she thought to herself Paul will go mad.

'By the way what is Lucy's address?' he asked her and Francesca had to say she did not know. She was not directly her friend, but a friend of a friend.

'So she's a friend of a friend? Who is the friend that she's a friend of?' he asked and Francesca felt her face flush with embarrassment. This is not going too well she thought.

'Well actually she and her boyfriend are friends of my boyfriend Paul' she told him, hoping he did not ask many more questions.

'Right so maybe your boyfriend Paul Blake will know her address do you think? I mean if they are friends of his' he asked looking her straight in the eye. She seemed very nervous to him and come to think of it, she had seemed nervous before when she had been asked certain questions. He just felt some things did not add up.

'I don't really know if he will have her address or not' she told him starting to shuffle around in her chair. It was plain as day that she was nervous about something.

'Right OK what about your boyfriend Paul's address could you give us that?' Alex asked.

'I am not sure he lives somewhere in Stone. To tell you the truth I have only been to his place a few times' she replied, and Alex looked at her in surprise.

'You mean to say you and your boyfriend have been together for what did you say nine months, and you don't really know his address' he told her lifting a eyebrow in surprise.

'Well the thing is we usually meet somewhere else so I have never needed to have his address' she told him suddenly feeling stupid. She could see his reasoning but in reality she had only ever been taken to his place at night and only ever stayed the one night. It made her realise that she did not know much about him at all. It was also ironic that she should have once thought that he would pop the

261

question to her. How could she have been so stupid? And now if anything their relationship had cooled even more, and she was also pretty sure that if her boyfriend got even a hint that she had discussed him with the police, then they would be finished. Yet what could she do? She had to tell the truth, especially if it would help to find Jennifer.

'I see Miss Davis. Can I ask if you have a contact number for him? I am pretty sure you must have? How else do you get in touch with each other to arrange to meet' he asked her with a wry smile and Francesca's stomach did somersaults. She had been cornered now. She had to give the DC the information he wanted. As he had a little sarcastically said to her, she must have a contact number for him or how else did they arrange to meet. What on earth will she tell Paul when she meets him later? She needed to tell him something. He would get angry again with her, for sure and say she had broken her promise to him not to get involved. But surely this was different? Jennifer was missing, and she could be in grave danger. Surely this time he would understand, but as much as she tried to tell herself he would understand she knew that he wouldn't. Instead he would be mad with her and might even end their relationship.

'Of course I have a contact number for him, but I am just not sure I should be giving it to you, not without his permission' she answered him feeling like an idiot.

'Well its like this Ms Davis, we need to speak with your boyfriend in order to get Lucy's address off him. Now I know you can't really remember too much about that night, but Ms Sudbury definitely said in her statement that she was speaking to a girl named Lucy at the club. We now need to follow this up, since Ms Sudbury is missing. Maybe this girl named Lucy can help us in our inquiries' he told her with a serious look in his face. Some things were just not adding up and he was going to find out what was going on or his name was not DC Alex McKenna.

Chapter 27

Paul had at first arranged to meet Francesca at the pub again, but after she had finished at the police station she had sent him a text.

'Hi Paul not feeling too good. I have got one of my bad headaches is it possible to skip the pub and maybe go to my place, or yours?' then she pressed send. A few minutes later he texted back.

'Hi Babe are your parents at home or out tonight?'

She had not felt in the mood to drink. She had also not told him that she had been to the police station or been asked to give DC McKenna his contact details. In fact in theory what she had actually done had stressed her out. Instead of giving him Paul's phone number she had in her phone, she had changed the number of one of them to read two instead of four. She had totally panicked and that was when she decided to do it.

She knew that when the DC rang the number she had given him, it would just either ring someone else or the number would not be recognised. She was taking a big risk with this, knowing full well that she could get into trouble. However if the DC got back in touch with her, which she knew he would then she would just apologise and give him the right number, but first she needed time to speak to her boyfriend and tell him what had happened. Francesca answered his message.

'No they will be home tonight' she told him.

'In that case we will go to mine because Jack is away' he replied.

'OK' she replied. This would give Francesca time to go home and change and maybe grab something to eat since he was meeting her in a hour's time. She had been glad when he had said they would go back to his place, because this time she would take more notice of where he lived. She had felt a complete idiot when she told the DC that she had not known his address. What must he have thought of her?

Paul was late when he picked her up and looked mithered, but was in a good mood. He gave her a big hug and even opened the car door for her to get into, which pleased Francesca since he seemed to be back to the Paul she had fallen in love with.

'How are you babe? How's that headache of yours?' he asked her looking concerned. If only he was like this all the time, Francesca thought to herself as she slipped her seat belt on.

'I will be fine, just had a busy day at work that's all' Francesca smiled back.

'I will sooth away your headache' he told her as he pulled off and headed along Trentham Road towards Stone. He had a lovely smile that always melted Francesca's heart.

'Why don't you close those pretty eyes and relax' he told her. But all Francesca wanted was to see where they were going.

'Why are you so stressed out anyhow, and don't give me the hard time at work bull. I mean we all have to work hard it's life' he told her and she thought she heard a slight hint of annoyance in his tone. So she decided to just close her eyes and pretend she hadn't heard him.

'That's better babe you rest' he told her picking up speed and overtaking another car. The other car picked up a bit of speed too, but he went even faster overtaking and peeping his horn angrily.

'GET OUT OF THE WAY IDIOT!' he shouted, and drove on past him.

Francesca's stomach turned over, but she said nothing just kept her eyes closed, right up until he stopped the car and turned the engine off.

'We are here' he told her. Francesca opened her eyes and smiled at him. She needed to tell him about having to go to the police station after she had finished work and that the DC wanted his contact number, whether he was angry or not.

DC McKenna had Mr Smyth brought into one of the interview rooms again. This time he was hoping that he would cooperate. He was still refusing a solicitor saying he did not need one because he had done nothing. He sat down and Alex sat opposite him, while a PC stood by the door. He was told that it would be in his favour this time if he answered all the questions, and that the sooner he did so he might be allowed home.

'For the purpose of the recorder can you please state your name and address out loud?' he asked him.

'Walter Smyth 1a Parkside Road' he replied sheepishly, wanting the interview to be over. He was tired and knew that they had been to his apartment with a search warrant.

'Mr Smyth when was the last time you saw or heard your neighbour Ms Sudbury?' he asked.

'I can't remember, maybe a week ago. I don't see her much, I mind my own business' he told him.

'You mind your own business? So you have never said anything untoward to her at any time?'

'No I have not, why should I have? I told you I mind my own business' he insisted.

'So you have never fantasised about her in any way?' he asked.

'No I haven't' he replied.

'OK. Can you explain what this is all about then?' Alex asked putting the photographs that he had taken a picture of as evidence on the table, in front of him.

'Never seen them before' he told Alex and looked away. Alex could see he was visibly shaking but carried on.

'So you say you have never seen these photos before, yet these were taken from the bedroom wall of your apartment. Can I ask who the other two girls in the photo are?'

'I told you I never saw them before' he insisted.

'OK now I want to ask you about something else that happened about seven years ago?'

'What's that then?' he asked and Alex continued.

'Well seven years ago you were arrested and cautioned because you were found to be stalking a young girl of similar age to Ms Sudbury were you not? The girl in question was Mary Travis. Is this true?'

Walter knew that it was no use denying it because it was still on record.

'Yes it's true. I was arrested back then but it was all lies....she told lies' he told him.

267

'There was also a witness to say that what Mary Travis said had been true and that you did follow her at various times' he continued.

'All lies I never did' he insisted.

'Mr Smyth when we entered your apartment there was a nasty smell coming from the bathroom, what was the cause of that smell?' he asked. He wanted to give him time to tell him about why there had been a dead cat underneath his floorboards.

'That would be the drains....maybe blocked' he told him, trying to sound convincing.

'The drains, are you sure? So the smell from your bathroom would not be because you put the body of a dead cat underneath the floorboards?' he told him and Walter Smyth went white and unexpectedly and to Alex's surprise started to sob.

'Mr Smyth can you please answer the question. Did you or did you not put the body of a dead cat underneath the floorboards in your bathroom?' he asked him again.

'I did. I did not want her buried in the ground outside, I wanted her with me always, my cat my Honey' he sobbed and Alex passed him a tissue, while he just kept sobbing.

'Interview with suspect Walter Smyth suspended for time being.'

After Mr Smyth was taken back to the cell, Alex called Max in and replayed the recorder.

'What do you think Max?' he asked and Max stroked his chin listening to it.

'Interesting! He denies the photos?'

'Yes and also says point blank the last time he saw Ms Sudbury was a week ago.'

'Do you think he is capable of doing anything to her though? I mean don't get me wrong he is not innocent by a long chalk. In my opinion he is a dirty little pervert, but I am not sure...and unless you charge him soon you will have to let him go.'

'I know that Max.'

'I spoke to Ms Sudbury's friend Miss Davis too, there is something not right there either if you ask me. I mean if you were going out with someone for nine months would you know what their address was?' he asked him.

'Of course I would unless I was stupid' he sniggered.

'Well I tell you Max she says she did not know and so I got his mobile number off her, but she was reluctant to give it to me at first' he told him.

'Are you going to question him?' Max asked with a frown.

'Yes I think so. I also want this girl named Lucy's address, and according to Ms Sudbury's statement that time, this Lucy was at the club that night' he explained.

'I want some questions answered and I intend to get them.'

Francesca decided to put her phone on silent while she was with Paul. She did not want any distractions, and she had an inkling that DC McKenna might ring her back if he could not get through to Paul with the number she had given him. She was going to wait until the right moment to tell him, if there was a right moment.

The house where Paul shared with another guy was quite posh looking on the outside. Francesca had thought. The two previous times she had been there she had not really taken much notice, but this may have been because it was dark when he had brought her there. She wondered what the friend he shared with did for a living. On entering Paul quickly shut the door to the lounge and led her straight to the kitchen, which also had a dining area where there was a wall mounted TV. The kitchen units were a sort of medium white wash and there was a breakfast bar. Francesca perched herself onto one of the high stools while Paul put the kettle on.

'Tea or coffee babe' he asked her.

'Coffee please' she replied.

'What does your friend Jack do for a living' she asked him. She was not sure whether Paul had told him that the house belonged to Jack and that he was just paying rent while he was living there.

'Oh this and that. He's away quite a lot, so I get the place to myself like tonight' he smiled getting out two mugs from one of the cabinets.'

She watched him make two mugs of coffee. He looked like the old Paul and maybe she would be able to tell him about DC McKenna after all without him jumping down her throat.

'Is it OK if I use the bathroom?' she asked taking a sip of the coffee.

'I would rather you did!' he told her and continued 'I don't want you making a mess on the floor tiles' he joked and Francesco laughed.

The bathroom was very big and she remembered using it to have a shower the previous time she had been there. It had a big corner bath too, big enough for two, and one whole wall had mirror wall tiles on it. There were two bathroom cabinets, one of which was clearly locked and the key was not there. She looked inside the other one, finding were men's toiletries and various other items. When she came out of the bathroom she noticed that one of the bedroom doors was wide open. She presumed it was Jack's room because it was not the room she had stayed in with Paul. Francesca was tempted to take a peek but then changed her mind and instead went back down the stairs to the dining room where Paul was still sitting, drinking his coffee and doing something on his mobile phone. He put it down when he saw her and smiled.

'How's your headache now?' he asked.

'Not so bad Paul' she told him.

'Do you fancy watching a film?' he asked suddenly turning the TV on. Francesca wondered why they never went into the lounge to watch it, but strangely it was either here or to his room.

After a while he switched it off and told her he was beat maybe they should just go to bed and cuddle, and Francesca agreed, because a cuddle was better than nothing, besides what better place for her to tell him about DC McKenna.

'Paul' she began as they lay in bed with her head on his chest where she could hear the beat of his heart.

'Yes Babe....what is it?' he asked kissing the top of her head.

'Today I was asked to go to the police station again. DC McKenna wanted to ask more questions.'

She felt his whole body stiffen

'Questions? What about?' he asked her becoming more alert.

271

'About Jennifer again and that night in the club, what else' she told him.

'Don't get cocky, how would I know! I thought you promised me you would not get involved?' he said sounding a bit annoyed.

'I didn't want to be involved, I was asked to go in, so what else could I do, and what I want to tell you and please don't get angry but he wanted your contact number.'

'WHY THE BLOOMING.........' 'I hope you never gave it to him?' he told her moving her off his chest and looking at her.

'That's what I want to tell you. I gave him the wrong number, well the right minus one digit, but it was awkward for me, and if he dials it he will know it's not the right number' she explained.

'Good! I don't see what I can tell him about your loony mate anyhow, she was gone before I got there that night.'

'I know that and I told him that too, but he thinks you will know where Lucy lives and....' she explained but Paul jumped out of bed annoyed.

'Lucy? Didn't I explain to you not to involve her?'

'Paul I am sorry but in the statement Jennifer made, she told them that a girl named Lucy was at the club. I told them that I had too much to drink that night and could not really remember' Francesca told him swallowing hard. She was afraid this would happen but she had to tell him.

'Then keep it that way, I don't want Lucy getting involved OK!'

'What are you saying Paul? That I have to lie to the police at all costs, just so your friend Lucy does not get involved?' Francesca was starting to get annoyed too now.

'Look and listen to me OK....and listen good. That's right you will do all you can so that Lucy or I do not get involved is that clear? Is that clear?' he repeated, his eyes blazing and looking at her with complete hate.

Francesca did not know what to think, at first she had felt scared but then she had felt angry with him.

'If you want me to lie to the police for you then at least you need to give me a good enough reason for doing it. Is that clear?' she threw back at him. Paul softened a little.

'OK let's just say I am not exactly kosher with the police. Nothing bad before you start thinking things but a little dealing in things that the police would not be happy with' he explained.

'Do you mean drugs? Paul please say you are not dealing in drugs for goodness sake?' she asked getting afraid.

'NO NOT DRUGS of course not, babe would I get involved in anything like that? And if you think that I would then you don't know me, and we might as well finish now' Paul told her looking serious.

'Then what if it's not drugs, and is Lucy involved too?' she asked again.

'It's nothing to do with drugs just a few stolen things that I sell on OK and that is all you need to know. Look babe it's nothing serious, I just don't want the police sniffing around OK?' he explained but Francesca wondered how she could avoid not giving his real mobile number out if he asked her again. She did not want to partake in anything dodgy and lying to the police was not her forte either.

She had never been a perfect person but she could say hand on heart that she had never stolen anything in her life and she had never dabbled in drugs either. She knew that was a slippery slope that she would never have gone down. Even when her friend Jennifer had gone off the rails for a few years she had not followed her. Alcohol was the strongest thing she had ever taken, she had never even smoked, although Jennifer was guilty of the odd funny cigarette while she had worked at the gentlemen's private club, but even she had come to her senses.

'OK but I don't like lying to the police. What if the DC pulls me into the station again and asks me more questions, and asks for your number again, what then?' she asked him.

'You could tell them we split up, so you no longer have my number. In fact delete it now from your phone. Where is your phone? he asked irritated again.

'No Paul....please, how will we keep in touch?' she asked him as he was rummaging through her bag looking for her mobile and Francesca was trying to stop him.

'It's the only way babe, and by the way if you don't agree then we are truly finished, so it won't be a lie will it?' he told her and tears stung Francesca's eyes as he grabbed the phone and turned it on.

'Paul Please don't....how will we keep in touch?' she asked.

'Simple I text and withhold the number' he told her. Already a message had come up on her phone.

'What's this?' he asked her showing her the message. It was from the DC asking her to call him back as soon as she got the message about the mobile phone number she had given him which was not operational.

'I told you I gave him one wrong digit, he has obviously cottoned on and that's why he left the message. What do I do now?' she asked and Paul looked really angry and continued to find his stored number and deleted it in front of her. Francesca was so upset she just burst into tears.

'Like I said just tell him that we have split up and that you were so annoyed with me you deleted my number....simple' he told her with a smug look on his face.

'You are horrible to me, I will never be able to text you now' she told him still crying.

'If you do as I say I will get another mobile number and then you will be able to contact me again. Just be patient for a few days until he's satisfied with your explanation, OK?' he asked her and attempted to stroke her hair. But Francesca was still upset and moved away.

'I am tired and my headache is coming back, I think I want you to take me home?' she told him sulkily.

'Well you will have to get a taxi home if you go now because I intend to stay in bed, and if you do go, then it's your choice but then we are finished' he told her smugly and turned on the TV in the bedroom. Francesca felt cornered, she loved him and did not want them to finish, no matter how nasty he was to her, but she did not feel like staying the night either. However she knew she had no choice, so snuggled down beside him.

'That's better babe, and don't worry I will get another number within a few days for you OK. Now I am going to fetch a beer, I'll be right back' he told her jumping out of bed.

Francesca did not like the thought of lying to the police and telling them that she and Paul had split up but knew it was what she had to do, in order for them to stay together. She just wondered what she was getting herself into, or even more worrying what was Paul really into that the thought of the police bothered him. She realised that she did not really know much about this man she was so in love with. How on earth could she have ever thought he was going to pop the question to her?

Francesca had a troubled night of tossing and turning while Paul seemed to drop off after a few beers. They never made love but then they never had, just a lot of kissing and cuddling. Francesca was beginning to think that she was not desirable enough, and that thought made her depressed. He was totally sound asleep snoring loudly.

She got out of bed and went to the bathroom, not that she needed to go, but it was something to do and take her mind of her over active mind. Coming out of the bathroom, she saw that Paul had closed Jack's door firmly shut. It had been open when they went upstairs the first time. She listened to see if Paul was still snoring and when she could hear him she opened Jacks bedroom door as quietly as she could and crept inside.

It was dark in there except for the light of the moon shining in from outside, it was quite a tidy room for a man she thought as she looked around. There were pictures on the wall, strange pictures of men in different outfits that looked like leather or PVC and they were in different positions. One was kneeling down on all fours. She looked away disgusted and thought she had better go in case Paul caught her prowling about, and then she felt herself kick something on the floor, something light. She bent down to pick whatever it was up and gasped. There was a sound in the other room, and it must have been Paul getting out of bed.

Chapter 28

The room was pitch black even though Jennifer was sure it was daytime. Where was she? She had not got a clue and it appeared that she had been tied up. Her legs were tied at the ankles and also her wrists were tied together. It was like being in a bad dream. Maybe if she closed her eyes again she would wake up from it. The air smelt musty but warm. She needed to go to the toilet badly. Where was she and why was she here and why had she been tied up like some prisoner?

All she could remember was a text message from her friend saying she wanted her to go and meet her. She remembered texting back to say couldn't it wait until the morning when she called to take her to the airport.....OH NO the airport! She was due to fly out to see her grandparents. Her grandpa was seriously ill and she needed to catch the plane, she needed to be with her nan, she was expecting her, she would be worried, had she missed it? Please God she thought, don't let me have missed it.

Her head felt muzzy as if in a fog and she could hardly think straight.

'PLEASE SOMEONE... ANYONE HELP ME' she shouted. But everywhere was deadly silent.

Think.....Think...think she told herself, try to stay calm and just think. Then it all came flooding back. She was supposed to have met Francesca and when she had got to the place that her friend had said she would be waiting for her on the text message, Lucy had been there instead saying that Francesca was in a right state because she and Paul had just split up. Yes that was it then but everything else was vague. Where was Francesca? She can't even remember seeing her. But how did she get here in this room? Her eyes were wet with tears, she felt scared out of her mind, and felt that something bad was going to happen to her. Why oh why did she go out again? She should have stayed in and made Francesca wait until the morning.

'PLEASE SOMEONE HELP ME' she shouted and tried to wriggle her wrists free, but the rope was too tight. It was just cutting into her flesh, and the more she tried to loosen it the more it cut into her. She felt sick and the urge to go to the toilet was just too much. Hang on, she told herself, someone was bound to come soon. Who could have done this to her and why?

Then she heard noises, like a car drawing up on gravel, a car door shutting and footsteps growing nearer and nearer until a key was being turned and then Jennifer braced herself as the door swung open. A tall figure dressed in dark clothing just stood there looking at her from the doorway. But the most terrifying thing was the mask he was wearing, it was from the scream painting by Edvard Munch. He was wearing a ghost-face mask. She felt frozen to the spot and even though she tried to open her mouth, nothing would come out. Instead she felt a slow trickle run down her leg. She could no longer wait and to her embarrassment she wet herself.

The tall man in the scream mask laughed out loud.

'Have you ever been so scared that you wet yourself?' he asked her and continued 'I think so.'

Jennifer suddenly felt angry, angry at this figure who found it so funny.

'Who are you? What do you want with me? Why am I here?' she asked feeling humiliated.

'Tut tut Jennifer or should I call you Katie?' he said sarcastically and continued 'I ask all the questions and you answer is that clear?' he told her and took a big carving knife out of his coat.

Jennifer gasped and it was then that she realised she was looking at The Prince of Mystery, whoever he was.

DC McKenna was in his office bright and early. It was now over a week since Ms Sudbury had gone missing. He had spoken to his superior DS Miles Hunter who was leading the case, and he was happy for him to continue with the search, since he had been the one who had initially interviewed Jennifer in the first place. Her father had sent a photo of her to them via email, and it had been circulated to the police team which specialised in trying to find missing people. They had even done a small piece in the Evening Sentinel, which was titled 'Local woman missing', and asking anyone who might have seen her to come forward. They had examined the apartment above Jennifer's and nothing untoward had been found. They had also granted Walter Smyth police bail for the time being, because apart from the pornographic photos on his wall they had not found anything else, although Alex thought he was not completely innocent. They had established that he was slightly subnormal though, and thought that he would benefit from contact with a social worker.

'Any news on the Sudbury case?' Max asked walking into the office with two mugs of coffee.

Alex screwed his face up.

'Nothing. A dead end so far, although I am going to go back to the club and ask around to see if anyone knows the girl Lucy that Ms Sudbury named in the statement, and I also want to question some guy named Paul' he told him.

'Right, didn't you get a contact number for him from Miss Davis?' he asked.

'Well as such, but the strange thing is the number just keeps ringing out. I tried to get back in touch with Miss Davis to ask her to repeat the number she gave me, but the answer phone just switches on, so I left her a message to contact me again, but no word as yet' he told him.

'Do you think going back to the club is your best bet then' he said to him taking a sip of his coffee.

Alex took a sip of his coffee too and pulled his face.

'Still terrible coffee, but cheers anyway' he told him.

Alex then made a quick call to DS Miles Hunter to update him on the case, and also to put to him about him going to the club again later to make more enquiries. He intended to ask a colleague, DC Isabelle Flack to accompany him. The superintendent had given him the go ahead, and just as he had put his phone down, his mobile phone rang. It was the Nursing Home about his nan. They told him that she had become very agitated with some of the staff there and had tried to go outside the main door, with her coat on, and when two members of staff had tried to stop her, she had raised her walking stick up to them as if she was about to hit them with it. She was obviously in her dementia state, because the gentle Maisie that Alex knew could never hurt a fly. He told them that he would call in later and visit her.

What a horrible illness dementia was, he thought to himself. In her usual state of mind his nan could not be a more helpful or kind person, and everyone that knew her had loved her. Yet here she was with hardly a soul to visit her anymore except for him. People seemed to forget all the good things about her. Yes there had been the odd friend or two that had kept in touch, but gradually they had all dwindled away until there was no one. It was sad to see. His nan was also going through a series of test to see if she had Alzheimer's disease, because it was clear that the dementia was getting worse.

By the time Alex arrived at the home Maisie was back to her usual self, and in fact she had been a little upset when they had told her that she had tried to go out of the main door and that was why they were confining her to certain areas of the home. She had no recollection of it, and when she saw Alex she burst into tears.

'Gran how are you today?' he asked taking her by the hand.

'Alex I am so glad to see you. They say I tried to hit Tracy one of the girls' she told him dabbing her eyes with her handkerchief.

Alex led her to her room and they both sat down near the big picture window overlooking the garden. He was feeling slightly annoyed that someone had told her what she had tried to do, especially after she had calmed down and gone back to her lucid self. They were all supposed to have had training on dealing with dementia. That was one of the reasons he had chosen this home because it had good recommendations in dealing with both dementia and Alzheimer's disease. He felt it could and should have been handled differently. He tried to change the subject and talk about the garden, asking his nan to name the various flowers and shrubs that they could see. Maisie loved the garden. She had always been a very keen gardener in the past, and would spend hours in it, bringing it to perfection. She knew almost every plant and shrub by name.

When Alex had been younger she had tried to get him interested, and even gave him a plot of garden all to himself to grow things, but alas he really did not seem to have green fingers.

After a short while Margaret one of the senior care assistants knocked on the door and then popped her head in.

'Maisie how are you feeling now dear' she asked looking at Maisie and then at Alex.

'Ah Margaret, I would like a word about my gran before I go' he told her without smiling. Margaret nodded and then asked if they would both like a cup of tea. Alex looked at his gran who smiled.

'Yes please Margaret and could we have some chocolate biscuits too?' she said to her.

'Of course dear I will be right back' and then she went out of the room, closing the door behind her.

So it just took a offer of a cup of tea and a few chocolate biscuits to make things right. Alex did not think so, and he intended to tell Margaret that before he left. They chatted for quite a while and

Alex felt relieved that she seemed to have forgotten her earlier ordeal. She seemed a lot happier in herself and talked about her past and the garden. On leaving Alex saw Margaret waiting for him and she decided to take him through to the office so they could talk privately.

'Sit down Mr McKenna' she told him.

'First of all I want to apologise for what happened' she told him and then continued 'it appears that your grandmother got very agitated and put her coat on and was trying to leave the main building, when one of the girls Tracy who has only been with us for a few months apparently tried to stop her. However instead of coaxing her she grabbed her arm and that's when she said your grandmother raised her walking stick shouting to let her go. Another care assistant intervened but by then she was in such a state of panic it became impossible to calm her down' she told him.

'Yes so I gather. I understand how difficult it must be in those circumstances, but what annoyed me Margaret is that after my gran calmed down and became lucid again she was told by Tracy I think, how bad she had been and that she had tried to hit one of the girls. As I said I realise how hard it is trying to pacify someone when they are like that, but after the situation has passed then surely it would have been in my grandmother's best interest to let it go, and not say anything about what happened. When I arrived she was clearly lucid but very upset' he told her and Margaret could only nod in agreement.

'We will have a word with the girls in question Mr McKenna and I can assure you this will not

284

happen again' she told him, and Alex smiled and thanked her and then left.

Alex had arranged to meet DC Flax back at the station that night and they would drive together to the club. He intended to find out all he could about the girl Lucy and Paul. There had still been no answer to the mobile number that Miss Davis had given him, and he had also left another message on her own mobile but had not heard back from her.

Alex and Isabelle drove to the club in the one car this time. He couldn't help noticing that she looked nice, her shoulder length fair hair was done in a French plait, not that Alex knew much about hair styles, and she was wearing a nice pencil skirt and semi casual blouse.

'So can I ask what the score is so far?' she asked him as he drove. She then continued 'I mean are there any suggestions on where she could be?'

Alex briefly looked at her then looked away and back to the road.

'Not a lot, although I have a few hunches. I want to talk with two people, one is a girl that Jennifer mentioned in her statement, someone called Lucy, short bleached hair and lots of piercings and the other is a friend of hers a guy named Paul, who happens to be the boyfriend of Miss Davis, only from what I gather she can't know him too well' he told her.

'Oh why is that then? she asked him looking puzzled.

'Well put it this way, when I asked her for his address, she was not able to tell me, and she said they had been together for over nine months.'

'Wasn't able to or didn't want to?' she told him with a wry smile.

'Yes that could be it too, that's one of the reasons for our tonight's mission to the club' he said with a smile.

'OK fair enough. Let's hope we get the information needed' she said to him as they approached the car park.

The pub had a constant stream of young people going inside.

'Looks like there might be something on tonight' Alex told her parking the car.

They both went inside and headed for the bar, although they were both off duty so to speak and were using this time to gain information they decided not to drink anything stronger than a fizzy orange and half a pint of shandy. The club was in full swing and there were a lot of youngsters to mid thirties people in. There was a band that was due to play called Encore

They looked at each other when after a while a young girl approached the bar with short cropped bleached blonde hair and tattoos and piercings.

'What will it be Lucy?' the barman asked.

'Shall I speak to her?' Isabelle asked putting down her drink, to which Alex nodded 'why not.'

They could have gone into the club and flashed their ID cards and got quickly to the point, but instead Alex had thought of a better way around it, and that was to just mingle and see what information they could pick up first, and if this was the Lucy they wanted to talk to then they had struck gold without even trying.

Chapter 29

Francesca just could not believe what she was holding in her hand and when she heard a noise that sounded like Paul getting out of bed she quickly dropped it back onto the floor again, and kicked it under the bed. If she had anywhere to put it she would have taken it with her, just to make completely sure it was what she thought it was, but all she was wearing was a thin t-shirt. She got out just in time and made for the bathroom, when Paul appeared on the landing.

'What's up babe can't you sleep?' he asked her with a yawn.

"I just needed to use the toilet' she told him and preceded to go into the bathroom and close the door. She learned on the back of it and gave a big sigh of relief. That was close, she thought to herself. She just could not believe what she thought she had seen which was Jennifer's mobile phone. She had recognised the front cover because it had a Union Jack on it. What did not make sense was why it had been in Jack's bedroom. She knew she could not ask Paul about it because he would be angry and ask her why she was in there nosing around in the first place, and of course it might not even be Jennifer's mobile phone. The Union Jack covers were very popular she knew that, but if it had have been Jennifer's phone then it would mean that this Jack knew where she was.

The following morning Paul insisted on dropping her off earlier than usual and this time Francesca didn't object too much.

'When will I see you again?' she asked him opening the car door. He had been fairly quiet on the journey back as if he had a lot on his mind. He looked at her and was deep in thought.

'Listen babe don't take this the wrong way but I think we should cool things for a week or two' he told her and Francesca's heart sank. He was going to finish with her, she was almost certain of it. Tears pricked her eyes and threatened to fall.

'Why Paul? Please just say if you want to end things. Don't keep me hanging on like a puppet on a string, it's not fair on me' she told him still holding the car door open.

'Oh babes don't be like that, it's not that I want to finish, but I think it's best if we don't see each other for a while, especially while that DC is sniffing around. Besides I have to go away for a week' he told her reaching for her hand. Francesca did not know what to think. Why did he continue to play these mind games with her?

'Where have you got to go?' she asked him.

'Oh just something to do with work that's all, should be back in a week or so.'

'And will you get a new number so that you can text me it?' she asked him with a heavy heart. She felt like her heart was breaking. It was awful loving someone the way she did, and not having that someone feel the same way about you. She could never do this to him. Paul sighed heavily.

'Yes I will get a new number to you, but let's leave it a bit, just until I get back from my trip OK?'

He stroked her arm lovingly.

'Just trust me babe OK, this is for the best and when I get back I will make contact with you' he explained. But Francesca was not sure anymore. He felt cold towards her this morning and it was cutting her up inside, messing with her emotions. She just did not know what to think now, but all she did know was that their relationship as it stood was destroying her. She got out of the car to go.

'Francesca....babe give me a smile before you go.....please?' he asked her. Paul could see she was upset and didn't want to leave her like this, but Francesca slammed the car door and walked away. Deep down she knew in her heart that this was it. Paul had no intentions of getting a new number for her. She hated the thought of it, but what could she do. She felt a strange feeling come over her as she heard his car suddenly start up make a roaring noise and then drive away. Tears started to fall, silent at first until they became heavy and were streaming down her face as if they would never stop. Why did love hurt so much, she sobbed?

The club was in full swing and Encore had just started to play and seemed in good form. DC Alex McKenna and DC Isabelle Flack had decided to visit the club off duty. Alex thought it was a stroke of luck when the girl Lucy appeared on the scene, and when Isabelle agreed to speak to her he had agreed.

She sidled up to her and smiled as the barman handed her a drink.

'Hello my names Izzy' she said and then nodded towards the band Encore ' they are good aren't they' she said to her.

'Lucy, pleased to meet you, have you been here to see them before? I can't remember seeing you around' she replied.

'Oh yes I have been quite a few times but not recently, are you with someone?' she asked.

'I am waiting for my boyfriend how about you?' she asked her.

'Yes me too. Can I ask if Paul will be in tonight?'

'Paul? Paul who?' she replied with a frown.

'Paul Blake' she continued.

'How do you know him then?' she asked and so Isabelle just smiled and took a sip of her drink

'Ah you know' she told her.

'The Manchester club?'

'Yes that's right' she agreed with her, without even knowing what she was agreeing with.

'Funny you don't really look the type' she laughed.

'What is the type then?' Isabelle asked her, hoping she would let slip something else.

'You know.....well you do if you have been there?' she said to her suddenly becoming a little suspicious. Isabelle stayed silent.

'Look who are you anyhow?' Lucy asked again.

'I told you my names Izzy' she repeated but at this stage Lucy decided she was not taking the bait and decided to leave, when DC McKenna decided it was time to step in.

'Hello Lucy can I have a word with you. I am DC McKenna and this is my colleague DC Flack' he told her flashing his ID card.

'What the! What do you want with me?' she asked him angrily and gave Isabelle a dirty look.

'I thought you might be a copper, can smell them a mile off' she told her.

'Just a few questions that's all' Alex asked.

'Well I don't have to answer any of your questions,, whatever they are' she told him aggressively.

'Well you can either answer them here or down at the station which is it to be?' he said to her.

So not wanting to make a scene Lucy found a table at the far side of the room out of the way and sat down.

'Look can you hurry it up, you are spoiling my night here. I came to listen to the band not talk to bloody coppers!' she spat aggressively.

'OK but first of all do you know anyone named Jennifer Sudbury?' Alex asked while Isabelle looked on.

'No can't say that name rings a bell. Why do you ask?' she replied.

'Because the lady in question Jennifer Sudbury has been missing for over a week' he told her.

'Well its nowt to do with me is it?' she told him giving him a look.

'Well it's very strange.'

'What is?' she asked.

'That you say the name does not ring a bell, because two weeks ago she was at this very club and in her statement she said she saw you and spoke to you.'

'Look I cannot remember anyone of that name. I see lots of people in here don't I and speak with a lot of people too. It does not mean I know them' she continued.

'Well let me see if I can refresh you memory at all. Do you know a Francesca Davis?' he asked

'Yes I do know someone named Francesca' she told him.

'Good, because Ms Sudbury - Jennifer is Francesca's friend. They both came into this club around two weeks ago' he told her.

'I think I know who you mean now. There was another girl in here with Francesca, but I can't say I got talking to her except for the odd word or two. She was also with a guy' she explained.

'Can you describe the guy for us?' he asked.

'No, not really, never saw him before in my life' she told him.

'What about Paul, Francesca's boyfriend?' he continued.

'What about him?'

'Well did he see the guy do you think?'

'I wouldn't know. I don't think he would have though because he came to pick Fran up.'

'Do you know Paul's address, or have a contact number for him?' he asked getting a notebook and pen out of his pocket.

'I think Paul's in Manchester now. I'm not sure of his address' she told him not wanting to say too much in case she got into trouble, but realising she had to say something. Isabelle looked at her and spoke.

'You mean the club you told me about in Manchester. Can you tell us what it's called?'

'OK but you have not heard it from me like OK?' she told them.

'OK if you can just give us the name of the club he goes to in Manchester' Alex said to her.

'It's a sort of fetish club called the Torment Club in Brevelle Gardens near to the city centre. That's all I know. Now can I go now? I am missing the band' she asked.

'There is just one more thing. Can I have a contact number for you in case we need to talk to you again.'

'Bloody hell. I have told you all I know. Why do you need my number?' she swore.

'It's in your own interest that you give it to us Miss' Alex stated.

'My name is Lucy Griffin' she told him.

'And your phone number and address preferably' he asked again. This time Lucy gave it to him reluctantly and then got up from the table and went back to the bar. Alex watched her then turned to Isabelle.

'I think we are finished here for the time being, although I would like to find out more about this place the Torment club that Paul Blake goes to.'

'Let's get out of this place, the noise is deafening me' he told her and Isabelle smiled.

'Don't you like heavy metal then Alex.'

'Is that what it's called?' he replied and they both got up to leave.

Back in the car they discussed the case as he drove her home.

'I wonder if Miss Davis knows about her boyfriend going to the Torment Club in Manchester?'

'It's hard to know, but it's not something I would like to find out about' she told him pulling her face then smiling.

She had a nice face and an even nicer smile he thought. He liked the way she wrinkled her noise when she smiled up at him. He knew that she was single and around five years younger than he was. Why was he even thinking that way, because did not intend to get involved with anyone else especially from work. He had heard it from others in the force that the two just did not mix. Pleasure was best left outside of work.

Chapter 30

This was a living nightmare Jennifer thought as she sat there sobbing, tied up with the heavy rope to both her ankles and wrists. She ached all over and had felt so humiliated that she had actually wet herself in front of her captor. She had not got a clue how long she had been in the room for since she did not have a watch or even her phone, but it seemed like a very long time.

Every now and again the captor who had kept her prisoner would come in and talk to her asking questions that did not make any sense at all. Sometimes he would bring her a glass of water or some other drink, and after she had taken a few sips he would take it away again, taunting her. The same with the food he offered feeding her a mouthful at a time. It was like he enjoyed the fact that she was thirsty and hungry, but only allowing small amounts to be taken at a time just enough to keep her alive. She wondered why she was being kept prisoner there, what the motive was. Why he had not just killed her and had done with it. Why was he torturing her the way he was? He had brought a bucket into the room for her to use as a toilet but only while he was there was she allowed to use it and he untied her legs and wrists momentarily.

At first she had refused to use the bucket, but he had laughed at her and told her she had no choice, and would learn. In the end what else could she do. She decided that unless she wanted to sit in her own urine and faeces the bucket was the only thing she had. He also bought a bowl, some soap and a towel so that she could wash, but he regarded that as a treat and he only brought it occasionally.

Sometimes she became so confused that she thought she saw other things too. It felt like her mind was playing tricks with her. She soon realised that the room she was being kept prisoner in had no windows, just the door that her captor came through and always kept locked.

After what seemed to be forever, she heard the sound of a car again driving on gravel followed by the same familiar footsteps that she soon got to recognise as his.

'Katie oh Katie' he called out as he entered with the scream mask firmly over his face ' I smell your fear.'

'I am not Katie. Why do you call me that? Why am I here?' she asked him.

'Less of the questions and speak when spoken to' he replied giving her a big hard slap with his hand that caught her lip on her tooth and she tasted blood.

'PLEASE my family will be worried about me, I need to let them know I am OK' she told him but he just roared with laughter that seemed to echo around the room.

'Someone will report me missing and eventually find out where I am and come after you' she told him angrily.

'Your family don't give tuppence for you, and why should they? You are nothing but a dirty little whore who needs teaching a lesson. No one misses a whore' he told her.

'What do you mean?' she asked feeling frightened again but the captor continued 'wonder what daddy would say if he knew what you really were?'

'What do you mean and why do you keep calling me that? I am not a whore?'

'I told you KEEP QUIET...and no questions. You will know soon enough' he explained and then took what looked like a calving knife out of his coat. Jennifer gasped when she saw the blade glisten.

'What are you going to do? PLEASE ' she screamed.

'It's for me to know and you to find out, and you will soon enough.' he told her.

He knelt down beside her and pulled her head back by her hair until she cried out with pain and then he pressed the blade to her throat.

'QUIET I told you' he said pressing the knife harder and harder until Jennifer could feel it cutting into her throat. She felt frozen to the spot and was visibly shaking. Was this the end? Was he about to kill her? she thought as she felt the sting of the knife cutting deeper into her throat.

The following day at the station DC McKenna reported his findings to DS Hunter and they discussed the case at length. He had telephoned Miss Davis to ask her to call back into the station as soon as she could, because there were more questions that he wanted to ask her.

Francesca knew it was about the wrong telephone number that she had given him, because although she had seen his message on her mobile phone, she had not returned his call yet, and when he had eventually got her on her lunch break she had agreed to go in to see him again after work. She had left her phone on just in case Paul had phoned her to say sorry, and also to give her his new mobile number, but he had not and Francesca was feeling very empty inside. She did not want him to finish with her, even though she knew it was inevitable that he would, given the way he had said to cool it for a few weeks.

Just as she had promised Francesca called into the station and Alex took her into one of the interview rooms with another DC sitting in.

'Sit down Miss Davis and thank you for coming in to see us again' he told her. Then he sat opposite her.

'Have you had any news about Jennifer?' she asked.

'No, not yet. Now what I have called you in for is about the mobile number you gave me' he began.

'Oh yes did you manage to get in touch with Paul?' she said putting up a pretense that she had not known the number was wrong.

'No that's just it, I think you may have given me the wrong number by mistake' he told her with a wry smile and looking her directly in the eye. She felt herself flush slightly by the way he seemed to look right through her as if he knew what she had done.

'Sorry no I don't think so' she told him.

'Well in that case can you check it on your phone for me, and read the number out again please' he told her getting out a pen and paper.

'I.....I can't I'm afraid' she replied.

'Sorry? Why is that?' he asked her with a frown, while Francesca sniffed as if she was about to cry.

'Well it's like this DC McKenna, Paul and I split up the other day and so I no longer have his number' she explained as he looked on confused.

'Can you explain what happened?' he asked her, but Francesca just started to cry. He handed her a tissue.

'Come on Miss Davis I know you are upset but something just does not add up here' he told her.

'What do you mean' she replied wiping her eyes.

'Well as I said something does not make sense. Can I ask you a question?'

'OK go ahead.'

'Were you aware that your boyfriend Paul Blake went to a fetish club in Manchester? In fact I have been told he is probably there now' he continued.

'No of course not. Who told you that?' she asked looking both shocked and hurt at the same time and then thinking maybe he was talking about his friend Jack, because that would explain about the posters on the wall in his bedroom. In fact maybe she should mention that.

'I can't tell you where we got our information from, but I assure you we have been told that it's true' he explained. Francesca did not know what to think.

'He never told me about any Fetish club. I don't think it's Paul you have been told about, maybe they meant his friend Jack' she explained.

'Jack who? Do you know his surname?' he asked her.

'No I don't. All I know is he has a friend name Jack.'

'And why do you think that the information we have been given is about this Jack? Do you know something you are not telling us?' he questioned her, but all Francesca could do was shrug. How could she tell him she was in his bedroom and saw the pictures on the wall, and about the phone she found on the floor that she thought could be her friend Jennifer's.

'Come on Miss Davis I think you know more than you are letting on, I hope you realise that it's a very serious offence to hold back information from the police' he continued and folded his arms like he had all the time in the world. Francesca sat silently.

'You could be here a long time, you know. Why don't you just tell us what you know and you can go home. And if you and Paul Blake are finished then what have you got to lose anyhow?' he told her.

Francesca was scared, scared that she might get into trouble, and scared of telling on Paul just in case he contacted her again. She missed him very much and did not really want them to finish.

'You may as well tell me. Paul is not thinking of you, especially when he is away in some fetish club in Manchester, and I assure you that the person I spoke to was speaking about Paul Blake and not Jack' he told her and tears pricked her eyes.

She was upset that Paul could do this to her.

'OK I thought it might be Jack you were talking about because of all the funny posters on his wall.'

'What wall are you talking about?' he asked.

'His bedroom wall. I went into his room while Paul was asleep, I was curious and I saw these photos of men on his wall' she told him.

'OK. Can you describe them to me?' he asked her.

'Not really. I was shocked and did not really look that much. Just men with chains on them in different positions' she said.

'Now we are getting somewhere. Where do this Jack and Paul live? I thought you said you did not know where he lived?' Alex said with a frown.

'I don't ....I didn't, it's somewhere in Stone. I had my eyes closed.'

'Had your eyes closed. You do realise all this sounds strange. I mean you go to your boyfriend's house in Stone and you say you close your eyes. Why is that?' he asked.

'I had a terrible headache and did not want to go to the pub so instead we went up to his house or rather the house he shared with Jack. On the way he told me to relax and close my eyes, which I did. I must have dozed off slightly and when we arrived I woke up' she told him.

'I see. Well it's still very strange, especially when you gave me his contact number and said previously you did not have his address, and then the number you gave me for him was also wrong. You then ignore the message I left on your phone and now this evening you are telling me you no longer have his number because you spit up from him! You would not be telling me porkies would you Miss Davis?' he said.

'No of course not. You have to believe me, it was exactly how I said.'

'OK so tell me this Miss Davis, what made you go into this guy named Jack's bedroom?' he asked to which Francesca burst into tears. She explained that sometimes Paul could be a bit cool with her, and she was just curious about his friend. So when he was sleeping, she needed to go to the bathroom and she saw Jack's bedroom door was open a little and was curious. He then asked if she had seen anything else untoward in the room and after hesitating she decided to tell him about the phone on the floor that looked similar to Jennifer's.

'What made you think it looked like Ms Sudbury's?' he asked.

'It had a Union Jack cover just like the one I had seen her with' she told him.

'And did you not mention what you had seen to your boyfriend Paul?'

'No I was too scared to. I mean if I had he would have known I had been nosing around in his friend's bedroom, and I had no right to be in there had I?' she told him.

'OK, well if Paul gets in touch with you I want you to let us know straight away, or you could find yourself in some very serious trouble' he told her.

Francesca could only nod. She knew if she was not careful she could be tarred with the same brush as Paul if he was doing something illegal.

Chapter 31

That day DC McKenna updated DS Hunter on the progress of the case, and volunteered to give the Manchester Club a visit. Manchester police had been aware of the Torture Garden Club but as far as they knew it did not get any complaints in spite of its name. It was both a straight, bisexual and gay fetish club that had a combination of both fantasy and SM body art and drag with rubber and leather. It was where clients of various ages, sex and gender acted out their fantasies. It also had a strict dress code and no one was allowed into the club unless they abided with this code. Therefore it was out of the question for them to go there normally dressed or undercover. It would have to be strictly on duty only. DS Hunter decided he would get the Manchester police force involved and ask them to pay a visit as soon as possible.

The results they got from their visit were eye opening, although they did not manage to speak with either Paul Blake or Jack, because apparently they were told that they had not been there all week. The Manchester force were told that Jack and his lover Paul Blake were known at the club as regulars. Jack was known to be bisexual while Paul was definitely gay. Jack was the dominant one of the two according to a few people they spoke to there. A guy named Gareth who was dressed in drag said he would see them at least once or twice a week, and knew them by name.

DC McKenna couldn't understand why if he were gay that Paul also had a relationship with Francesca. It made no sense at all, and made him suspicious that there must be an ulterior motive for his connection with Francesca. He intended to find out one-way or another what this motive could be. He also thought that he should ask Francesca if she had known that he was gay, since in Manchester it was common knowledge. He also needed to bring the girl Lucy in for questioning as he thought she knew more than she was letting on.

Both the Manchester police and the Staffordshire police had put an alert out for the two men, not that they were suspects at this moment in the case, but just that they were wanted to help with their inquiries concerning the continued disappearance of Ms Jennifer Sudbury.

Mr Beaumont had been on the telephone to the Staffordshire police almost every day asking if they had any news about his missing daughter. He was still in France with his mother, who had taken the whole thing quite badly. It was one thing to lose your husband, but to not know where your granddaughter was either was just too much to bear, especially for a ninety year old. He had informed the police that his father Jean-Paul had died and the French police were now classing it as a murder inquiry. They had an alert out for a black sports car. No other witnesses had come forward, and so the black sports car was all they had to go on.

Mr Beaumont and his mother had put Jean-Paul's funeral on hold, just in case Jennifer was found. They knew that she would be devastated if it went ahead with out her, but they also knew that it could not be put on hold for very much longer. So if there was still no news soon they decided it would have to go ahead without her and when Jennifer was found they would then hold a memorial Service. It was all taking its toll on both of them and DC McKenna could only sympathise. The sooner this case was sorted out the better, he thought.

Clive Beaumont hated to see his once active mother looking so frail. It had really taken it out of her both with the death of his father and also the disappearance of his daughter. He was beginning to feel old himself too, more than his sixty-four years.

He also had the added burden of not knowing his eldest daughter Nicole's forwarding address and telephone number. He had asked his mother about it but she had been vague and had told him that Nicole had been very difficult to live with. She had not told him the real reason and that she had just left in a huff, but she knew that she had to say something soon though because he was getting more inquisitive as the days went by. When Clive had finished talking to the Staffordshire police again about the whereabouts of Jennifer, he told her that he was also thinking of reporting Nicole as missing. He just could not understand why Nicole had not been in touch with him or forwarded a telephone number at least.

'I may mention something about Nicole mother' he told her.

'Clive I honestly don't think you should, it's obvious that Nicole does not want to be found. It's her choice' she told him feeling more than a little annoyed.

'Why do you say that? I mean don't you think it's strange she never gave you her mobile number or tell you where she was going?' he asked. But Maggie shook her head.

'No I don't Clive and OK I suppose I do need to tell you about Nicole, you are her father after all, and maybe I should have told you before now but I was so angry with her' she began.

'What is it mum? What happened?' he asked her looking confused.

'Well Clive it's like this, we found out that Nicole had been stealing money from us.'

'Oh surely not. Why would she do that?' he asked looking shocked.

'Well that's what me and your dad thought at first, then we checked our accounts and bank statements, and over a period of three months she took hundreds if not thousands. We confronted her, of course we did and she denied it. In the end she overhead us talking about changing our will to only include Jennifer and you of course. You would get this Villa but Jennifer would get the rest of our money, which as you know is a tidy amount over the years, and enough to buy Jennifer a house of her own. Well she went berserk as we expected she would and packed her stuff and left' she told him at which Clive looked on sadly. Then she continued 'Were you aware that she was using?'

'Using?' he asked looking puzzled.

'Yes, you know drugs' she told him.

'NO NO of course not. My goodness I had no idea, how do you know?'

'We didn't at first until one day your father caught her. She denied it of course because Nicole got into the habit of lying to us, until it became second nature to her. I am so sorry to have had to tell you this Clive' she said to him with a tear in her eyes. He looked at her sadly.

'I never knew. What do I do? I thought Nicole was OK, thought she was staying with you until she had finished the job she came over here to do. Well that's what she told me' he said putting his head in his hands.

'I am sorry Clive but your dad and I always knew she was a bad apple' she replied then continued 'believe me I don't get any joy out of thinking this about my eldest granddaughter, but there have been times when I sometimes wondered if she were related to us at all' she said.

'How could I have been so blind? Oh I know she could be quite an handful when she was growing up yes, but I would never have thought Nicole would have got involved with drugs, not drugs for goodness sake. This leaves me in a very awkward position now if I do want to report her missing if you see what I mean' he told her.

'Yes I do see what you mean, and that's why I had to tell you what happened in the end' she replied.

'I am sure Nicole being Nicole will eventually get in touch with you anyhow, especially when she needs something' she said.

'That's just it, I hope she does get in touch with me and before it's too late. You hear so much about addiction and how it turns peoples lives into living hell. Some of the addicts end up homeless and living on the streets.'

Clive felt sad that Nicole had become what she had, but she was still his daughter and he loved her no matter what.

They decided that they would hold Jean-Paul's funeral on the following Tuesday even if they still had not had any news about Jennifer. They had kept it on hold for long enough, especially as it was the custom in France and other continental countries to bury their dead quickly. So after much discussion they agreed they needed to get it over and done with. The French police had told them that they did not need his body to bring charges if they made an arrest in the future.

'What will you do mum, will you stay over here or sell the Villa and come back to England?' he asked her and Maggie closed her eyes momentarily. She felt weary and was feeling her age.

'I am ninety Clive, it no longer matters and one day the Villa will be yours to do what you want with. In the meantime I shall just stay put. I have good neighbours and people I know here, and where would I go if I came back? I no longer have friends back there, and besides I can't see myself going through all the rigmarole of buying another house can you?' she told him.

'You know I would help you if that was what you wanted though don't you?' he replied.

'Yes I know that, but this is my home now and I think it's where I want to be, in fact I am sure it's where I want to be, and spend my last days here' she continued.

'OK mum if you are sure that's what you want, but I am only a phone call away if you need me' he told her, and Maggie smiled. If only that was true, she thought to herself, remembering how often she had been unable to get in touch with him because he was working. It had been the same for Jennifer too, but she did not say anything.

'Let's hope we have news about Jennifer soon' she said feeling sad that it was taking so long.

'Yes, well it would be great if she is found before next Wednesday' he replied. And at the back of his mind he was not sure if she would ever be found, he hated to think it but he did.

The following day DC McKenna was about to arrange for Lucy Griffin to be brought in for questioning when he heard a scuffle going on outside and when he looked he could hardly believe his eyes. Lucy had been arrested on suspicion of drug dealing. She was struggling with two police officers and shouting and swearing obscenities.

Apparently there had been a tip off from an anonymous caller, who had not left their name but just gave details where she could be found, and sure enough they saw a guy handing her some money. As soon as the guy saw the police car he was away and although they gave chase they were unable to catch him. All they had was Lucy with a wad of notes on her person.

'Well, well Miss Griffin we meet again' Alex told her with a wry smile. This case was being given to Max but Alex immediately asked if he could sit in and Max agreed.

After reading her rights and asking if she required a solicitor, to which she refused saying she did not need one because she was innocent Lucy Griffin was taken into one of the interview rooms.

'For the purpose of the recorder I am DC Max Brennan and my colleague is DC Liam Denvers and sitting in on this interview is DC Alex McKenna with suspect Lucy Griffin arrested on suspicion of dealing in drugs.'

Will you please give your name and address for the purpose of the recorder?' he asked her.

'Lucy Griffin, 33 Turner Street' she said reluctantly and with a scowl on her face. She knew from experience that the fastest way to get out of there was to cooperate, and if she didn't then they would only hold her in custody.

'OK, first of all were you dealing drugs?' Max asked looking her straight in the eye.

'No of course not. I don't do drugs, I am a good girl I am' she said calmly and sarcastically.

'Then why were you taking money from a guy at the corner of Caroline Street?' he asked her.

'He was paying me for something I sold to him a few days ago' she replied.

'And what was it you sold to him?'

'A stereo car radio CD. I no longer have a car so decided to flog it' she replied.

'How much did you sell it to him for?'

'Dunno, couple of hundred' she told him.

'Couple of hundred? That's a lot of money for a second hand one is it not?' he continued.

'It was bloody expensive when I bought it' she replied.

'Even so, OK can you give me the guy's name and address that you sold the stereo to?' he asked her not convinced

'Not really, he was just some guy I met in the pub a few days ago' she replied.

'So you are expecting me to believe this cock and bull story about meeting a guy a few days ago in a pub, and you sold him your car radio CD and then today he paid you for it, yet you did not have his address. How did you know he would come back to pay you?' he asked.

'I trusted him. I have seen him around a lot and knew he was trustworthy so took the risk' she said.

'OK so if it was all very innocent as you would have us believe, then why was the guy running away? He ran away as soon as he handed you the money and the moment he saw the police car' Max put it to her, and she shrugged.

'I don't know do I? He maybe hates coppers like me' she told him then continued 'one of your female officers searched me and never found any drugs did she?'

'Maybe that's because the guy that ran off had them' Max told her.

'I told you I never gave him any drugs. I don't deal with drugs. I told you what happened and that's the truth' she replied.

'The truth? I don't think you would know the truth if it hit you in the face Miss Griffin' he continued but he knew they had no evidence and would have to let her go at some stage. There had been a body search and nothing had been found. Also the guy who ran away had not been caught. Max decided to end the interview and hand her over to Alex for more questioning concerning the Sudbury case.

'Miss Griffin we meet again. What I want to talk to you about is Paul Blake' he said to her.

'What about him?' she asked looking at her fingernails as if she did not have a care in the world.

'Well for a start we know he is gay and the person he is with is called Jack' he told her to which she pretended to look confused, but Alex knew it was just pretense because it was her that had told Isabelle about the club in Manchester.

'I thought he was going out with a girl name Francesca' she told him.

'So you had no idea that Paul Blake was gay....and think about this one carefully because one wrong answer could cause you to spend the night in one of the cells' he warned her.

Lucy wondered who he had been speaking to. If he knew that Paul was gay, and it was obvious he did, then it was no use denying it any more.

'OK, yes I had a feeling he was' she confessed.

'And did you ever wonder why he was going out with Francesca then? I mean why was that?'

'Goodness knows. I'm not his keeper, maybe he fancied a change' she told him sarcastically.

'Maybe...or could there just be another reason he wanted to go out with Francesca?' he continued.

'Like what? she replied shrugging again.

'Perhaps he had other reasons. Francesca is Jennifer's friend, is she not?'

'So what? I don't know what you are meaning' she replied.

'Oh I think you do Miss Griffin' he replied then continued' I wonder if Paul Blake and his boyfriend Jack know where Jennifer is? You would not happen to know as well would you?' he said to her.

'Look I am not involved in the disappearance of this Jennifer, you can't pin that on me' she told him starting to panic.

'I never said you were Miss Griffin, but you know as well as I do that withholding information from the police is a criminal offence don't you? So what you think? Do you think he knows where Jennifer is?' he asked her but all she did was stay quiet.

Chapter 32

It was late Monday afternoon when Francesca met Lucy by chance coming out of the Royal Anchor. She was on her way home from work and was in deep thought about Paul, and wondering if he would contact her. She still had deep feelings for him, even though he had treated her quite badly by deleting his phone number from her phone, and then telling her they should cool it for a few weeks. But never less it still hurt and she was missing him like mad.

'Well well if it's not gay Paul's little girlfriend' she told her gloating and sidling up along side her.

'What do you mean? Paul's not gay! Why are you saying that?' she asked crossly.

'Because it's blooming well true, that's why. Didn't you know? I am sure you must have known, I mean he hardly would have made love to you would he? Not when he had a boyfriend' she continued.

'Shut your big mouth! You know nothing about Paul and me' she told her feeling hurt. She could not understand why she should be saying all of this either.

'Oh but I do you silly little bitch, you don't think he wanted you for your body do you. Open your eyes, he is well and truly 100% gay whether you like it or not' she told her menacingly.

Francesca felt sick. Maybe that would explain why they had never done more than kiss or cuddle. How could he have done this to her, more to the point why would he?

'I don't know why you are saying these things but you are wrong' Francesca insisted.

'Oh so you think I am wrong do you? ' Lucy spat, then take a look at this photo.' She scrolled down to a photo that she had on her mobile and pushed it under Francesca's nose. She laughed at the look of horror on Francesca's face. It was a photo of Paul with another man kissing and in the background was Lucy.

'See I told you so. You must have known or else you were walking around with your eyes shut' she told her mockingly, and Francesca just carried on walking so that Lucy did not see the tears that were forming. How could Paul have done this to her? Then a very frightening thought crossed her mind. She thought about all the times they were together, the times when she had even thought that he might pop the question. They had never been sexually intimate and Paul put it down to being because the time was not right. At first she had thought it was out of respect for her because he was a gentleman. A gentleman! It made her laugh now she knew the truth. But the most frightening thing was that whenever they were together he would ask lots of questions about her friendship with Jennifer. He told her it was because he wanted her to be able to tell him everything, and not have any secrets at all. He said when two people were as close as they were, then they should never have secrets. What a laugh! Paul had kept the biggest secret of them all. He had stolen her heart and abused it. She did not think she could ever trust another man in all her life. How could she? She had definitely not known that Paul was gay, yet he was. So what else had he kept from her?

She decided that she would drive to see if she could find this place in Stone where Paul and his boyfriend were living and confront him. She wanted to see him squirm when she told him that she knew. She wanted to drive up there and knock on his door and look him straight in the eye and tell him what a dirty lousy bastard he was. Then she was going to be the one to tell him he was ditched. She had a brief idea where he live and it would only take a bit of driving around to find the right house. She was sure of it, and that was what she intended to do. Then she would go to the police station and give DC McKenna his address.

It took just fifteen minutes of driving around for Francesca to find the right house, but when she eventually turned off her engine and got out of her car, she was having a few second thoughts. Maybe this had been a silly idea after all to confront him, she thought to herself. It might not even be safe, as Paul could turn very nasty especially if he had something to do with Jennifer's disappearance. Maybe she should have just gone to the police instead. She stared at the house that appeared to be in complete darkness. There were no car or cars in the driveway. Maybe Jack was still away, and maybe that was where Paul was. He had told her that he had to go away for a week. Maybe he was really going to be with his lover Jack. The thought made her feel quite sick.

She approached the front door to check out the number of the house. It was number eight.

There were only four houses to the block and they were in a rural area of Stone. Paul's or rather Jack's was the end house. At least the journey was not wasted, she had found his address this time and she intended giving it to the police DC.

There had been no one at home, and part of Francesca was glad. She was still stinging from seeing the photo that Lucy had shown her. How could she have been so stupid? She intended to make him suffer like the way he had made her suffer. She was going to go and see DC McKenna first thing tomorrow morning and tell him everything she knew about him.

It was pitch black in the room and Jennifer did not know how long she had been left for this time. The last time she had thought that her captor was about to kill her. He had held the knife to her throat and started to cut until she had felt the sting of the blade cutting into her flesh. Her whole life had flashed before her and everything both good and bad that she had ever done she seemed to see in her head, like little pictures, as if she were viewing a cine camera. She was sure she was going to die.

Then out of the blue, as if he had suddenly had second thoughts he had withdrawn the knife and howled with laughter. Then he had come right close to her face and sniffed at her, and said to her 'your fear.....I love the smell of your fear, and can almost taste it.'

She had withdrawn like an injured animal shaking uncontrollably. Then he had told her that she could not die not yet and that she would know why very soon.

She had no sense of time in the room because there was no clock. It was always pitch black there because there were no windows that could let light come through. She did not know if it was day or night but then half the time she was sleeping anyhow. She was sure now that some of the liquid drink she was given had a sleeping draft in it, because soon after she had taken it she had felt very drowsy. Jennifer had thought about refusing to drink it, but her mouth was so dry she would drink anything. Besides what did she have to stay awake for, only the darkness of the room and the loneliness of knowing there was no sound there.

She wondered when he would be back to taunt her again, her captor. There was no way of knowing until she could hear the sound of tyres on gravel and the sound of his footsteps. Jennifer's stomach hurt from hunger, although she thought she would not be able to eat anyhow. She was sure that her stomach had shrunk from the lack of food, not eating even a mouthful for what seemed like days.

She thought about her life and why it had come to this, being kept a prisoner. Then she thought about her grandpa and hoped he had survived. She had no way of knowing. Tears pricked her eyes as she thought of him, and her lovely nan. She was sure she would never get out of the room alive. Sometimes she wished he would just kill her, at least she would be put out of her misery. This way it was a living hell. She drifted back into sleep seeing shadows in her subconscious. Faces appeared, people she recognised and strangers. She had no way of knowing what was real or what was just inside her head.

Then she heard it the sound of the tyres on gravel and then coming to a complete stop. She heard his footsteps coming closer, but wait she thought, there were more than one set of footsteps this time. She was sure of it, unless it was her mind playing tricks on her again, but no there were definitely two sets of footprints this time. Then they got closer still and she thought she heard whispering. After a minute or two she heard the sound of the key being turned in the lock and the door began to open.

It was the day of Jean-Paul's funeral and there was a vast gathering of both old and new friends, plus neighbours. There were also people that Maggie did not even recognise who had come to show their respects. They all gathered into the small Church in Agay for the funeral service. Clive walked beside his mother almost holding her up. If she had looked frail before she certainly looked far worse now, if that was at all possible. She looked gaunt and she had clearly lost weight from hardly eating when she had sat for hours at a time with her husband, willing him to survive. Maggie was dressed all in black and was wearing a hat, and she clung to her son as she was led to the front of the Church where Jean-Paul's coffin was. They both took their places and the service began. Several people gave various tributes but for Maggie it was all a blur, and then the Minister stood up to say a few words. He was speaking both in his native tongue of French and also a little English for the sake of those that did not know much French.

It was after the service had finished and hymns were sung that Maggie just could not hold her grief in any longer, and she let out a sound that sounded at first like a wounded animal that filled the entire Church. All the pent out feelings and emotions had come to a head. She was grieving both for her beloved husband Jean-Paul and also for her granddaughter Jennifer. She just could not stop the tears and her anguished cries, and Clive was at a loss at what to do.

Jacques and his wife Fleur came to their aid and Fleur put her arms around Maggie and just sat there holding her tight, letting her cry and release all the tears until after what seemed to be a very long time Maggie stopped. It was as if all the tears had suddenly dried up again, and she then felt very numb inside, as if she was not really there, but in a film that she watching. It had been a strange sensation and one that did not feel real. Everything else passed in a blur, until at last the funeral came to an end and it was time to go home again.

Clive wondered how his mother was going to cope when he went back. He did not want to leave her, but at the same time he needed to go back to England. He wanted to do his own search for his daughter Jennifer, although he knew he had not really got a clue where he would even start. But he had at least got to try. He felt helpless being stuck there in France, with her missing in England.. He intended to stay for another day or two, then book a plane ticket to go back home again.

It was not his job he was thinking about this time, he had already been in touch with his boss who surprisingly told him to take as long as he needed off. No this time he wanted to go strictly to look for his daughter. He had discussed it with his mother at length before the funeral and she had understood and agreed that he should go. She had told him she would be fine, and not to worry about her. But now he was not so sure if he could leave her in the state she was in. Even though he knew she had her neighbours Jacques and Fleur to keep an eye on her. It was hard to know what to do for the best; he would just have to take one day at a time.

Chapter 33

DC McKenna was surprised to hear that Francesca wanted to speak with him, and he arranged with her that she should call in after work to see him. He had actually been thinking about her and wondering if he should bring her back in to see if she had any other news about her boyfriend and to ask her if she was aware he might in fact be gay.

There was an alert put out by both the Staffordshire police and the Manchester police, to bring both men in if they should appear. However they had only had descriptions of them from a few people at the Manchester club, they did not yet have any photos of Paul or his friend Jack. Alex was becoming more suspicious of the two and wondered if there was indeed a connection in the disappearance of Ms Sudbury. No one at the club knew their address in Stone where Francesca said she had gone to either, so that could not be checked out. It seemed like Paul Blake and Jack Twist had just vanished.

When Francesca appeared Alex lead her through to one of the interview rooms, and asked a woman PC to sit in. He noted that she was very pale looking with dark circles under her eyes, as if she had not slept. He smiled at her and asked her to sit down

'Well Miss Davis what can we do for you?' he asked.

'I have been thinking a lot just lately about Jennifer and what could have happened to her, and to be very honest I still don't have a clue as to where she is, but as I said I have been thinking and I feel that there are a few things you ought to know' she began and Alex listened carefully.

'OK Miss Davis we would appreciate anything you can tell us. Is it something that's happened recently?' he asked.

'No! Well nothing like that exactly, but as I told you before Paul and I have split up.......' she hesitated and Alex thought she was about to cry, but he did not speak.

'I....I found out he was gay! You would have thought I would have known wouldn't you? I mean how stupid is that? I feel so, so stupid' she told him, sniffing.

'How did you find out?' Alex asked.

'Someone showed me a photo of him with his boyfriend, and let's say what they were doing in the photo was obvious they were more than friends' she told him.

'And you honestly had no idea? Alex put to her.

'No I definitely did not. I mean, I would not have gone out with him in the first place if I had known he was gay. I could kick myself for being so silly' she explained.

'So why do you think he wanted to go out with you?' Alex asked.

'Well as I said I have been thinking and I know I should have wondered all of this before, and you will probably think I have been very naive, which I know I have, but Paul was always asking me questions when we were together' she told him.

'Questions? Questions about what exactly?'

'About my friend Jennifer.'

'Right, can you tell me what questions he asked. In fact could you make a statement saying just that? Alex asked her and went to fetch the appropriate paperwork.

'Yes of course that's why I am here.'

'Right Miss Davis let's get all of this down shall we' he told her.

'So what questions did he ask about your friend?'

'Lots of things, like how we met, was she ever married before, where did she live, all sorts of things. He told me that if we were going to be an item then we should have no secrets, which thinking about it was big considering the big secret he kept from me. He also asked me if Francesca had any fears, what she did in her spare time, and if she had any hobbies' she explained to him, and Alex wrote all of this down.

'Were you not suspicious why he wanted to know all these things?' he asked her.

'No not really, I just thought as he told me if we were going to get closer in our relationship then I needed to show I trusted him, except sometimes it did get on my nerves. All the questions. He even told me not to get involved that time when she reported waking up in the apartment and not knowing how she got home. He said it was for the best I didn't get involved' she explained.

'But really you were involved weren't you? I mean you were there that night in the club?'

'Yes I know that, but I honestly did not know what had happened to her, she just left and when I could not find her I left a message on her mobile phone, asking her to ring me when she got home safely' she told him.

'Do you think Paul had anything to do with what happened to her?' he asked.

'I don't know. All I know is he came to pick me up to give me a lift home that night, but at that time Jennifer had already left' she replied.

'What about his friend this Jack? Did you see him?' he asked.

'To be very honest I did not even know what his friend Jack looked like until I saw him in the photo yesterday, so no I don't think he was there, but as I said before I had had an awful lot to drink that night.'

'Who showed you the photo of Paul and his friend Jack?'

'It was Lucy. I met her yesterday and she was horrible to me, and told me I should have guessed he was gay. Then when I refused to believe her, she showed me the photo on her phone of Paul and Jack kissing.'

'Are you are talking about Lucy Griffin?' he asked.

'Yes Lucy Griffin.'

'And you know her as a friend of Paul's?'

'Yes that's right, well she's a friend of Jacks.'

'OK what else can you tell me about Paul Blake?'

'Well last night I drove up to Stone, I was determined to confront him, well both him and Jack. So I took a drive up to Stone and drove around until I found the house he lived in' she told him with a faint smile.

'And did you find it?'

'I did yes' she told him with a smug look on her face.

'And were you able to speak to Paul or Jack?' he asked her.

'No there was no one at home, the house was in complete darkness when I got there.'

'I see, so would you mind giving me the address?'

'Yes of course it's number eight Sheridan Heights' she told him.

'Thank you Miss Davis you have been very helpful' he told her writing the address down.

'What will happen now? To Paul I mean' she asked him.

'Well both he and his friend will be brought in for questioning. In the meantime we will be sending someone around to the house to see what is going on there' he told her then he asked her to sign what she had told him on the statement, and he then signed his own name.

'Miss Davis as I said you have been very helpful, and if there is anything else that you remember, please don't hesitate to let us know' he told her standing up.

'Do you think you will find Jennifer?' she asked him.

'I certainly hope so. Maybe now we will start to get to the bottom of things.'

'Can you let me know please?' she asked walking over to the door. 'Jennifer and I are best friends' she told him.

'Certainly. Rest assured we will let you know in due course, and thank you again Miss Davis for coming in to see us' he replied.

'Not at all, it's the least I could do' she told him then she left. DC McKenna got straight onto DS

Hunter with the information about Paul Blake and gave him the address.

'I think we should bring him in' he told him and he agreed that he was now a suspect in the Sudbury case.

Jennifer braced herself as the door unlocked and her captor came in. She thought that she had been mistaken at first by the sound of the footsteps, when she had thought that she had heard two sets.

'Hello Katie or should I say Jennifer I have someone here to see you' he told her in a menacing voice, and when Jennifer saw who it was she gasped with shock.

'It can't be? It can't be you' she said to the woman that followed him in. She looked different somehow, her hair was shorter untidier and she looked very thin, thinner than she had ever seen her before. She wore a tee shirt that showed all the needle marks in her arms, where she had clearly been injecting herself. But there was no mistaking it was Nicole.

'Hello little sister' she said sarcastically.

'I don't understand.....why? Why are you doing this to me?' Jennifer said to her with tears in her eyes.

'Cut the crap you whore why do you think?' she almost spat angrily.

'I don't know why. What did I ever do to you?' she asked her sadly but Nicole just laughed out loud.

'What did you ever not do to me? Daddy's precious princess, you are the one he only ever cared about. You killed my mother, if it was not for you she would still be alive' she told her.

'That's not my fault I never asked to be born' she replied with tears streaming down her face.

'You were born though and my mum died, she gave her life so you could be born, and what a whore you were' she continued.

'What do you mean?' she asked.

'What do I mean? I know full well what you did in that club, shame dad never knew what a whore you were' she spat.

'Nicole please don't be like that.....please?'

'You even turned nan against me. It wasn't enough that you got all the attention from dad was it you bitch, you had to turn nan against me too.'

'I don't know what you mean, I never turned her against you….ever' she told her feeling confused. She felt sick to the stomach that her sister was in on all of this.

'Oh but you did you LIAR, why do you think she wrote me out of their wills, hers and grandpas?' she told Jennifer. Then it dawned on her that she did not know that her grandpa was in hospital seriously injured.

'You do know that grandpa is in hospital don't you Nicole?' she told her.

'Of course I do you silly whore. Who do you think put the old fool there?' she confessed.

Jennifer could not believe her ears, and looking at the mad expression on her face she realised it could well be true.

'Why? Why would you do that?' she cried.

'Well it was not me exactly. Let's say we got someone to do it for us' she told her gloating.

'You are mad, completely mad, but you won't get away with this, you do know that don't you?' Jennifer told her.

'Oh why is that Jennifer? Don't you think I have already got away with it? No one will ever find you here' she continued, while Jennifer struggled trying to get free.

'What are you going to do with me?' she asked and Nicole just laughed.

'You will know soon enough, let's just say after we give you a drugs overdose you will be well and truly beyond saving my little sister.'

'You wouldn't, not murder? Surely you wouldn't stoop that low, not even you?

'Ah but I forgot to tell you....grandpa's dead......next is nan, after you of course.'

Jennifer screamed, as she felt so distraught.
'Please God someone help me.'

Chapter 34

It was decided that the house in Stone should be thoroughly searched with or without the two suspects being present. A search warrant had now been issued, as it had been sought straight after the statement made by Miss Davis.

DC McKenna along with DC Brennan and two other police officers had driven to the house where it still appeared no one was at home. A neighbour came out to see what was happening when they heard the sound of breaking glass. They spoke to one of the officers, while DC McKenna forced an entry and went inside.

'What's going on? Has something happened?' the neighbour asked looking alarmed by the sight of the policemen and the sound of breaking glass, but only a minimal explanation was given, and then the neighbour went back inside his house.

They all split up and went into separate rooms doing a thorough search of each, putting anything they thought looked suspicious into bags. There were two computers, one in the bedroom and another in the dining room. Both needed passwords to get on to them, so they had be taken into the station to be examined as well.

No phone was found in the bedroom where Miss Davis had said she had seen one under the bed.

Alex still felt sure that they would find something if they searched long enough, and hoped it would be the phone that Miss Davis had thought was her friends. They were almost finished and the phone had still not been found. All that remained to be searched was the outside of the house, but then Alex caught sight of a notepad on a table in the lounge. He picked it up to examine it more closely. There was nothing written in it except an imprint of something that had been written on the page above which had obviously been torn out. He put it down again dismissing it at first, but then he picked it up and looked at it again. With a frown he decided to take it back to the station with him for a closer examination.

'Alex take a look at this' Max said coming into the lounge where he was standing, and showing him the phone that one of the officers had found discarded in the rubbish bin outside.

'Looks like the one Miss Davis was talking about don't you think? Union Jack cover, but it's been battered by something, all the screen is cracked and it looks like it's unusable to me.'

Alex took a quick look and pulled his face.

'We'll take it back anyway and then check if the sim is still in, but I doubt it somehow' he said, and then he spoke into his radio to the superintendent telling him that they were finished at the house and were coming back to the station.

On arriving back at the station there was an announcement that one of the suspects Paul Blake had been found just outside Manchester and had been arrested on suspicion of the abduction of Jennifer Sudbury and they were bringing him in for questioning.

'Let's see what he has to say about it all shall we' he told Max with a wry smile.

Paul Blake was led struggling into the Police station by two Policemen and then read his rights and had both his fingerprints and mug shot taken. He was then taken into an interview room where DC McKenna and another colleague were waiting for him.

'Well, well Mr Paul Blake sit down. You have a lot of questions to answer' Alex told him, but Paul refused to sit telling him he requested his solicitor to be present, and that he was not saying a thing. So Alex decided he would have him put into one of the cells until he calmed down and also until his solicitor appeared.

'We will let him stew in the cell until his solicitor arrives. In the meanwhile let's see what we can find out on the two computers and the mobile phone we bought in' Alex told his colleague who agreed.

Jennifer was devastated to hear about the death of her grandpa from Nicole. She just could not begin to imagine how her nan would be feeling. She only hoped her father had flown out to France to be with her. Shortly after appearing with her captor she had left again, in spite of Jennifer's pleas, asking her sister to not go through with all of what she was planning. She even told her that she could have all the money that her nan was planning to leave to her, and that money meant nothing at all to her. But Nicole had laughed and then spat in her face and told her she would have the money anyway.

After Nicole left her captor came back into the room with a glass of what looked like milk for her, but Jennifer refused point blank to touch it, in case it was drugged. However he forced it down her throat wile she spluttered and coughed.

'Who are you anyhow and why are you helping Nicole? What's in it for you?' she asked him breathless from the struggling.

'My, my Jennifer or shall I call you Katie....don't you know me yet?' he said to her then continued ' there is a lot in it for me. For one thing I get to feel your suffering. Fear can be your friend if you let it' he told her.

'What are you talking about?' she asked.

'Let me give you a clue Katie. Would you rather be buried alive or locked in a dungeon?' he asked her and then he roared with laughter.

'I don't believe it. You are Prince Of Mystery....but tell me how did you know my online name was Katie? It's not possible' she told him starting to cry again. Just then Nicole came back into the room.

'That's where you are wrong little whore of a sister. Remember you told your friend Francesca Davis?' she told her gloating.

'Francesca wouldn't do that to me, she's my friend' she replied, but deep down it was all making sense now why Francesca had not stuck by her. Goodness, she thought sadly she was in on all of this too but why?

'So you see you stupid little bitch you have no friends, neither will anyone miss you. And even if they search your apartment looking for clues, they will eventually find that photo of you that you told Francesca about, and will know what you are really like, and if they don't then there are more copies of it. I wonder if our father would like to receive one?'

she continued laughing and mocking her, until Jennifer wished that they would just get it over with and kill her once and for all.

She felt degraded and helpless. Every part of her body ached. She felt she had not eaten for days yet she no longer felt hungry.

'What will you do with me?' she asked tears rolling down her face.

Nicole came closer and looked at one of her arms.

'Untie her' she told Prince of Mystery who proceeded to untie her wrists but left her feet still bound.

Jennifer felt scared to death at what was about to happen and pulled away as Nicole grabbed her left arm.

'Just a tiny prick and it will be all over' she told her with hate in her eyes, as she pulled out a syringe filled with some drug.

'NICOLE PLEASE DON'T......NO NO' she struggled even though she felt weak. Then Nicole backed away and told The Prince of Mystery to tie her back up again.

'Just for the time being, but tomorrow all of this will be over completely' she told her, and all Jennifer could do was recoil like a wounded animal and cry. She was never going to come out of this alive, she thought to herself. Tomorrow she would be dead unless someone found her, but she couldn't think how they would.

There was a urgent meeting called to discuss the Sudbury case and all the evidence was bought up by DS Hunter and DC McKenna. One of the computers was going to be used as evidence as IT forensics were able to find conversations between someone at the house using a pseudonym and Ms Sudbury. Also the mobile phone was being examined further.

Paul Blake was still refusing to talk except through his solicitor who told the DC that his client was pleading innocent of any crime, and so Paul was kept in the cell. DC McKenna came up with a plan to bluff him into talking by telling him they were able to find out that the mobile they had found at the house was indeed Ms Sudbury's, and he told Paul that he would go down for a long time if he didn't start talking. But Paul was still denying his involvement, even though there was evidence of a conversation that took place from the Stone house via the computer.

Alex was at a loss. He wanted to find Ms Sudbury and knew that time might be running out for her. Something was bothering him about the notepad that he had retrieved from the house. Although there was no writing on it, there had clearly been something written from the imprint it had shown.

He sat at his desk looking carefully at it for a long time, trying to fit the missing jigsaw puzzle together. He saw the imprint of an O then it looked like W and at the end was S. He called in DC Brennan and asked him what he thought.

'It could be anything' he shrugged not looking too impressed. Then Alex had another idea as he took out a soft lead pencil, and rubbed gently over the surface of the paper, until the indentation became highlighted.

'Max look at this now' he told him with a big grin on his face. Highlighted on the paper was 'The Old Warehouse.' Max looked at it closely.

'Think we should check this out just in case' Alex said to him.

'It could be something or nothing, but if I am not mistaken it's the old deserted warehouse just outside Stoke' he told him and then continued 'I think I will pay Paul Blake a visit in the cell first though.

'Blake get up' he called to him as a policeman opened the cell door, and then he went inside.

'What now?' Paul Blake asked rolling his eyes.

'I have already told you already, I have nothing to say to you.'

'Well I have something to say to you Blake, something you already know anyhow.'

'Oh! what's that then?' he muttered not looking too impressed.

'We think we know where your boyfriend is hiding Ms Sudbury.'

'Don't have a clue what you are harping on about' he replied.

'Ah that's interesting, since we got this little piece of information from the house where you live in Stone. A bit careless wasn't it?' he told him then continued 'she's being held at the Old Warehouse isn't she?' Alex said to him and the look on Paul Blake's face told him everything he wanted to know, without him even saying a word. Paul Blake went as white as a sheet. Alex smiled

'Thank you Blake' he said to him and then left.

Without another word Alex got straight onto the phone to DS Hunter and told him exactly what he had found out. DS Hunter gave the go ahead to carry out the investigation at the Old Warehouse, and called for backup to surround the area.

Jennifer felt sick to the stomach at everything Nicole had told her. She also felt a numbness that she had never felt before. She knew that she was just waiting for her untimely death, and it must now be very close by. Nicole had said tomorrow, yet how could she even begin to measure time in this awful hellhole?

She felt real fear but yet a strange calmness had come over her. Maybe it was due to the lack of food in her stomach but she suddenly felt like she didn't care anymore. Anything would be better than this living hell that she had been plunged into.

She had never really been much of a praying sort of person, but she did believe in God and the only hope for her now was God's divine help to bring someone to her rescue. She knew that deep down good always did overcome evil in the end, but in her case she did not think anyone was going to find her, not now. Her life would soon be over, and she was just waiting for the sound of the car on the gravel, the footsteps and the turn of the key in the lock of the door. It all came sooner than she expected, for she could suddenly hear the sound of a car on gravel, two sets of footsteps getting closer and closer until the door opened.

'Well Jennifer what is your last request before you die?' her captor asked mockingly and Nicole laughed.

'PLEASE NICOLE....DON'T DO THIS' she pleaded with her sister. Then she said that someone would find out what she had done, and she would not be able to destroy the evidence if she injected her with an overdose.

'Ah but there will be no evidence, because after I inject you, this place will be blown to smithereens' Nicole told her smugly.

'How?' Jennifer asked.

'Well you may as well know, we have set an explosive device to go off in approximately twenty five minutes from now, so you see we don't have much time......untie her Jack' she told him.

'NO... NO PLEASE' Jennifer cried out struggling.

But it was too late Jack had untied the strong rope that bound her wrists.

'PLEASE NICOLE YOU CANT DO THIS, YOU WILL NEVER GET AWAY WITH IT' she screamed.

'Oh but we will. By the time the device goes off we will have left here, and all that will remain will be a mass of debris' she told her enjoying every minute of it.

'Why Nicole? Why do you hate me so much? All I ever wanted was your love as a sister, my big sister' she told her sobbing.

'SHUT UP and stop struggling'

'What about my last request? He said I could have one' she told her looking at her captor and trying to buy time.

'OK what is it? But be quick there are only twenty minutes left' Nicole told her frostily.

'I would like a cup of coffee and a sandwich' she said to her and Nicole nodded to Jack.

DC McKenna and DC Brennan were the first to arrive at the Old Warehouse just outside Stoke closely followed by a back up Police car. On first impression the place looked deserted, and Alex wondered if he had got it all wrong. They decided not to park too close to arouse suspicion in case anyone saw them, so walked a little way on foot.

'Max it looks like someone is inside, and take a look at this' he said to him as he approached a black sports car' then continued 'wasn't it a black sports car that the French Police were after in connection with the hit and run accident?' he asked looking around the car to see if there was any damage but it all looked OK.

'I am going to call for more help. My hunch is that Ms Sudbury is being held here' he told Max who agreed. After radioing in for extra backup they decided to try and get inside.

Within five minutes the place was surrounded by police officers from the armed SWAT team in Stoke. Just then Alex and Max heard screams coming from the building.

"OK whore you have one minute left to finish that coffee. Sorry there was nothing to put in a sandwich, but you will never need to eat again after I inject you with this' Nicole told her holding the syringe up for her to see

'What was that noise?' Jack asked looking around suddenly.

'I didn't hear anything' Nicole replied, grabbing hold of Jennifer's arm and plunging the needle into it. Jennifer struggled with all the strength she had left and pushed Nicole to the ground.

'THIS IS THE POLICE. THE PLACE IS SURROUNDED COME OUT WITH YOUR HANDS IN THE AIR ' Alex shouted outside the building, with Max and a few other police officers from the armed SWAT unit pointing their guns alongside him. Jack panicked and tried to escape through the back corridor, while Nicole limped after him.

'The bomb it's been set' Nicole told him 'we need to get out of here and quick.'

'Come on Nicole let's try the back way. We need to go fast, there can't be long left now ' he replied.

DC McKenna rushed inside the room and saw Jennifer lying on the floor half dazed. He grabbed hold of her and quickly carried her outside to safety, while two armed police officers attempted to go after Jack and Nicole.

'Be careful....bomb inside' Jennifer whispered with what breath she had left, and Alex shouted a warning about the bomb and called for everyone to evacuate. The two police officers from the SWAT team heard and quickly ran back out again getting clear of the building.

Then it happened, there was a massive bang, and the building exploded and burst into flames. Alex could only look on in complete shock, realising the suspects Nicole and Jack were still inside.

'Phew that was a close shave Alex. You took a risk there, going in and getting her out' Max told him.

'We better get Ms Sudbury to hospital as soon as possible. It looks like she's been injected with drugs, and I'm not sure how much, but her eyes are rolling around the back of her head' he told Max and called for a ambulance.

Epilogue

Two weeks later Jennifer Sudbury boarded the flight to Nice from Manchester airport. She was looking forward to seeing her nan again. There was to be a memorial service for her Grandpa Jean-Paul and her father Clive was planning to fly back out as well. Clive had been devastated to hear that Nicole had been involved in the whole thing and still could not get his head around it. Part of him blamed himself, maybe he had not been a good enough father - had he shown Jennifer more love than Nicole? He would never know now what tipped Nicole over the edge to plan such an evil thing against her own sister and indeed his father. Nicole had been blown up in the explosion, along with Jack. Jennifer had spent a few days in hospital recuperating because of the drugs her sister had injected her with, but fortunately for her not all the drugs in the syringe had gone into her blood stream.

Paul Blake was charged with his involvement in the abduction and attempted murder in the Sudbury case, and would go to prison for a long time. Lucy Griffin was also arrested and charged, even though her involvement was not in the abduction but she was charged with being an accessory to the crime.

Francesca was also questioned further, but released with no charge. The only crime she had really committed was giving out information to someone she thought she trusted. She and Jennifer were back together as friends again after a tearful reunion.

It turned out that the main people who had plotted the whole thing were Nicole and her close friend Jack. After realising she had been taken out of her grandparents will she had become bitter. She had always blamed her younger sibling for the death of her mother, but the writing out of the will was just too much for her. Jack had then knocked Jean-Paul down and left him for dead. Then their plan was for them to eventually kidnap and torture Jennifer. Jack moved to a Northern town in Staffordshire and set up home in Stone. He also joined a fetish club, as he was a sadomasochist. It was there that he met Paul Blake. Their friendship grew and it was not long before the plot thickened and he became part of the plan. He moved in with Jack Twist and sought out Francesca, an easy catch, who fell deeply in love with him. Francesca talked to him about everything, including her friend Jennifer. He found out about her online name of Katie, and Jack then became Prince of Mystery. He was also the second guy Luke Miller who had asked for her mobile phone number.

DC Alex McKenna sat in his office reflecting back on the past events of the Sudbury case. Were there one or two things he could have done better, or differently perhaps? he asked himself. Could they have found her sooner? He had been pleased they had found Jennifer in the end, and most of it had been due to him solving the puzzle of the indented writing on the notepad. That had most certainly been his breakthrough. He knew he had taken a risk running headlong into the warehouse unharmed, but that was who he was, and what he was about. He was highly respected as a dedicated and long-standing detective, and he hoped it would always be that way.

Made in the USA
Middletown, DE
26 July 2017